SEAL of BRAVERY

IRON TIDE BROTHERHOOD
BOOK TWO

JESSICA ASHLEY

B.A.D. PUBLISHING CO
believing in the power of reading

SEAL of Bravery
Iron Tide Brotherhood, Book 2
By Jessica Ashley
Copyright © 2026. All rights reserved.

This book is a work of fiction. Names, characters, places, businesses, and incidents are products of the author's imagination or used fictitiously. Any resemblance to actual persons, living or dead, places, or actual events is entirely coincidental.

No part of this book may be reproduced or transmitted in any form by any means, electronic or mechanical, including photocopying, recording, or by any information storage and retrieval system without written permission of the author, except for the use of brief quotations in a book review.

This book was not created with the use of AI and is not to be used to train any kind of AI technology.
Scripture used in this novel comes from HOLY BIBLE, New Living Translation®, NLT®.
Used by permission. All rights reserved worldwide.

Edited by The Editing Soprano
Proofread by Love Kissed Books, LLC
Proofread by Dawn Y.
Cover Design by Covers by Christian
Photographer: Wander
Model: Martin C.
Alternate Cover Design by Qamber Designs

SEAL of Bravery
Iron Tide Brotherhood, Book 2
By Jessica Ashley
Copyright © 2026. All rights reserved.

Edited by The Editing Soprano
Proofread by Love Kissed Books, LLC
Proofread by Dawn Y.
Cover Design by Covers by Christian
Photographer: Wander
Model: Martin C.
Alternate Cover Design by Qamber Designs

Iron Tide Brotherhood Chronological Reading Order

While the books in the Iron Tide Brotherhood series are written in a way that you *can* read in any order, I do recommend you read in this order to avoid any possible spoilers.

Happy reading!

1. SEAL of Honor
2. SEAL of Bravery
3. SEAL of Courage
4. *Coming soon*
5. *Coming soon*

SEAL of Bravery

Demolition is his specialty. But nothing prepared him for the single mom next door.

Former Navy SEAL Garrison "Demo" Holt came to South Carolina to rebuild his life after his military career went up in smoke. Now a counselor for troubled teens, he's determined to protect those who can't protect themselves—even if it puts him back in the line of fire.

Katelyn Ellis has spent years keeping her son safe by staying invisible. She knows what happens when the wrong people notice you. The last thing she needs is her protective, former-military neighbor getting involved—especially when someone from her past is still hunting her.

But when danger closes in and a violent coastal storm shatters the fragile safety she's built, Katelyn has no choice but to trust Garrison.

As threats escalate and secrets unravel, Garrison

becomes the only thing standing between her family and deadly revenge.

A swoony small-town romantic suspense featuring a protective hero, a courageous single mother, and a powerful story of faith forged in the fire.

AUTHORS NOTE

You know those moments where you find yourself sitting behind the wheel of a car that seems destined to run off the road?

Maybe you aren't even the one driving it, but you're an unwilling participant in an event that is going to shake the very foundation of your life.

You know, the kind of thing that leads up to a moment when you find yourself standing in the middle of a hole, shovel in hand, and instead of trying to get out you just keep digging?

Yeah, me too.

I can't even count the number of times I've been standing there, holding that shovel, *knowing* without a doubt that I should set it aside so I can get out of the pit, but I just keep digging because that's what I know.

It's what's comfortable.

What feels safe.

Because man is it easy to want to cling to that illusion of control when everything else is spiraling.

In the world today we are told to be stronger. That we can manage everything ourselves, all we have to do is keep trucking forward.

After all…everyone has the same twenty-four hours in a day, right? *(Hearing this brings me a huge wave of frustration because everyone's twenty-four hours looks INCREDIBLY different.)*

Why can't you take on another sport?

Or classroom activity?

Or…INSERT RANDOM THING HERE?

The noise is SO LOUD. Deafening.

And sometimes, standing in that pit feels a lot more comfortable than making the conscious choice that it's too much.

That we can't do this alone.

That we *need* to set that shovel aside, give up control, and just get out of the pit.

Because the fact is…NONE OF US CAN do it alone.

And I know that's a hard truth to swallow, especially in a world that is constantly telling us to do more.

To be more.

To have more.

Even sitting here at my keyboard, I'm exhausted. Not because I've done anything particularly difficult today, but because my to-do list is constantly growing and expanding in my mind.

All of those millions of tiny things that society tells me I should be doing.

And as I sit here, I'm reminded that the only thing we HAVE to do, is turn our eyes to God.

Then Jesus said, "Come to Me, all of you who are weary and carry heavy burdens, and I will give you rest." *(Matthew 11:28)*

When we take a minute to do that. To bring our burdens and really sit *with* Him, the noise of the world is drowned out by His peace.

Pure, wonderful peace.

Because we're not focused on all the millions of things we should be doing, we're focused on Him. On the fact that we are already enough because we are His.

The fact is, NOTHING we do here will get us into Heaven. None of those endless tasks, to-do lists, or activities will lead us into eternity with God. *(Ephesians 2:8-9)*

You know what will? Faith in our Lord, Jesus Christ, and the sacrifice **He made for us.**

The dishes can wait (*I know, it makes my eye twitch to say it, too*).

The laundry won't fold itself, but it'll be there later.

That extra sport? Classroom activity? Not mandatory.

We. Are. Enough.

Because HE IS EVERYTHING.

So let's throw down that shovel.

Pray and let Him lift us out of the pit.

Let's remain rooted in Him even as the world tries to blow us down with the hurricane of things meant to keep us so occupied, that we can't see the firm foundation we are already standing on. *(1 Peter 5:10)*

Because, darling, we were fearfully and wonderfully made. *(Psalm 139:14)*

The same God who created the mountains and each and every star, formed us in our mother's womb. *(Psalm 139:13)*

NOTHING this world throws at us can change that.

NOTHING that happens to us in this world will diminish that light.

(Ephesians 1:13-14)

We are not powerless because He is standing with us.

So let us pick up God's armor and stand firm in His truth.

-Jessica

To those carrying heavy burdens.
You don't have to do it alone.
Matthew 11:28

CHAPTER 1

KATELYN

By the time I've reached the last flight of stairs leading toward my apartment, the double shift I just pulled at the diner hits me like a tidal wave. My feet throb with every step, and I know they'll likely be swollen by the time I do manage to get my shoes off.

If only I could get away from my fear of elevators, then I could have saved myself a lot of pain. Unfortunately, that fear outweighs any desire I have to be off my feet right away. Besides, it only takes a few extra minutes to make the climb.

And, stairs are good for you, right? Isn't that what the experts say?

My final text from Thomas came in two hours ago, so I know he's already home and in bed, sleeping in preparation for school tomorrow. Though, I suspect that's only because he made it a point to be in bed before I got home in order to avoid the conversation we are absolutely going to have about his struggling grades.

Stormwatch Landing was supposed to be a fresh start for us. In a lot of ways, it has been. But moving constantly has caught up to my thirteen-year-old, and his grades are suffering for it.

No more. It's the promise I made to myself when we moved to this small South Carolina town. We will be here until he graduates—no matter what.

I sigh as I step onto my floor, then head down the hall. Unease trickles up my spine when I notice the door to my neighbor's apartment is cracked open. He seems to be a kind man, though we've shared nothing but a wave here and there.

Mainly because, whenever I see him, my entire nervous system goes straight into overdrive. The guy is attractive with a capital "A". Make that all caps. As in: should be on the cover of every magazine everywhere.

Considering my luck with handsome men, I've done everything I can to avoid him. Including hiding out whenever I hear his door open or close. Even if I'm already on my way out. Because, in my experience, they have heavy hands and very little internal substance. Thomas's father ensured I understood that.

Still…why is his door open? I cautiously approach, trying to look through the crack in the door without actually peering inside.

And then a knocked-over teacup catches my attention. I

move in a bit closer, and my gaze lands on what I can see of a Bible lying open, halfway dangling off the coffee table as though it had been tossed there.

More unease slices through me, and I know, without a doubt, *something* is wrong.

"Hello?" I ask as I knock on the ajar door. "Are you—" The door swings open, revealing a battlefield inside.

Adrenaline surges through my system as I race inside, looking for my neighbor. What if he's hurt?

What if the person who made this mess is still here?

I pause long enough to withdraw my phone and preemptively dial 9-1, not finishing the call just yet. "Hello?" I move farther into his living room, then come around to the side of the couch. As I turn toward the hallway and spot the bare-chested man face-down in a pool of his own blood, that adrenaline kicks into overdrive.

The scene is straight out of a horror movie, right down to a man wearing a ski mask, lying directly behind my neighbor. His eyes are the only part of his face that's visible, and they're frozen open, staring at the ceiling.

Dead.

My stomach twists, and panic pulses through me as I fall to my knees beside my neighbor while dialing the last 1 and hitting Call. I put it on speaker and set it on the floor next to me as the nurse I've tried so hard to bury surfaces.

"9-1-1, what's your emergency?"

"My neighbor has been attacked. Male, mid-thirties," I trail off as I feel for a pulse, then breathe a sigh of relief when I feel the faint thump against my fingers. "Faint pulse, thank God."

"What is your location?"

I rattle off the address. "I'm going to roll him over to see where the blood is coming from." Both of my hands are already slick with his blood as I slide them beneath his muscled chest and waist. With great effort, I manage to roll him over.

It takes me all of a heartbeat to find his injury. I find a massive, jagged wound in his side, and the blood has begun to slow, which means he doesn't have long.

"Nasty stab wound," I tell the dispatcher.

"We have help on the way."

"Thanks." I rip the sweater over my head and press it to his side, then glance over at the other man. "There's another man here, but—" Maintaining pressure with one hand, I reach over and feel for a pulse on the other man.

There is none.

"The other man is dead."

"There's another man?"

I nod, then realize she can't actually see me. "He's wearing a mask. I just found them this way. My neighbor is breathing, but—" I scream when a large hand grips my wrist. My gaze lands on my neighbor's, his dark eyes wide and pleading.

"Help. Her," he chokes out.

I scan the room. "I don't see anyone else. I can't leave you to look, or you'll bleed out. Help is coming, okay?"

Her. Who is "her"?

His eyes roll back in his head, and I press firmly onto his injury as the blood continues to pound in my ears.

"No, stay with me. Are you there?" I try to wake him, but his head lolls to the side.

"Ma'am, are you still there?" the dispatcher asks.

"Yes, sorry. I'm here." My throat tightens. Is there someone else here? Someone else who needs help?

"Did I hear that right? Is there someone else there?"

"I don't see anyone else," I say. "And I don't want to risk leaving him to check. He's going to die if I release the pressure." Tears swim in my eyes. *Please don't die.* There's so much blood.

So. Much. Blood.

Panic begins to push through my rational mind, and even though I know I'm safe, my body's fight or flight kicks into gear, and I want to run away.

Far and fast.

"Stay right there. Help is on the way."

"Okay. Please hurry."

My gaze drops to where his hand has gone limp on my wrist. His chest is slick with his own blood, and it saturates the diner uniform I'm wearing, staining the rust-colored skirt a shade darker.

Those eyes flutter open again, but they're glazed over and staring straight up at me as though he can't really see me.

"I'm here," I tell him. "You're going to be okay." *Please be okay.*

"I—" he starts, but his eyes roll back into his head, and he falls silent again.

"Stay with me, okay?" I say again. "Please stay with me."

But he doesn't stir again. In the distance, sirens grow closer, but his breathing grows more shallow.

Because I don't know what else to do, and he'll need a miracle to survive, I lower my head and pray.

"Our Father, Who art in Heaven, hallowed be Thy name."

CHAPTER 2

———

GARRISON

THREE WEEKS LATER

The ache in my side isn't unfamiliar, but man, is it frustrating. I'm genuinely beginning to regret not taking Sawyer up on his offer to crash in my guest room so I wouldn't be alone my first night home from the hospital, but after having absolutely no privacy for the last two weeks, I'm more than ready to be alone.

Freshly showered, I make my way down the hall, stepping carefully around the dark blood stain still saturating the carpet. It's been partially cleaned, but I'll likely have to have it cut out and re-carpeted to fully remove the evidence of my near-death experience two weeks ago.

My living room has been re-set at least, my Bible placed back on the coffee table. The mug Tessa had been drinking out of when she was abducted has been washed and put away, thanks to my friend, Anastasia Knox. So, there's that.

I glance around, grateful to be home. My gaze lands on the door I left partially cracked in my desperate attempt to wash myself. Instead of closing it right away, though, I continue into the kitchen.

Pain management and water. Then I'll close the door.

Man, what I wouldn't give for some real pain meds. But with addiction in my bloodline, the last thing I want to do is tempt that monster. So in lieu of something stronger, I reach for a bottle of Advil sitting on my counter and open it up, dropping two into my hand. The tiny blue gel caps will hopefully take the edge off enough that I can sleep. Then tomorrow, I'll get started on getting back to my normal life.

First up, checking in on the community center. I've been assured things are running smoothly in my absence, and I'm sure they are, but seeing it for myself will put my mind at ease.

With the community center on my mind, I reach up to pull a glass down. I move too quickly, though, and pain shoots through my side. A hiss escapes through clenched teeth as the glass falls and shatters against the tile floor of my kitchen.

Shards fly in all directions, leaving me standing—barefoot—in the center of what might as well be a minefield.

Fantastic.

"You have got to be kidding me." With a frustrated sigh, I band one arm around my injury, then carefully cross toward the living room to grab my phone. There is absolutely no way I am going to be able to get on the ground to clean that up easily. Which means, as much as I don't want to admit it, I need help.

Besides, if I can't even get a glass down from the cabinet, then I'd say I'm probably in some serious trouble here, and dealing with Sawyer's sarcastic comments is likely going to be worth the extra help.

I've nearly reached my phone when the front door swings open.

Did he somehow read my mind and show up?

As dark as it is, I can hardly see, and before I can reach for the light, my hand closes on a soft shoulder.

A woman screams, and spray hits my face.

I snap my eyes shut as they ignite, and I let out my own painful cry. Tears stream down my cheeks, and breathing becomes an impossibility as all oxygen vanishes from my vicinity.

"What is—"

My back hits the wall hard enough to knock what little air is in my lungs out, and I fall to the ground, coughing as I frantically try to breathe. Fire spreads through my lungs, and I struggle to draw in even a single clear breath.

Head swimming, I can't see.

Can't feel.

I'm helpless against the assault on my senses.

"Oh no! I'm so sorry!" a woman cries out, her voice panicked. "Come on. We need to get you to fresh air!" She pulls at my hand, and I struggle to my feet. An arm comes around my waist, and she guides me out into the hall, but my balance falters.

The coughing turns to choked gasps, and panic sets in as I realize just how much trouble I'm in if this collapses my lung again. My heart hammers so hard against my ribs I'm sure it'll shatter them.

"Thomas, open up!" the woman calls out as she beats on what I imagine is a door.

I can't see a single thing.

Nothing but darkness.

"Mom, what—"

"Help me get him into the kitchen; then call 9-1-1."

9-1-1? I just got out of the hospital. "No. No ambulance," I try to argue, but my voice is barely audible. It comes out as a slur of unintelligible grunts.

"We have to get you help," she says, tone steady as she leads me through what I'm assuming is her apartment. She could be leading me right off a cliff, and I wouldn't be able to do anything about it.

My eyes are burning.

My lungs are on fire.

Is this how I go out? A Navy SEAL and demolition expert taken out by a can of pepper spray wielded by his gorgeous neighbor? If that is who came into my apartment. I can only assume at this point it was her. We didn't walk far enough for it to be anyone else.

"Head down so I can rinse your eyes," she says. Her

fingers thread through the hair on the back of my head as she guides me forward. I obey, not really having much of a choice. Besides, if she can get me relief from this agony, I'll take it. Cold water hits my eyes. It stings, burning my already sensitive eyes like tiny granules of glass behind my lids. I grind my teeth together, focusing only on staying upright.

At least the pain in my side is muted, thanks to the agony I'm suffering internally.

Seconds pass, and soon, slow relief creeps in. I groan as the pain in my eyes slowly ebbs. As time keeps on ticking, my breathing becomes a bit easier, but when my head swims and I sway, I know I'm not out of the woods yet.

"Are they on their way?" she asks.

"Yes. A few minutes out," her son replies.

"I am so sorry," she mutters to me. "I thought you were dead. They told me you were dead. I thought you were an intruder. When you grabbed me, I panicked—"

"Death would be preferable at this moment," I groan, unsure if she even hears me. Did I even say it out loud? I have absolutely no clue.

My legs give out, and I fall over, darkness stealing the small sliver of light that rinsing my eyes gained. I don't even feel the impact of the floor, nor the pain that should have followed.

The last thing I hear is a woman's scream before the entire world goes silent.

Light assaults my sensitive eyes as I open them and stare up at a stark white ceiling. Fluorescents hang directly above me, mounted on the tiled ceiling, and the all-too-familiar beeping of machines pulls my attention next.

I'm back at the hospital. *Fantastic.*

"He's awake!" A teenage boy I recognize instantly comes into view above me. Thomas Ellis. He spends the occasional afternoon at the center—or at least he has since he and his mother moved in next door to me three months ago.

His wide blue eyes are staring down at me, a relieved smile on his face. "Mr. Holt, it's good to see you awake," he says.

"Thank the Lord," a woman replies, her tone soft but slightly strained. My gorgeous neighbor comes into view next when she steps up beside my bed. Her blonde hair is pulled back into a tight ponytail, her hazel eyes focused intently on me. They're rimmed with red, likely from the pepper spray.

"Are you okay?" she asks. "Thomas, call the nurse."

Before I have the chance to argue that I just need a moment, Thomas has already pressed the call button on the side of my bed.

My head is throbbing, the pain in my side coming back with a vengeance as each second passes by.

"What happened?" I manage.

"My mom pepper-sprayed you," the boy says with a smirk at his mother.

Her cheeks turn a deep pink.

"Yup. I remember that." I try to sit up, but fresh pain shoots through my side.

"No, you need to stay down." Slender hands grip my right shoulder and gently press me back down. Her touch ignites something else in my blood, despite the lingering pain from my initial injury and being pepper-sprayed. I still beneath her hands and let her guide me back down onto the bed.

"You know, I'd hoped not to see you for quite some time, Garrison," Doctor Alex Jones comments as he comes into the room.

"You and me both, Doc," I groan.

"We'll give you some privacy." My neighbor—Katelyn, if I'm remembering right—takes her son's hand and pulls him toward the door. As soon as it closes, I shift my attention to the doctor.

"Good news. The lung didn't collapse again, but you did set yourself back on the healing process quite significantly."

Fantastic. "What am I looking at?"

"We need to keep you for a few days so we can monitor your oxygen levels, but—"

"I want to go home. Is a stay necessary?" I'd *just* gotten free of this place. Am I really going to have to stay longer?

Anxiety is already threatening to get the better of me. I hate hospitals.

With a passion.

The stench of death clings to every inch of the halls. Something no amount of sterilization can remove.

Alex hesitates a moment. "Since your lung didn't collapse again and you're able to breathe freely on your own, I could send you home tomorrow. But the only way I'm okay with it is if you agree to absolutely *no* heavy lifting. No exertion of any kind. Just rest."

"Deal."

"And, you need someone to stay with you."

"Done," I agree without hesitation. If it means I get to go home, then I'll allow the good doc himself to follow me home.

"If you feel off in any way, you don't hesitate to call."

"I can do that." Excitement pushes past some of my exhaustion. Home. My bed. My shower. It's within reach—again.

The door opens, and Sawyer breezes in, a sucker in his mouth and a grin on his face. *I am never going to hear the end of this.*

"I told you I should have stayed with you," he says as he stops beside my bed. The humor leaves his face. "You going to live?"

"That's what the good doctor here says. I get to go home tomorrow."

"With restrictions," Alex adds. "And supervision."

"Well, I'm happy to be your delightful new babysitter," Sawyer comments as he pulls the sucker from his mouth. It's a habit he's taken up recently. Something I'm pretty sure has everything to do with trying to distract himself in any way, now that the woman he's secretly in love with is in a serious relationship with an FBI agent based out of Savannah, Georgia. "We can even braid each other's hair. I also happen to give an amazing manicure."

"Fantastic," I reply, already regretting my decision. "Maybe Cowboy is up for staying."

Sawyer snorts. "Why do you hurt me when I show you nothing but love?" He turns to Alex. "You can count on me." Sawyer offers a mock-salute, then drops down in a chair by the bed. The same one Katelyn was sitting in when I woke up.

I have to admit, I'd much prefer her to be there again. Even given the fact that she pepper-sprayed me in my own apartment.

"Great. Then tomorrow we'll look you over, and as long as everything looks good, you can head home."

"Thanks, Alex," I say.

"You're welcome. How's your pain?"

"Manageable."

"You're sure you don't want anything? I wouldn't let them when you were brought in, but if you're hurting—"

"Nah, I'm fine," I reply, although it's far from the truth. I hurt worse now than when the blade first pierced my skin.

"Then I'll be back to check on you later." He offers me a friendly smile before leaving the room.

I can feel Sawyer staring at me, so I turn toward him, only to see a bright grin on his face. "Want to tell big brother what happened?"

"First of all, we're the same age. Second, not really. Who called you?"

"Rose. She tried Zane first, but since he and Tessa are out of pocket on their honeymoon boat trip, I was next on the list."

I'm not surprised that Rose made the call. She's a nurse here at the hospital and a surrogate mother to all who come into this place. Since I imagine my neighbor had no idea who to call, she took it upon herself to notify someone.

Zane Knox, a man I served under when I was a Navy SEAL, married his high-school sweetheart last week in a private ceremony right here at the hospital. Afterward, they'd taken off on a sailing trip eighteen years in the planning.

"Fantastic. Weston and Ryker weren't available?" I ask, honestly wishing any other member of my team could have come. Weston Hayes, AKA Cowboy, and Ryker Granger, AKA Tank, are both quiet men, and neither of them would be giving me a hard time right now.

Probably.

"You know you love me," Sawyer replies. "Seriously, though, what happened? Rose said something about you being pepper-sprayed?"

"My neighbor thought I was dead."

"So she pepper-sprayed you?" His grin is infuriating. "That seems like a perfectly logical way to treat someone coming back to life."

"She heard me break a glass in my apartment and came in. It was dark. She wasn't expecting me—and, well. You know the rest." I close my aching eyes and lean back against the pillow.

"So," he says, trying to keep his voice steady but failing. I can hear the laugh he's trying to hide. "You were pepper-sprayed in your own apartment. That's got to be a first."

"She kept apologizing. It was an accident."

"One we will no doubt laugh about weeks from now." Sawyer stands. "I am glad you're okay. I need to check in with Anastasia; she was worried about you, too. I asked, and you don't have any dietary restrictions. Want a coffee?"

"Please."

"You've got it." Sawyer pauses by the bed, his expression and tone turning serious. "Stop almost dying, Demo. You're shaving years off my life."

I grin up at him. Sawyer might be the most sarcastic man I've met, but he has a huge heart, and there are very few others I'd trust the way I trust him. "I'll work on that."

"Good. I'll be back in a few." He leaves the room, though the door remains cracked. Just as I'm closing my eyes again, a faint knock draws my attention.

"Come in." My throat burns as I call out, but seconds

later, Katelyn moves through the doorway, and my body warms for a different reason. Which, in my current predicament, makes absolutely no sense.

She's *gorgeous*. The kind of understated beauty that steals my breath—a poor choice of words at this present moment, but it's the truth.

More than once over the past few months since she moved in, I've lingered outside my apartment, hoping to pull her in for a conversation. But her hours are all over the place, and I started feeling like a creeper, so I gave up and just decided that, if a conversation was meant to happen between us, it would.

Bright hazel eyes stare back at me as she comes to stand beside my bed. "An apology doesn't make up for it, but I am so sorry."

"It's okay. Thanks for saving my life. Again. You're the one who found me before, right?" That's what they'd told me, at least. That my neighbor found me lying in a puddle of my own blood, clinging to life, and called the emergency in.

She kept pressure on my wound, unyielding despite being inches from a man I'd killed just before getting stabbed.

"I did what any normal person would do." She takes a seat in the chair.

"The doctor told me, if you hadn't gotten pressure on the injury when you did, I would have been dead before the paramedics arrived. So, thank you," I say again. "Ironically,

I planned on coming by tomorrow and bringing you cookies or something. Are cookies enough for saving someone's life these days? I forget."

My joke earns a slight smile, and my heart leaps at the sight of it. When her expression turns somber again, the entire room darkens as though someone took the sun out of the sky. "It's my fault you're lying here again. I'm so sorry," she says again. "When I heard the glass break, I thought someone had come back to steal from you since—well, you were supposed to be dead."

"So you went in armed with pepper spray to stop a robbery?"

"I had 9-1-1 dialed and ready if need be."

The fact that she was so willing to put herself at risk makes my stomach churn. What if it hadn't been me? What if someone else had decided to take advantage of my not being home? Stormwatch Landing is a safe place, but it's not without its problems.

"They had to tell everyone I was dead," I tell her. "I'm sorry for the lie. I imagine you probably wouldn't have assumed someone was breaking in if you'd known I was alive."

Her eyes darken slightly, and if I'm not mistaken, there's a hint of pain hidden in them. Darkness she likely tries really hard to ignore. "I really am glad you're okay."

"That makes two of us." Exhaustion is already pulling me under again, but I don't want this conversation to end. Not when I've been trying to get her attention for the last few months. "Well, you've saved my life twice now, and we haven't even properly met yet. I'm Garrison Holt."

"Katelyn Ellis. And since I'm the one who nearly killed you that second time, I shouldn't get the credit."

"I'm giving it to you anyway," I reply. "How did you know what to do to rinse it out, by the way? Do you have a lot of experience with pepper spray?"

She shifts in her seat, a telltale sign of discomfort. "Just intuition." She stands. "I need to get my son home. I left my number with your nurse, so if there's anything you need, please let me know. I want to help. It's the least I can do."

I hate that she's already leaving, but I can also see her flight response in action. The fact that she is taking the blame for my being back in the hospital clearly has her spooked. "Thank you, Katelyn. Seriously, it's no big deal at all. Just an accident."

She smiles, but it doesn't reach her eyes. "You're welcome, Garrison. I hope you feel better soon."

CHAPTER 3

KATELYN

"I can't *believe* you pepper-sprayed him," Thomas jokes as we climb the steps to our apartment. "I mean, do you even know *who* he is?"

"Do you?" I ask, unsure if I should be amused or concerned that my son seems to think the guy next door is the coolest person he's ever met.

"Uh, yeah. Everyone in school talks about them. Plus, I've met him a few times after school at the community center."

This is the first place my son has managed to make friends, and those friends spend their afternoons playing basketball at the community center next door. "Who is 'them'?"

"The whole team," he replies, his tone annoyed as though I should have already known. "Garrison, that guy who came to see him today, and the others. They're Navy

SEALs. Like, the ones you see in awesome action movies, Mom. Just living next to the guy got me cool points."

I stop and turn toward him. "Navy SEAL?" He nods. "It's not just a rumor?" *Did I seriously assault a member of the United States Military?* Oh, this just keeps getting better and better.

I can see the headlines now. *LOCAL MOM ASSAULTS VETERAN IN HIS OWN HOME.*

Thomas grins and shakes his head. "Didn't you see the size of him? I mean, the guy must work out all the time." My son keeps walking up the steps, clearly unconcerned with the fact that I'm reeling.

A Navy SEAL?

Right next door to me?

Thomas is right; the guy is built like a soldier, all solid muscle and broad shoulders. I'm still not quite sure how I managed to hold his weight long enough to keep him from getting hurt when he collapsed right before the paramedics arrived, but I know I'll be feeling it in the morning. Maybe even later tonight after the adrenaline wears off.

"He's a cool guy, though. Super nice."

"He seems that way." *Here's hoping he doesn't press charges.* I hadn't had the courage to ask him outright, but based on the way he thanked me, I'm going to assume he won't—hopefully.

The last thing I need is my name on an official police report.

"I heard he can kill a guy with just his pinky finger,"

Thomas says, wiggling his own in demonstration. "That he and the others once went into a fully armed compound and —" As Thomas continues, my thoughts drift back to Garrison in that hospital bed. On how pale he'd looked, how vulnerable despite his size.

I'd genuinely grieved when I went to see him and they told me he hadn't made it. My heart hadn't wanted to believe that a man who had been so kind to my son, who'd seemed to have made such an impact in so many lives, was taken from this world in such a horrific act.

And then I pepper-sprayed him.

I fight the urge to groan. Why hadn't I just paused a moment? Asked a question? Knocked before entering? Embarrassment heats my cheeks.

Maybe I'll make him cookies or something. My way of trying to make nice so he doesn't decide later on to have me arrested for assault.

"Are cookies enough for saving someone's life these days? I forget." Garrison's attempt to lighten the mood pops into my mind, and I can't help but smile softly. He'd seemed in high spirits. And maybe if I play off his joke, he'll stay that way.

We reach the landing, and Thomas is still telling likely fictitious yet heroic stories of bravery in the face of danger, even all the way up to our door. I pause and take a deep breath, my gaze landing on Garrison's apartment door. It's been closed, but unless someone else came by to lock up, it's unlocked.

My thoughts drift to the broken glass and the lingering effects of the pepper spray. He certainly won't be able to clean it up, and I'd hate for him to come home, try, and collapse again.

"Head on inside and get ready for bed, okay?"

"What are you going to do?" Thomas asks as he unlocks the door with his keys.

"I'm going to head over and open some windows to make sure Garrison—Mr. Holt— doesn't come home to the stench of pepper spray in his apartment."

"Want help?"

I smile at my boy, so proud of the man he's becoming—even if he does struggle from time to time. His heart is good, and the rest will fall into place. "That's okay. You head in and get your homework done. I'll let you know if I need help."

"Sounds good." Thomas heads into our apartment, so I push open the door to Garrison's.

The stinging stench of lingering pepper spray immediately assaults me, so I cover my nose and mouth with my arm, then head over toward the patio doors and throw them wide open. Fresh air coming in, I head back inside and turn on the ceiling fan before I get to work cleaning up the broken glass in his kitchen. Thanks to the fact that he's incredibly organized, it doesn't take me long to find the broom.

As I'm putting it away, my gaze lands on the blood-stained carpet.

My heart begins to race as I recall what he'd looked like lying there.

He'd been pale—far too pale to be alive. Or so I thought.

And there had been so much blood, as evidenced by the massive stain right in front of me.

I shiver, then shake my head, trying to clear an image that will likely never fully go away. Did it hurt him to see it when he got home earlier? To know that he nearly lost his life in that spot?

At least, blood is something I'm well-versed in cleaning up. I may not be able to take back the fact that Garrison is back in the hospital because of me, but I can hopefully make his return easier.

Leaving the balcony doors open, I head back next door to my apartment. It's not much—but it's home. The small, single-bedroom apartment is exactly what I'd needed when I drove clear across the country for a fresh start.

One that both Thomas and I desperately needed. The couch folds out to my bed, and I'd insisted on Thomas taking the back bedroom. He thinks it's to give him space —and it is. Partially.

The other reason is far too sinister to share with my son. A boy who, at the age of thirteen, has already had way too much of his innocence stolen.

I walk into the small laundry room off the kitchen and grab my bottle of hydrogen peroxide, a cleaning cloth, and a protein bar, then head for the front door. Thomas's bedroom door is closed, and his music is blaring, so I don't bother letting him know I'm headed back over. Hopefully, he's in there doing his homework. If not? Well, that's a conversation for tomorrow. Because tonight, I just don't have it in me.

Once back inside Garrison's apartment, I apply the hydrogen peroxide to the blood stain, though I'm not confident it will get all of it out. Not when there's so much and it's already set. Still, I'm hoping that I'll be able to at least get most of it. That way, he doesn't feel like he needs to be down on his hands and knees to clean it.

The apartment door opens, and I jump as a striking woman with blonde hair pulled back into a tight ponytail strolls in. She sees me and freezes, looking just as shocked as I am. I recognize her from town, but I don't know her name.

And then it hits me—she's come into the diner with Garrison and his friends before. My cheeks heat. I'm *mortified.* How did I not know he had a girlfriend? Of course he has a girlfriend! A guy like that? No way he's single. And here I am, scrubbing the floor of his apartment. Will she think—

"I'm so sorry. I was—the door was—I'm sorry." I grab my hydrogen peroxide, then start for the door.

"No need to apologize," the woman says, her expression shifting from shock into a friendly smile. "Wait, you're the one who found him the night he was—" She swallows hard and points to the blood. "You saved his life."

"Yeah. Katelyn," I tell her. "I live next door. I also happen to be the one who pepper-sprayed him earlier," I blurt. "I thought someone was robbing the place, and—well. Anyway, I was just trying to clean up a bit." I'm blabbering, a nervous habit of mine. As much as I know I need to slow down, choose my words more carefully, I can't seem to stop.

"That's really sweet," she replies, her smile widening. "I'm Anastasia Knox. I own the coffee shop in town. You work at the diner, right?"

"I do." I swallow hard. "Sorry, I can get out of your way. I was just trying to help."

"Oh no, you don't have to leave. I'm just here to grab him a few things." Anastasia sets her purse on the couch, then moves past the stain and down the hall. I don't miss the way she avoids looking down at it as she walks past it. Definitely can't blame her there. It hurts me to see it, and I don't have any personal ties to him.

Unsure what else to do, I drop down and start blotting at the peroxide I'd put on the carpet. The blood saturates the cloth as I dab at it. Now that I know it works, I saturate even more of the stain. If it keeps this up, most of the blood will be gone. A bit of relief surges through me.

So the peroxide can set, I wash my hands, then step into the doorway of the bedroom. Anastasia is packing a black duffel bag as she hums happily, moving around the space as if she lives here, too.

Does she?

"So, is he going to be home soon?" I ask.

"Doctor said maybe tomorrow. Though if it were up to me, he'd be staying until he was completely healed. Stubborn men, am I right?" She hoists the duffel bag up, then turns to face me. Standing this close to her, I can see a fresh scar on the side of her cheek. A puckered, red line that spans from nearly the corner of her mouth back toward her jaw.

His words from that night come back to me. *"Help. Her."*

Is this the "her"?

"Thanks so much for cleaning that up," Anastasia says. "I tried, but didn't have much luck."

"Hydrogen peroxide is the trick," I tell her.

She shivers. "Let's hope I don't have to remember that. Seriously, though. Thank you, Katelyn."

"It's the least I could do. I did put him back in the hospital."

Anastasia smiles softly. "It was a total accident. Water under the bridge. You have to come by the coffee shop. Let me treat you to a coffee and a muffin as a thank you."

Now I smile, appreciating her kindness. I'm not sure I would have known what to do if I found a strange woman in my boyfriend's apartment, but Anastasia doesn't seem like the jealous type. *Whew.* Let's just add drama to the list of things I've had enough of in my life. "That's really not necessary, but thank you."

"It's *absolutely* necessary. I'll see you tomorrow?"

I swallow hard. "Uh, sure. Maybe."

"Great." Anastasia smiles again, then reaches into her pocket and withdraws a set of keys. After working a silver one off, she offers it to me. "Here's the key. Can you lock it up for me? I need to get this over to him, then get back to the shop to get everything ready for tomorrow. Nothing like being the owner and only employee."

"Uh, sure." I take the key.

"Great. Thanks. And, Katelyn?"

"Yeah?"

"Don't beat yourself up over the pepper spray. Garrison's the most understanding guy in the world, and he's not at all upset."

"I do feel guilty, but thanks for saying that."

"Anytime. See you tomorrow at the coffee shop!" she calls out as she leaves me standing in the apartment. I stare down at the key in my hand. Who would give a stranger a key to her apartment? Do I just have that *"I won't steal anything"* face?

Turning, I survey the place. It's decorated plainly but organized, and a black leather-bound Bible sits on the coffee table. There are no pictures on the walls, but there are mix-matched frames on various shelves of the bookcase.

Before I study those closer, though, I do another round of cleaning on the stain, then wash my hands. After drying them on a towel, I cross over to the shelves to get a closer look at what things a man like Garrison Holt would put on display.

Random books, ranging from non-fiction to fiction, line the shelves, but it's the pictures that really capture my attention. Garrison wearing a military uniform, standing in front of a bunch of small children. There's a little girl in his arms, and she's laughing and looking up at him like he's her entire world.

Honestly, they're all looking at him like that.

Then there's a photo of him standing in front of a group of teenagers outside the community center. He's smiling widely, and each of them—even the ones you can tell are trying to fight it—has a grin on their face.

Is that who Garrison Holt is?

A man who loves working with children?

A man who does good in a world riddled with evil?

Swallowing hard, I turn away and head back toward the stain. *Stay focused, Katelyn.* The guy wouldn't want me going through his stuff, and neither would his incredibly sweet girlfriend.

So, even though I would love to know more, I focus only on what I came here to do—make things easier for him when he comes home.

By the time I get back to my apartment, I'm exhausted. My arms are sore from scrubbing, but I'm more than happy with the results. I'll check back in tomorrow morning before my shift, but I was able to get most of the stain up, leaving only a dark shadow.

Thomas is sitting at our small dining room table, math book open, with an apple in his hand. He glances up at me. "That was a while."

"I cleaned up the blood." I throw the now-empty bottle of hydrogen peroxide into the trash and add it to the running grocery list pinned to the refrigerator.

"That was nice. You okay?"

"I am." I smile at him, forcing the exhaustion down. "How are you doing?"

"Fine. Almost done."

"Yeah?" Joy warms my chest. He's been working so hard to get settled in this new school, and I know keeping his grades up has been a struggle since even before our world was turned upside down. With them falling the way they have lately, seeing him actually put forth effort makes me happier than I can say.

"I can't go to baseball camp if I don't get my grades up." He grins at me. "That's fueling my motivation."

My stomach plummets because financially? I'm not entirely sure how I'm going to swing the cost of the five-day baseball camp he wants to go to over spring break in just over a month, but I know he's desperate to go. "It's a good motivation to have," I reply as I head into the kitchen for a glass of water. Hopefully, the liquid will ease my dry throat.

How am I going to afford four hundred dollars? The payment is due in less than two weeks, so I'd better figure it out soon. Maybe I can find out if anyone else in town is hiring. Another job won't hurt. Who needs sleep?

He writes something down on his paper, then closes the binder and math book. After stretching, he grabs both and stands. "I'm going to head to bed. Practice starts first thing in the morning."

"You said you need to be at the school by six?"

"Yeah. I can walk if I need to. I know it's early."

"Absolutely not," I reply. "It's not early at all. I am so excited for you, sweetie."

"Thanks, Mom." He smiles at me, a wide, bright smile that intensifies the fear in my heart. Because if he knew just how impossible it's going to be for the camp, uniform, and equipment, I know he'd give up on his dream to play baseball.

"You're welcome. See you in the morning."

"See you in the morning. Love you, Mom." He kisses me on the cheek.

"I love you, too, honey. See you in the morning."

With one final smile, he heads into his bedroom and closes the door.

As soon as I'm alone, I wrap both arms around myself and struggle to keep my emotions in check as I fight the horrible thoughts that we were better off before.

We weren't.

Financially, we had it all. A house far too big for three

people, a fully stocked refrigerator, a private chef, three maids…but physically? Mentally? We were drowning. It was only a matter of time before Victor put his hands on Thomas or did to me in front of our son what he already did in private.

The fists weren't worth the financial stability that came with them. Even if it means I get another job, I'll do it. Whatever it takes to make sure my son has everything he needs. That he *never* feels the absence of a man who never even wanted to be a father and certainly didn't let me forget it.

After turning off the lights to the kitchen, I head into the living room and remove the couch cushions to pull out my bed. That way, it's ready as soon as I'm out of the shower.

God's got this, I remind myself. He'll show me the path, and everything will be fine. But deep down, those thoughts that I'm not good enough for God, my son—for anything—threaten to drown me.

CHAPTER 4

GARRISON

"Remember what the good doctor said," Sawyer says. "Absolutely no heavy lifting." He sets my bag down on the floor just inside my apartment as both Ryker and Weston—the other two members of my team—lurk just behind me as if I'll take a fatal fall at any moment.

Granted, considering my luck lately, that doesn't seem like too far of a reach.

"Yeah, I've got it. I'll be fine." My mood has been sour since I woke up this morning, though I'm attributing that to the lack of sleep as the nurses came in to check my vitals every hour or so. To say I'm relieved to be home—again—is an understatement.

At least, the place smells better. Seems the pepper spray faded away while I was gone. Likely because I'd completely forgotten to close the door. I'll have to thank

Anastasia for locking up for me when I see her next. She'd dropped my bag off during the only small window of actual sleep I'd gotten last night.

"Elijah will be here tomorrow morning to do a security install," Ryker tells me.

Elijah Breeth, a former Army Ranger who now works in private security, designed a system that his company, Knight Security, uses exclusively. Even though they're based out of Maine instead of South Carolina, he'll be able to monitor all our security systems remotely and alert us if there's an issue.

Me nearly bleeding to death on my floor prompted us to beef up security all the way around. Though, I seriously doubt we'll face another issue like what landed me in the hospital the first time. Especially since we no longer do shadow work for the government.

Still, if it weren't for Katelyn, I wouldn't have survived, and that's enough to have us installing systems everywhere that matters. On our homes and the homes of Zane's mother, Linda, and his sister, Anastasia.

Katelyn. She was another reason I couldn't sleep last night. Anytime I tried to close my eyes, I'd see her haunted eyes in my mind.

There's pain there. And a lot of it.

Who put it there?

How can I help her move past it?

Easy there, Holt. She's not a client. Even as I try to correct myself, though, the desire to help her lingers. But

Katelyn is not a troubled teenager weighted down by a changing world. She's a woman. A mother. Two things I know nothing about.

"Apartment's clear," Weston announces as he comes down my hall. I glance over toward him, and my gaze lands on the area where I nearly bled to death—only to find the blood stain nearly gone.

It's then I also realize that the glass I broke in the kitchen is also gone.

"Who cleaned up?" I question.

"Anastasia said that your pretty neighbor was here when she came to get your stuff." Sawyer wiggles his eyebrows. "Okay, I added the pretty part."

"Katelyn?" I question.

Sawyer nods.

"Wow. She didn't need to do that." I study the stain. What was once an obvious reminder of the night that nearly claimed my life is now little more than a subtle shadow. How long had it taken for her to clean that up?

"She probably felt guilty for pepper-spraying you," Weston comments as he crosses his arms and leans back against the counter. His sharp tone holds no hint of a joke. Which is not surprising. Of all of us, Weston struggles the most with forgiving. Something that likely has a lot to do with his dad abandoning them after Weston's sister had been murdered. It tore their family apart and pulled both Weston and his mother away from their faith in God.

She has since found her way back, but Weston hasn't occupied a pew since the day they buried his sister.

"I think it's great you have a neighbor so willing to rush into danger for you. Plus, she's gorgeous. My neighbor is seventy-two and yells at me for breathing too loud when I unlock my door," Sawyer comments dryly.

Ryker snorts.

"Seriously, though. And I do *not* breathe loud. Being silent was in my job description."

A sort of grieving silence falls on the room at his words. Transitioning out of the military is rough on everyone, but we weren't even granted that opportunity. After being blackmailed into working for a branch of the government that doesn't exist on paper, the rug was ripped out from under us when we were handed our service record DD214's and a "Thank you for your service," before being shown the door.

Don't get me wrong, we're all beyond grateful to be granted the opportunity at normal lives, but the transition has been hard. We went from having a clear purpose to planning futures we weren't sure we'd have.

Of all of us, Zane is handling it the best. Though I have a feeling that has a lot to do with his new wife and their sailing trip around the world.

"You want to head over to the diner for dinner?" Weston questions. "I can bring you back here before I head to the ranch."

"Nah. I think I want to just stay in."

"You've got it. Anastasia went grocery shopping this morning," he says. "Your fridge should be stocked with some quick meals. Call if you need anything, and don't leave the door unlocked. Can't have you getting pepper sprayed again. Doc says your lung can't take much more."

"Thanks for the reminder," I retort as I slowly lower myself down onto the couch. It may be two weeks old, but the knife wound in my side still feels fresh. Though that could have a whole lot to do with the fact that I pulled it so badly yesterday. It's a miracle I didn't tear anything open.

The moment I'm resting back against the couch, my muscles go completely limp. Exhaustion tugs at my senses, and I yawn.

"We'll get out of your hair. Are you sure you're okay if I head home and grab some things? I won't be gone long."

I nod. "I'll be fine. SEAL of honor," I add, holding up my hand.

Sawyer rolls his eyes. "You'll never make that a saying."

"One day, all the kids will be saying it."

Ryker chuckles as he heads for the door. "I'm off tonight, so if you need something, let me know."

"Thanks, Tank. I will."

He nods, then slips out into the hall. Weston and Sawyer both offer me waves before following him out. Before I even have the chance to pull myself up to lock it, I can hear the faint scrape of a key being slid into the lock moments before it turns on this side.

Alone at last, secured in my apartment, I take a deep breath and let the silence sink into my mind. It's the first time I've been alone in weeks. Sure, there were those couple of blissful hours before I ended up back in the hospital, but even then, I was haunted by the blood staining the floor. By the image of the man I killed, lying dead on the carpet just beyond it.

Now, thanks to Katelyn, even that's gone. I have to find a way to make it up to her. Maybe flowers? Or are those too romantic? When I'm on my feet, I could make her a lasagna and take it over for her and her son.

Or is that too suggestive, too?

With another yawn, I close my eyes and settle further, sinking into the couch as best I can. All while images of Katelyn play through my mind. Someday, I'll find a way to thank her for cleaning up my apartment.

One way or another.

Subtle scraping pulls me out of sleep. Before I'm even fully awake, the adrenaline is already surging through my system. I reach beneath the cushion of my couch for the knife I keep there, then pull it out and get to my feet. As I do, I move toward the door, keeping enough distance that I can pull back if it's Anastasia, Sawyer, or someone else coming to check in on me, but close enough that I can use the element of surprise if it's an unwanted guest.

Though the latter is highly unlikely since they caught the guys who tried to kill me the first time.

Still, the fight or flight in me is heavily weighted toward fight, so I wait.

Lord, please grant me calm.

The door swings open, and through the dim light from the hallway just outside the door, I can make out a soft, feminine figure.

"Hello?" she calls out.

I flip the lamp beside me, bathing the room in light as I hide the knife behind my back. "Hey." The adrenaline already waning, my movements are slow. Jarred.

Katelyn blinks rapidly, her hazel eyes adjusting to the flood of light. Seconds later, her cheeks turn a gorgeous shade of crimson. "I am *so* sorry. I knocked, and no one answered. Your girlfriend left me with a key, so I wanted to come and leave you some of these since I figured you probably wouldn't be making meals anytime soon." She holds up a few aluminum trays stacked on top of each other.

"No need to apologize, come on in." As soon as she walks farther inside, I tuck the knife behind my television and follow her into the kitchen, one arm banded around my waist to apply slight pressure to my still-healing wound.

The clock says I've only been asleep about forty-five minutes, which means Sawyer is due here any minute.

"I really am so sorry. I keep barging in here like I own the place, and that's not me. I wasn't sure you'd be home yet, and I wanted to make sure that you came home to food.

Though I imagine Anastasia is taking care of you. Wow, I feel like a fool." She laughs nervously and sets the trays down on my counter. The color of her cheeks deepens, and I'm momentarily struck mute at the sight of her.

My chest tightens, heart pounding.

What is happening to me?

And then her earlier reference to a girlfriend hits me. "Anastasia? I don't have a girlfriend."

Katelyn's cheeks turn a deep shade of crimson. "I just assumed—wow, I am making the worst third impression ever." She holds out her hand. "Katelyn Ellis. I know we've already met, but maybe a do-over will help us both sleep better at night. Or, at least, it'll help me."

"Garrison Holt." I grin as I take her hand, enjoying the way mine envelopes her much smaller one. The touch feels warm. But it's more than that. There's a part of me that relaxes the moment we make contact. As though my soul recognizes that she's important.

I shake it off. That kind of stuff doesn't exist in real life…does it?

Withdrawing my hand, I plant it firmly on my counter as she stares back at me. "So, uh, what did you bring me?"

"Oh! Right." She starts unstacking the trays and setting them side by side on the counter. "Um, sausage, egg, and cheese biscuits. You can keep them in the freezer and pull them out one at a time for breakfast. Thomas loves them, so I brought you about a dozen of them. Then there's frozen burritos—bean and cheese."

She lifts the lid to one of the trays, revealing parchment paper-wrapped food stored in a freezer bag.

"Then, in this tray, I have a few freezer bags of meals I prepared. Teriyaki chicken and white chicken chili. Though, I just realized you may not have a crockpot to cook them in."

"I have a crockpot."

"You do?" She arches a brow, clearly surprised.

"Yeah. It's saved me from having to get takeout more than once."

She smiles, and it's like a hit to my gut because, while that haunted look is still there, her hazel eyes shimmer with relief. "Good. I know it's not much, but I wanted to help out. Especially since, well, you know."

"This is amazing. You have no idea." I smile back, and our gazes hold.

There's no way for me to even put into words the tension between us, but it's there. A delicate weight that feels so unbelievably right and is unlike anything I've felt before.

"Well, I'm glad."

"You really didn't have to do this, though." I start to run a hand over the back of my neck, only to be reminded by a sharp stabbing pain that lifting my arms is still not a great idea. Slowly, I lower it back down, hoping she doesn't take notice of my pain. "Oh, and thanks for cleaning up my floor. You really didn't have to do that, either."

"I don't mind. I've gotten good at cleaning up—" Her

eyes go wide, and she laughs awkwardly. "Messes. I'm good at cleaning up messes."

But I can read between the lines.

And as soon as she speaks those words, the haunted look becomes clear.

It's a look I've seen in the eyes of more kids than I care to count. That mask worn to hide fear. Pain.

Abuse.

Anger slips into my mind, momentarily blocking out anything else. Who hurt her? Is that why she's here in Stormwatch Landing? Is he locked up? Did she run?

Easy, Holt. That's not how you get answers.

I force that anger back down and take a deep breath. "Well, I appreciate it more than I can say. I was actually thinking about bringing you dinner. Maybe when I'm back on my feet, I can cook for you and your son."

"That's not necessary." She waves her hand in dismissal.

"Please. It's the least I can do. You did save my life, then cleaned up my apartment."

"After I nearly cost you your life. I'd say we're even." She smiles, but it doesn't reach her eyes.

"Please. I insist. I make a mean lasagna. It'll be a rain check for when I can actually stand that long, but I really would love to."

Katelyn draws her bottom lip into her mouth and chews on it, a move that has my body reacting in a way I would really rather ignore. *Keep it together, Holt.*

"You know what, sure. But just a heads up, Thomas will be prepared to ask you a million questions about your time in the military. Apparently, all the kids talk about it at school. You and your friends are local legends."

I laugh because I've heard the rumors. It's hard not to when most of those kids come hang out at the community center after school. I've even met Thomas a time or two. "Yeah, well, I can set some of those rumors to rest."

"You weren't actually a Navy SEAL?"

"No, I am."

She cocks her head to the side. "Are you still enlisted?"

"Once a SEAL, always a SEAL," I reply, feeling that familiar pang in my gut. I love my life now, and what I do makes a difference, but I always thought I'd get to retire as a soldier. Even though I've technically been out for six years, it still felt like I was enlisted until we were officially released two weeks ago.

"Got it." Katelyn offers me another smile. "Well, I'd better get going. I need to make sure Thomas is ready for bed." She starts toward the door, but I step in front of her.

The way she recoils confirms my suspicions, and guilt immediately snakes through me. "Sorry." I move out of the way without hesitation, putting distance between us so she doesn't feel caged in. "I just wanted to say thanks. For everything. You've done so much for me, and we don't even know each other."

"Kindness doesn't need familiarity," she replies. "I wanted to help, so I did. Goodnight, Garrison."

"Goodnight, Katelyn."

She heads toward the door and slips out. After crossing over, I open it and lean out, watching as she disappears into her place. Only when she's inside do I close and lock the door. As I head back into the kitchen to rinse dishes, I note that the spare key I'd given to Anastasia for emergencies is sitting on the counter beside the trays of food. Even though I know it's foolish, there's a part of me that wishes Katelyn had taken it with her.

CHAPTER 5

KATELYN

As I push into the bustling coffee shop, my nerves are at an all-time high. I'd prayed about it last night, though, and this place popped into my mind. And after walking past it three different times this morning, I finally have the courage to come inside.

She'd offered me a coffee, but I'm coming here for a job.

Heart in my throat, I move up to the counter. Anastasia is smiling and taking the order of someone in line. There's a thin coat of sweat on her forehead, but she doesn't look the least bit overwhelmed despite there not being a second barista working alongside her.

That's good, right? Is that why You wanted me here, Lord? Because she needs help?

Anastasia's gaze lands on mine, and her grin widens. "Hey, Katelyn! Give me just a second." She takes payment then starts prepping the order. All while another five customers remain in line.

"Need a hand?" I ask.

She laughs softly. "If you are open to working the register, I'll owe you a lot more than a coffee," she replies.

"I can do that. I worked at a coffee shop all through college. So I can help with whatever you need." I move around the counter and wash my hands in the tiny employees-only sink just inside the room.

"Seriously?" Anastasia asks. "What perfect timing!" After embracing me quickly, she tops two paper cups with foam, then puts lids on top. "You grab the next order, and I'll get prepping it."

"You've got it." The anxiety eases as I step up to the register. *Maybe I won't have to beg her for a second job after all.* "What can I get for you?"

"A lavender honey latte, please," the woman replies. "Hey, I've seen you at the diner, right?"

"You have," I reply with a friendly smile. "That will be four-seventy-five."

The woman holds up a card and taps it to the reader.

"Thanks so much. We'll get right on that."

"Thank you so much!" she says happily, then moves down the counter to wait.

I glance over at Anastasia, who is already working on the latte, happily humming as she works. So, I turn back to the next customer, an aging man I've never seen before. "What can I get you?"

"A black coffee and a caramel macchiato with nonfat milk."

I ring him up, seriously hoping that Anastasia's comment yesterday about being the only employee was the cry for help I took it as. "You've got it."

"You saved me today," Anastasia says as she drops down in a chair and slides a muffin toward me. "Thank you, thank you, thank you."

I smile. "You are so welcome." I could honestly see being friends with someone like Anastasia. She's unbelievably kind and seems to carry this air of positivity around her. A light that cannot be stifled. Which is something I can seriously appreciate after spending so many years in the dark.

"So, I owe you a lot more than a coffee. And as soon as I get to my feet, I will make good on that." She yawns.

"Actually," I start, then clear my throat as I shift my gaze down to the muffin I've yet to touch. "Maybe we can consider today a trial run."

Anastasia turns to me, expression curious. "A trial run?"

You're in it now, Katelyn. Finish it out. "Sure. I'm working nights at the diner right now, but I'm looking for a job during the day. If you'd like an extra set of hands, I can—"

"You're hired." Anastasia slaps her hand on the table.

I jump, my heart racing. *Not in danger,* I remind myself as I take a deep breath. Most days, my fight or flight is weighted heavily in flight. Today seems to be no different.

"Sorry," Anastasia says with a laugh. "I'm just super excited. I was literally praying during prep this morning because my second set of hands had the audacity to move away last week, and I was about to start interviewing. Instead of letting me go through that nightmare, God sent me you." She beams at me as she gets to her feet, leaving me sitting there shocked.

Was it seriously that easy?

Did that just happen?

I'd prayed about the job, and this place popped into my mind.

She prayed for help, and I showed up.

I can't help but smile at the way God works. *Thank You, Lord.* I don't deserve it, but that doesn't stop Him from delivering me more blessings than I know what to do with.

Anastasia returns with a short stack of papers. As she takes her seat, she slides them over to me. "This is my standard employment contract with a background check."

Background check.

I take a deep breath.

Every time my name is run through the system, it's a risk. But I had to do it for the diner, and that ended up being okay. So, *have faith, Katelyn.* "You won't regret this. I promise."

"I know I won't." Anastasia smiles. "So are there any days you can't work?"

I shake my head. "Whenever you need me. I can get you my schedule at the diner; those days I'll need to leave by three to make it there by my shift at four-thirty."

"That won't be a problem at all," Anastasia replies. "We're typically slow in the afternoon, and I close at five every day. This is going to work out perfectly. God is so good." She claps her hands together and does a little dance in her seat.

"He is," I reply, feeling a bit of the weight settle off of my shoulders.

"I'll include today's pay in your check. I pay weekly on Fridays, and we split tips fifty-fifty when we're both on shift. Days where it's just you, you get one hundred percent, and same for me. Does that work for you?"

"That's perfect."

"Sweet!" Anastasia claps her hands together again. Her cell rings, so she pulls it out and checks it, her grin spreading. "Just a second." After answering it, she presses it to her ear and stands. "Hey, honey, how is your day?"

The bell above the door dings, and a man walks in, his expression neutral. When he sees me, he smiles, and it's when that smile reaches his caramel-colored eyes that recognition kicks in. I passed him when I left Garrison's hospital room two days ago.

"Hey, you're the pepper spray lady, right?"

Ouch. Not a nickname I wanted to stick. "Katelyn," I

reply as I get to my feet and move behind the counter. I'm not entirely sure I'm officially on shift today, but since Anastasia still hasn't come out of the back room, I figure it can't hurt to continue to prove my worth to her.

I need this job more than I need oxygen these days.

"I'm Sawyer," he says and offers me his hand.

Another one of the SEALs Thomas was talking about. Even if Thomas hadn't mentioned that one of Garrison's team members had been at the hospital, I would have called this guy as being one of them.

He towers over my five-foot-four height and is built like a soldier, just like Garrison. His bronze hair is cut short, and a black t-shirt stretches over broad shoulders. A pair of grease-smeared coveralls is folded down to his waist, though his hands have been scrubbed clean. "It's nice to meet you." Even though the contact of a man—any man—makes my stomach twist into nervous knots, I accept the handshake. "Garrison's friend, right?"

"His best friend," he replies, leaning in. "Some may argue that, but don't let them fool you." He pulls back his hand.

His charm disarms my frayed nervous system just enough that my smile isn't forced. "What can I get you?" I move around the counter toward the register.

Sawyer's gaze narrows slightly, but not in an untrusting way. More surprise. "Where is Anastasia?"

"On the phone. She hired me this morning."

"Good. She could use the extra hands. Um, I'll just take a black coffee," he replies.

"You've got it." I ring it up. "Seventy-five cents."

He offers me a five.

I make the change then hand it back to him, but he just shoves it into the tip jar, his gaze shifting over toward where Anastasia is standing on the phone. Her back is to us, but her body language is stiff. And if there's one thing I am better at than cleaning up blood, it's reading body language.

It's a skill one develops when they're forced to walk on eggshells.

Whoever she's on the phone with is not making her happy.

I pour Sawyer's coffee, then offer it to him, but he doesn't move. If Anastasia's body language is angry, his is just as serious. He's tense, as though he wants to rush over and rip the phone away to erase whatever is making her upset.

If I'd thought she and Garrison were an item before, I wouldn't have believed it anymore after seeing the way Sawyer watches her. Like a man focused on a priceless treasure.

Does she see it? Are they an item?

She hangs up the phone and turns toward us. When she sees Sawyer, her expression shifts so quickly that I nearly miss it. Unfortunately, I'm all too educated in what a mask looks like. Which is exactly what Anastasia slips into place when the smile replaces her frown.

"Hey, how's it going?"

"What's wrong?" Sawyer asks, setting his coffee aside and stepping forward.

"Nothing."

"Don't lie to me. What's wrong?"

Anastasia sighs. "Jack was supposed to come into town this weekend, but he just cancelled. Apparently, something came up with work." Her disappointment hangs heavy in the air around her.

"Sorry to hear that," Sawyer replies, lifting his coffee.

"You are not," Anastasia replies playfully. "You don't like him." She turns to me. "Jack is my boyfriend. He's an FBI agent out of Savannah, Georgia. We've been doing the long-distance thing for a couple of weeks now."

Ouch. The grin on Sawyer's face is so fake it makes my heart hurt for him. "Long-distance is hard."

"It is," she replies with a sigh. "And it's even harder when my friends don't like him," she adds, poking Sawyer in the chest with her finger.

Does she really not see that he cares about her?

"I never said I didn't like him. I just don't think he's good enough for you."

She laughs. "All of you have made it painfully obvious that no one will ever be good enough for me." Anastasia heads over behind the counter and washes her hands.

Sawyer's gaze lingers on her far longer than a friend's

would. "I'm headed back to work, but I'll catch you later?" he asks. "Dinner at Momma Knox's place?"

"Since she's *my* mom, I'll be there!" Anastasia calls out.

Sawyer turns toward me with a friendly smile that doesn't quite reach his eyes this time. "It was nice to see you again, Katelyn. I'll see you around."

"Yeah, see you around." I offer him a wave before he turns to leave.

As soon as the door closes, I turn back to Anastasia. "Do you need me to stick around today?"

"Nope. But if you can get that all filled out and be here for a shift tomorrow morning, that would be great."

"I can do that. What time?"

"Does seven work?"

"Seven is perfect."

"Great. I can typically handle the super early morning solo, but things pick up around then, and well—" She gestures toward the room. "You saw how that worked out for me today."

"I did." I smile, enjoying the way the oxygen fills my lungs fully for the first time in I don't know how long. "Thanks again for this. I cannot tell you how much I appreciate it."

"The gratitude comes on both sides, trust me. Oh, hey, the diner is closed tonight, right?"

"It is," I reply. "They're closing after lunch for some remodeling."

"Great. Then you're free for dinner?"

"Dinner?" I stare back at her like she just asked me to walk on the moon.

"Yeah. My mom does this weekly dinner, and there's always *so* much. Think you and your son can join us?"

"Oh, I—"

"I insist," Anastasia replies. "Jack was going to come, but since he's not going to be there, you can be my plus two." She beams at me. "I think she's making enchiladas, and they are seriously the best."

"I don't—"

"I won't take no for an answer." She withdraws her phone and pushes it at me. "Put your number in, and I'll text you the address. We're eating at six, but you can show up anytime after five."

I stare down at her phone, trying to decide what a legitimate excuse is not to go. I've worked hard to keep all attachments to a minimum. That way, should I need to cut and run, no one remembers me well enough to care that I'm gone.

But when no excuse comes to mind, I enter my phone number, save the contact, then hand it back to Anastasia, who shoves it into her pocket with a smile.

"Can we bring anything?"

"Just yourselves," Anastasia replies.

The bell dings overhead as three women walk into the café, all of them talking happily.

"I'll see you later, okay?"

"Yeah, okay."

Anastasia offers me a wave before taking the new orders, so I grab my stack of papers, purse, sweater, and head out the door, my mind reeling on all that's happened already. I mean, it's not even ten in the morning, and I have a job and a family dinner invitation.

A slow smile spreads over my face as I start toward the diner to help with a quick, short shift before they close the doors for the day. The sun is bright overhead, and the salty sea air hits my lungs just as it does every time I step outside. Somehow, though, today feels different—happier.

Hopeful.

Like maybe, just maybe, this could be a turning point for my life.

CHAPTER 6

GARRISON

"All done," Elijah says as he steps back from the alarm system panel he just finished installing. Complete with window and door sensors, as well as a hidden exterior security camera, my apartment is locked down tight—so long as I actually remember to arm it. Either way, this will send an alert straight to Knight Security, who will then patch it through to our entire team here.

Safety first.

"Looks a bit complicated." Personally, I've always been better with detonators than computers, though I can make my way through basic tasks.

Plus, I do love a good spreadsheet.

"It's not too bad," Elijah replies as he finishes putting his tools away, then closes up the box the system came in. "Now, I set the door and window sensors to silent, so they won't sound unless you arm the system. If you like, I can show you how to change that so they ding every time it opens. Personally, I didn't start using those until Charlie started walking. Now, they're nice," he adds with a laugh.

"I'm good with silence," I reply.

"I thought you might be." Elijah taps on the screen. "To arm it, all you have to do is press this blue button here at the bottom. That will lock down the system and activate the motion sensor on your door. To disarm, you tap the same button, then type in your code. That'll disarm the system before any alerts are sent."

"What will the motion sensor pick up? I'd hate for you guys to get alerts anytime someone walks by the door."

"Thought about that, too," he replies with a grin. "The only time it will go off is if someone tries to access your door directly. I might have hidden it across the hall so I could angle it on just your door. That way, there won't be any late-night walk-throughs sounding a security alarm. Now, the alarm itself is silent. You'll get an alert on your phone, but it won't make any loud noises."

"I appreciate that, too."

"I don't do it for every system, but with your military history, having any kind of shrill panic alarm can cause more harm than good." His gaze darkens a moment, and I remember that Elijah carries his own PTSD scars.

"Thanks so much for this," I tell him.

"Not a problem at all. I already put one up at Mrs. Knox's place and handled the coffee shop. I've got

Sawyer's shop next, then Ryker's apartment. After that, I'm headed back to Hope Springs."

"You sure you don't want to stick around for dinner? I know Linda would love to have you."

"I appreciate the offer, but I miss Andie and Charlie already," he grins. "Stupid in love, that's what I am."

"I don't consider that stupid at all," I reply. "And if you change your mind, you're more than welcome."

Elijah zips the large suitcase containing the rest of the alarm systems, then shoulders his bag of tools. "It's good to see you, Holt. Call if you need anything."

"Good to see you, too. And you be sure to do the same."

He offers me one final wave, then leaves the apartment, closing the door behind him. I flip the lock and stare at the security panel. I never thought I'd have one in my place. Ever. And, to be honest, if Elijah hadn't installed it, I doubt I ever would have agreed.

I haven't known Elijah long, but he and the other guys of Knight Security have become close friends ever since Dylan Hunt introduced all of us. We're spread out all over the country, with Knight Security being in Maine and the Hunts in Texas, but we manage to stay in touch.

It helps having other veterans to talk to. Others who know what it's like to go from having your day planned out for you to being thrust into civilian life. Something that has been a major adjustment for everyone on my team.

After downing some water and taking some Advil, I

head down the hall toward my room. The blackout curtains are already drawn, so I set an alarm to make sure I get up with enough time to shower before Sawyer picks me up for dinner at Linda's, then climb beneath the covers and close my eyes.

I've never been much of a napper, but apparently two near-death experiences in as many weeks will drain the energy right out of a person.

***

"Garrison Holt, you shaved ten years off of my life," Linda Knox scolds, her hands on her hips, as I walk into her house alongside Sawyer. As usual, she's wearing an apron covered in random chickens—a gift from Sawyer last Christmas, and her silver hair is pulled back in a loose bun.

"That's what I told him!" Sawyer exclaims as he kisses Linda on the cheek.

"Well, it's the truth." Her expression softens, gaze full of worry. "How are you, sweetie?" She pulls me in for a soft hug, which I happily return before kissing her on the top of the head and stepping back.

"I've been worse," I reply, then take a deep breath. Well, as deep as I can, since my lungs still burn once I hit a certain oxygen level. "What are you making? It smells delicious."

"Enchiladas and Spanish rice."

I grin at her. "My favorites."

"Absolutely," she replies. "Come on in; have a seat." Linda affectionately ushers me in and gently pushes me into the kitchen where Ryker is currently topping an apple pie with brown sugar crumbles and Weston is stirring something on the stove.

Both men glance over and offer me nods.

"What can I do?" Sawyer asks, clapping his hands together.

As Linda puts him to work, I glance around the small home. It's one half of a duplex that Linda bought after selling the home Anastasia and Zane grew up in. Since their father passed away when they were young, she'd said the house felt too empty once her kids were grown.

Still, this home has all the love Linda raised both her children with. It's no wonder her son is the best man I've ever known, and her daughter is one of the kindest souls to walk this earth. Genuine, happy people who do everything they can to show the love of Jesus to everyone they meet.

Honestly, she reminds me so much of the aunt who raised me that sometimes the all-too-familiar grief surfaces whenever I think of her. She'd been my lifeline in a time when I was ready to lie down and never get up.

There's a soft knock at the door, and before Linda can pull away from what she's showing Sawyer, I'm on my feet.

"I've got it."

"No, honey, you sit." Linda starts toward me, but I wave her off with a smile.

"I've got it, Momma Knox. Promise." With one more smile, I start down the small hall from the kitchen into the living room, then pull the door open.

When I see the petite woman on the other side, surprise and delight rush through me like a tidal wave. "Katelyn, what are you doing here?" I ask, looking between her and a smiling Thomas.

She seems just as shocked to find me here as I am to see her. That is if her wide eyes and flushed cheeks are any indication. "Oh, uh—Anastasia invited me," she stammers. "How are you feeling?"

"Who is it?" Linda comes up on my side before I get the chance to respond. "Oh! You must be Katelyn. Anastasia told me you were coming. Come in, come in!"

I step aside as Linda ushers them in.

"This is my son, Thomas." Katelyn gestures to Thomas.

"Thank you for having us, Mrs. Knox," Thomas says, offering her his hand.

"You both can call me Momma Knox," she replies with a grin. "Everyone else does. Come on in and have a seat. Do you want some sweet tea?" As she ushers Thomas off into the house, I shove both hands into my pockets.

"I seem to keep surprising you," Katelyn tells me with a smile.

Isn't that the truth? "I like surprises. Most of the time," I add quickly, then fall into step beside her as she follows the same route as Linda and Thomas.

We emerge in the kitchen, and Sawyer glances up and offers Katelyn a smile. "Hey, Pepper, it's good to see you."

Linda slaps him on the arm. "You do *not* call her that."

To my absolute delight, Katelyn laughs softly. "It's okay. Less than what I deserve after the damage I caused."

"Oh hush, it was an accident," Linda brushes it off.

Weston's expression tightens, but he finishes drying his hands and offers one to Katelyn. "Weston Hayes," he says.

"Katelyn Ellis. This is my son Thomas."

"We met," Weston replies with a partial smile. "Basketball last week."

"Ryker Granger," Ryker introduces himself.

"It's nice to meet you both," Katelyn says softly.

"These are the other guys I was telling you about, Mom," Thomas says, his smile wide as he practically bounces from foot to foot.

His excitement makes me grin.

"Oh? We were talked about?" Sawyer questions.

"Briefly," Katelyn replies as she shoots me an embarrassed smile. "After we got back from the hospital, Thomas told me that you guys were all SEALs. Apparently, you all have quite a fan club."

"I always did like being popular." Sawyer winks. "Guac is done!"

The front door opens, and a few moments later, Anastasia comes in, a beaming smile on her face. "Hello, everyone. You must be Katelyn's son," she says, offering Thomas a handshake.

The teen's cheeks flush as he takes her hand. "Uh, yeah, Thomas." He clears his throat. "Nice to meet you, ma'am." I fight my own smile as I note the not-so-subtle signs of a swiftly-developing crush.

I quickly glance at Sawyer, amused to see him hiding a grin.

"Please. Just Anastasia." She shrugs out of her light jacket and hangs it on the back of a chair before crossing over to give her mom a hug and kiss. "It smells amazing, Momma."

"Thanks, Babygirl. Why don't you get some sweet tea and have a seat? We're ready to eat."

As it always does, Sawyer's gaze lingers on Anastasia. That is until he realizes I've noticed. Then his smooth smile slips into place, erasing the longing that had been there only a heartbeat before.

"So, Katelyn, what's it like living next to Garrison? He a noisy neighbor?" He takes a seat right beside her, with Thomas on her other side. I take a seat beside him while Ryker and Weston help Linda place the food in the center of the table.

"Actually, we'd never even officially met until after I—"

"Pepper-sprayed him," Thomas interrupts.

Her cheeks flush. "Yes. Exactly. We seem to keep different hours." Her gaze momentarily shifts to me before turning back toward the others.

The grin Sawyer directs at me is evidence enough that

I'm wearing my feelings on my sleeve. *I'll be hearing about that later, for sure.*

"So tell us, what brought you to Stormwatch Landing?" Linda asks. "You both moved here recently, right?"

At her question, the light in Katelyn's eyes fades just a bit. "We've been trying to find a place to call home for quite some time." She wraps an arm around Thomas, who, for the first time since they arrived, keeps his eyes downcast, his mood falling just a bit.

"You've moved around a lot? That must have been hard," Anastasia offers.

"It has been," Katelyn replies. "But as long as we have each other, that's all that matters."

Thomas smiles up at his mom, but it doesn't reach his eyes. There's pain there, too—and it hurts me to see it.

"I love that." Linda's own smile is a bit softer now, and I imagine it's because she's likely picking up on the tension rolling off the two guests in waves. Secrets buried don't just linger silently; they fester, and when they become large enough, tendrils of that darkness find their way out one way or another.

And that's exactly what's happening here.

Whatever Katelyn is avoiding—it's big. Unfortunately, if there's one thing I know well, it's that the past has a way of catching up with you. One way or another.

"Mr. Holt! You're back!" Three teens rush forward to greet me at the door.

Jeremy Stewart, a seventeen-year-old who's been hanging around the community center since he was thirteen, is the first to reach the door. Followed closely by Jonathan Davidson, his best friend, and Derek Charleston, one of our newer teens. He and his family had just moved here the week before I ended up nearly bleeding to death.

"Hey, guys. I'm not officially back, so shh." I put my finger to my lips and move into the center. The pain in my side is certainly agitating today, but staring at the four walls of my apartment was just too much. Besides, the doctor only said no heavy lifting.

Walking is good for you, right?

"Should you be on your feet?" Jeremy asks, cocking his head to the side.

"As long as I don't lift anything, I'm fine." I head through the lobby and offer a wave toward Susie Marquez, our secretary. She's on the phone, but she offers a smile and a wave back.

"How are you feeling?" Jonathan questions.

"I heard you got pepper sprayed when you got home!" Derek adds.

Chuckling, I head down the hall toward my office. After unlocking the door, I push it open and take a seat—carefully—behind my desk. This place has been my second home since I took the job six years ago after moving here to be close to the rest of my team.

Since then, I've re-vamped the entire program and turned the dying community center into a thriving outreach program.

Being away from it these past few weeks has been harder than I was prepared for.

"Word travels fast, huh? Well, I did get pepper-sprayed," I tell the three boys as they all take seats in my office. Jeremy and Jonathan both sit across from me, while Derek plops down on the couch near the door. "My neighbor thought I was breaking into my own apartment."

"Seriously?"

I nod. "To be fair, she thought I was dead."

"*Dead*?" Jeremy says, his tone shocked. "Why did she think you were dead?"

"The doctors told her I was. It's complicated." I lean forward on my desk to alleviate some of the strain on my side. "How have things been here? Everyone staying out of trouble?"

Jonathan shares a look with Jeremy, and Derek pales slightly behind them.

"What's going on?"

"Kyle hasn't been in since you've been gone," Jonathan says. "We tried to get him to come to group, but he blew it off. We haven't seen him at school, either."

Kyle Harding. My chest aches for a new reason. He's been the one I was really worried about in my absence. He'd been a fresh face around here, brought in by our gaming competition three months ago. His home life is less than stellar, given his father's abandonment last year and his sister's ongoing medical needs. He's been struggling with anger issues and alcohol consumption.

A habit he picked up from his biological father before the man decided his daughter was more trouble than she was worth—his exact words to her mother—and bailed. Kyle's mom has been doing her best to manage everything, but reaching Kyle has been a struggle.

Which is where I came in. And I'd been close, too. I was finally getting him to open up.

"I'll reach out to him. Thanks for the heads-up."

"You won't tell him it was us?" Derek asks.

"Of course not. But telling me someone is struggling is a good thing. He could be in very real trouble."

Derek nods.

It's one of the biggest battles I've had to overcome in this place. Most of the kids that come here have been conditioned to keep their mouths shut. I've had to re-train them that, when someone is a risk to themselves or someone else, you have to tell someone you trust.

I thank God every day that I am that trustworthy person for a lot of these kids.

A timer goes off on Jonathan's phone, so he pulls it out of his pocket and turns it off. "Free period is over. Time to get back to class."

All three boys stand, and I can't mask the smile on my face. Even two years ago, getting these kids to go to class each day was a struggle. Now they're setting a timer to be on time.

Pride swells in my chest. *Thank You, Lord.*

"You're going to be okay?" Jeremy asks.

"I'll be kicking your butts on the basketball court in no time."

Jeremy snorts.

Jonathan laughs.

Derek shakes his head.

"You'll never beat us, Mr. Holt. Even when you're at your best," Jeremy replies.

"Yeah, you went and got stabbed to avoid our last game," Jonathan jokes.

I laugh, appreciating the lightness of this moment despite the dark topic. "Yeah, well, just you wait. I'll be back and better than ever."

As they leave, a silence settles around me, and I close my eyes.

I can still picture the day I walked into this place. The walls of this office were covered in peeling wallpaper, and the basketball hoops on the court were broken, the nets long gone.

Kids didn't want to be seen here, so they'd go out and spend their afternoons doing whatever else felt interesting at the time. And a lot of times, those interesting things were not at all what they needed to be doing.

What I don't think they realize, though, is how much they saved *me,* too.

When I moved to Stormwatch Landing, I'd been a shell. A soldier merely following orders. I hadn't *lived* in a long time. These kids breathed life back into me. They gave me purpose that went beyond simply following the next set of orders.

This is my happy place.

I may lay my head to rest in my apartment, but this community center is home.

There's a knock on my office door moments before it opens and Susie pushes it open. Her expression is grim, her eyes full of unshed tears.

"What is it?" I demand, pushing up as quickly as I can despite the agonizing pain in my side.

"I just got a call from Kyle Harding's mother. He's been arrested."

"For what?"

Her face pales. "He got caught with a knife at school."

***

"Thank you so much, Garrison," Ursula Harding cries as she reaches forward to hug me. I accept the embrace and wince silently when pain shoots through my side. Kyle's mother is still wearing her animal print scrubs, likely because she came straight over from Stormwatch Animal Hospital where she works as a veterinary technician.

"It's going to be all right," I assure her, sincerely

hoping I'm right. But bringing a weapon to school? Especially in today's world? That's not a minor infraction.

She nods and wipes her face. Ursula has been trying so hard to support her family ever since her husband left. But life has not been kind to them, not with Kyle behaving the way he has been and her younger daughter, Pauline, in and out of the hospital.

"I know it is. I just can't—why would he have a knife?" she asks, eyes wide. "What possible reason could he have for taking a weapon to school?"

I reach forward and pull open the door to the police station. "We'll get to the bottom of it, okay?"

She nods and takes a deep breath.

Captain Alan Leopold steps out of his office and greets us with a strained smile. I know that if he'd been able to avoid putting Kyle in cuffs, he would have, which makes me wonder exactly what happened that caused him to actually book the teen.

More than likely, Kyle argued and resisted, giving Leopold no other choice.

"Where is Kyle?" Ursula asks, her tone shaky.

"He's in our interrogation room."

"Interrogation room?" she repeats, her voice cracking at the end.

I wrap an arm around her for support.

"Can I see him?"

"Of course." He gestures toward the room, so I release her.

As soon as the door closes, I shift my attention to Leopold. "How bad?"

He runs a hand through his greying hair. "It wouldn't have been so bad if he hadn't been combative with the teacher. She tried to get him to turn in the knife, but he refused, saying that she was going to 'kill him' if she took it." Leopold lifts an evidence bag with a knife the size of my forearm in it.

That's not a knife an average person would be carrying with him. Not unless that average person was Crocodile Dundee. I cross my arms, trying to make sense of what Leopold is telling me. "Kill him? As in the teacher was going to?"

Leopold nods. "He flipped his desk over and stormed out, but the principal managed to keep him distracted until I got there. When he saw me, he lost it." He gestures to the bruise on his cheekbone. "Clocked me pretty good for being as young as he is."

Assaulting an officer.

Resisting arrest.

Possession of a weapon on school property.

These are no small charges.

Groaning, I run both hands over my face. This is bad. So bad. "What's it looking like?"

"I want you to talk to him first. I need to know why he had that knife before I take a stance on it. I'm willing to bet he'll be expelled, but before I decide what to move forward with, I want your opinion. Kyle was a good kid before his dad did a number on him. Used to mow my grass." He looks exhausted and just as tortured by this turn of events as I am. "I want to help him, but endangering the other students is not something I can let slide."

"I understand." In the last few years, Leopold and I have worked together on more than a dozen difficult cases involving teens and difficult households. He trusts my judgement, and I trust his.

If he's waiting to officially charge Kyle with anything, it's because he thinks there's hope for the kid. I can only hope he's right. *Lord, please let him be right.*

Turning away from Leopold, I head for the interrogation room and pull the door open. Kyle is staring away from the door, his expression hard, hands clasped in his lap. His mother looks back at me from where she's kneeling beside him. Her cheeks are stained with tears, and based on her expression, she's all but given up.

She stands and presses a kiss to the top of his dark hair. "I love you so much, Kyle. I'm so sorry." She leaves the room and closes the door behind her, so I take a seat across from him.

His shoulders are rolled forward, his expression downcast as he refuses to make eye contact with me.

"Hey, Kyle."

He doesn't respond.

"It's been a while. I apologize for that."

More silence, then he offers me a quick glance. "I thought you were dead."

An ache spreads through my chest in response to his broken tone. "For a minute there, I thought I was, too."

"Hmm."

"Want to talk about what happened today?"

"People overreacted."

"You brought a knife to school," I tell him. "I saw it. It's a big knife. You hunting crocodiles these days?"

"It's mine."

"It's a weapon," I tell him.

"I wasn't going to hurt anybody!" Kyle explodes out of his chair like dynamite. It scrapes against the floor and hits the ground as he pushes to his feet, hands fisted at his sides.

The door opens, and Leopold starts in, but I shake my head and hold up a hand. Slowly, he backs out. All while I remain seated, my muscles tense for a fight I sincerely hope doesn't happen.

While I don't fear what the kid could do to me on a normal day, Sawyer will never let me hear the end of it if I was pepper-sprayed by my neighbor and hospitalized after a teenager attacked me all in the same week.

Not to mention the damage it will cause to the fragile relationship I've built with this kid over the last few weeks.

"I don't believe you were going to hurt anybody, Kyle."

Tears stream down his cheeks now. His expression is broken and furious at the same time. "I wasn't gonna," he insists. "I needed it." His voice wavers, and he pokes himself in the chest.

"Why?"

He looks away from me and shakes his head.

"Kyle."

"No."

"Kyle. You can trust me."

He shakes his head, still avoiding eye contact. "It's only a matter of time before they come for me, too."

"Who?"

He shakes his head again and closes his eyes. His hands are trembling now, so he crosses his arms, trying to hide the vulnerability he's feeling. Unease slips up my spine, icy fingers that have the hair on the back of my neck standing on end.

"Kyle, who is coming for you?" I press. "Your dad?" According to his mother, Kyle's father hadn't been abusive. At least, not until Kyle confronted him the night he left. Their altercation came to blows, and the teen was seriously injured.

Once again, Kyle shakes his head. Only, this time, he opens his eyes and looks directly at me. "I'm sorry," he whispers. "It's all my fault."

"What's your fault?" Now, I stand and take a few steps closer. The cracks are there. The fissures in walls this kid has spent a lifetime building. First, to keep out his alcoholic father, then to shield his pain from a mother who is already carrying enough on her shoulders.

"They told me that Pauline would be okay. That they would make sure she was okay."

"Who?" I repeat, moving a little closer.

He turns to me now, dark eyes full of brokenness. "I'm sorry. I'm so, so sorry."

"Kyle, tell me what happened."

"They didn't say what they were going to do. I promise, I didn't know. I didn't know," he repeats as he takes a step back. "But it's not their fault. Please don't take it out on them. It was just my fault."

"Kyle, tell me what happened," I repeat again, my tone sharpening.

"Promise me you won't take it out on them."

"Take what out on who?"

"Mom and Pauline. It wasn't their fault. You should still help them."

"Kyle. Talk." Unease climbs up my spine at the fear on his face. Over the time I've known him, Kyle has never looked at me with fear. Anger, sure. Plenty of times. Distrust? Absolutely. But fear? I have never laid my hands on this kid, and I never will.

So why is he looking at me like I'm a bomb about to go off?

"I made a copy of your key," he whispers. "They told me they needed something from your apartment, but they said no one would get hurt." The tears continue to stream down his cheeks, and the fear turns to regret so potent it brings him to his knees.

All while I stand there, staring, trying to process what he's telling me.

"When I heard what they did to you, I knew they'd be

coming for me, too. I couldn't let them get me. I've been watching Mom and Pauline. Because I thought they'd come for them, too. I didn't mean to come to school today, but Mom was at work, and Pauline went, so I wanted to make sure I was there, too. I needed the knife to keep her safe." He wraps both arms around himself and begins to rock back and forth.

It's not alcohol that's been keeping Kyle out of school.

Or drugs.

It was fear for his family.

Even though it aches, I slowly lower myself to the floor beside him, then press a hand to his back. "It's okay, Kyle."

"No, it's not. They almost killed you! You almost died because of me! It's my fault! It's always my fault. I stole your keys. I made a copy. I put them back before you knew. And you almost died." His words are coming out in a panicked slur now, as he talks so quickly I can barely keep up.

I can't even fully process what he's telling me because my only priority is talking him off the ledge he's clearly teetering on. "But I didn't."

He shakes his head.

"Kyle, those men aren't coming for you. They were caught and arrested."

He shakes his head violently, his entire body trembling.

"They're not coming for you," I repeat.

"It was my fault."

"It's not your fault. You were trying to help your sister. I can't blame you for that."

"I'm so sorry," he cries. "I'm so sorry."

I wrap an arm around his shoulders and pull him toward me. Kyle collapses against me, and even though the contact sends a fresh wave of pain through my side, I don't move away.

The anger I feel isn't even directed at the kid but at the men who manipulated a troubled teenager who was just trying to help his little sister get the medical care she needs.

They took advantage of him, and it's a weight he's been carrying ever since. For *weeks*.

"I'm so sorry," he says again.

"I forgive you, Kyle," I tell him. "I know you didn't mean for anything to happen to me."

"They said you wouldn't even be there. That they just needed something and you wouldn't even miss it."

And you didn't question it because they dangled help for your sister in front of you like a carrot on a string. I bite back the response, though, because it'll do him no good. Not when he's already kicking himself enough.

"Listen to me." I push him back a bit to look at him. "You shouldn't have taken my key, but it is *not* your fault what happened to me, okay? That fault rests firmly on the shoulders of the men who attacked me."

"You've done nothing but believe in me, and I betrayed you."

"You made a mistake. Now we need to make sure that

the ripple effect doesn't cost you the bright future your mother, sister, and I know stands ahead of you."

He shakes his head. "It's all over."

"It's not," I reply. "All we're dealing with is a speed bump, okay? And what do we do with speed bumps?"

He closes his eyes tightly.

"What do we do with speed bumps?"

"Go over them slowly," he whispers.

"Exactly. It's not over until you give up. And I've got news for you, kid. I'm not giving up on you, so you're not allowed to give up on yourself either."

CHAPTER 7

KATELYN

Feeling light despite the exhaustion after my shift at the diner, pulling at my consciousness, I make my way into the front of the small apartment building. After checking the mail and seeing a couple of bills, I head for the stairs.

Movement in the corner of my eye stops me, though.

Panic shoots through me like a bolt of electricity, but it turns to concern when I realize it's my neighbor leaning back against the wall, his chin tucked to his chest.

"Garrison? What's wrong? What are you doing down here?" I shove the bills into my purse and shoulder it as I make my way over to him.

"Just taking a quick pause before getting on the elevator," he replies. When he lifts his head to look at me, I note the paleness of his face and the heaviness of his eyes. His shoulders are slumped forward, his smile half-hearted.

Immediately, I move into what Thomas calls "Nurse-mom Mode." Something he loves to tease me about whenever he gets the chance. It's served me well, though, especially over these past few weeks.

Garrison doesn't seem to be gasping for breath, so that's one concern I can set aside. But his pallor is bothersome. Reaching forward, I touch a hand to his cheek, my thumb running over the clammy skin just above the coarse hair of his beard. He stills at the contact, his dark lashes fluttering closed.

The stirring in my gut is as unmistakable as it is unwanted. "How long have you been down here?"

"What time is it?" His voice is weak. Not quite a whisper, but not nearly as deep as it usually is.

"Eleven fifteen."

He laughs softly, but it's humorless. "A while, then. Sorry." He pushes off the wall and starts toward the elevator but stumbles.

Rushing forward, I slip an arm around his waist to steady him. It's not lost on me that touching him doesn't make me want to hurl. Not like it does whenever any other man tries to touch me. *It's just because he needs help.*

"Thanks," he murmurs. "Sorry. Long day."

"It shouldn't have been," I reply, tone sharp. "You were supposed to be taking it easy." I make a mental note to let Anastasia know she needs to tell Sawyer he should check in on Garrison more often if he can. Will he even listen to his friend, though?

The elevator doors open, and a wave of panic hits me when Garrison moves forward and guides us both toward it. I start to fight, but I can't carry him, and he's in no shape to walk up the stairs.

Even knowing that, though, it takes every bit of willpower I have to force myself to step into the box.

The walls begin to close, and my own breathing turns ragged as the doors close in front of us.

No. No.

I'm safe.

He's not here.

Nothing is going to happen.

"Are you okay?" Garrison's deep voice roots me in the present.

"Not a fan of small spaces," I reply. Because that's an answer far easier than the truth. Explaining to people you nearly lost your life when your husband trapped you in an elevator with him and tried to beat you to death, all while your infant screamed in his stroller, tends to lead to more questions than I want to answer.

A shiver of relief runs through me when the doors open. I let Garrison set the pace as we move off the elevator and toward his door.

"Thanks. I'm okay now."

"Good. I'll make sure you get inside."

"Don't trust me not to make a run for it?" he asks.

The sideways grin he throws my way warms my insides, but the short trip down memory lane, thanks to that elevator, has given me the strength to beat that attraction back. I have no time for men and their broken promises.

"First of all, I don't think you're running anywhere," I reply.

"And second?" he asks, arching a brow.

"Well, let's just say I don't want to lose my job because I didn't take care of my boss' friend," I reply, only half kidding.

"Boss? I know Maddie, but I also know she won't fire you over me."

"Not her. Anastasia."

"Anastasia?"

"Would you just unlock the door so we can get you inside?" I take his keys from his hand and unlock the door myself, then step aside so he can move in. I remain close, though, just in case he needs me.

"When did you start working at the coffee shop?"

"She hired me yesterday. Today was my first day."

"Are you still working at the diner?" he asks as he takes a seat on the couch. Garrison runs both hands over his face and settles back. I try to ignore the way his shirt rides up just a bit, revealing a sliver of toned skin.

Why does he have to be so attractive?

"Yes. I work nights there. When was the last time you ate?"

"This morning? I had one of those breakfast sandwiches. Absolutely delicious, by the way." He leans his head back and rests it on the couch. "Sawyer ate two of them, too. He slept on my couch," he adds.

"Then left you alone all day?" I shake my head. "And that is not enough food. What have you been doing all day? Standing in that corner?" Did no one check on him?

"Sawyer has his shop to run. I'm fine. I just need to sit."

"You should have been sitting all day." I sound like a broken record at this point, but maybe one of these times it'll sink in. He should be resting. Not up and moving around.

"I had some things at work to deal with."

"No one else could cover?"

He looks up at me now, and a darkness passes over his expression. A haunted look that stops me in my tracks. "Not this. I promise you that I will be staying in tomorrow. And once again, I appreciate your help. I'm going to grab a shower, then go to bed." But he doesn't move.

I cross my arms. I should go. Leave him to whatever evening he has planned, but something keeps me rooted in my spot.

"Where is Sawyer? Is he staying here tonight?"

"Not tonight."

"You shouldn't be alone."

He opens his eyes and grins. "You offering to babysit?" When I don't respond, he laughs. "I'll be fine. Shower, then bed. That's all I need."

"You *need* to eat."

"I'll be fine." He flashes me a smile that's meant to be reassuring, but only solidifies just how tired the man truly is. "Thanks for being there. Again. One of these days, I'll have to make it up to you. I'd say we're up to at least three lasagnas."

Without waiting for me to respond, he pushes himself up off the couch, then heads down the hall with one hand on the wall to brace himself. I stare after him, trying to understand just what might have happened today that put that haunted look in his eyes.

Is it just that he's so tired?

The sound of the shower turning on tugs my thoughts from what he might have had to deal with today and places them firmly on the fact that he's *in the shower.* Heat rushes my cheeks, so I turn and leave his apartment, locking the door behind me and making a note to give him his keys tomorrow. If he's truly not going anywhere, he won't need them. Maybe this is the perfect way to make sure he does stay in.

"Hey, Mom," Thomas greets without looking up at me. Controller in hand, he's guiding a colorful car over a soccer field, trying to score points for the blue team.

"Hey, honey. Homework?" I ask half-heartedly because my mind is still on the man next door.

"No. Didn't get any today. But the craziest thing happened. Didn't you see the text?"

"Text?" I ask.

"Yeah." The game ends, so he gets up from the couch to give me a hug. "Kyle Harding got arrested at school today."

Fear for my son, even though he is standing here safely in front of me, pushes all thoughts of Garrison aside. "Kyle—you've mentioned him before."

"Only once. Kyle defended me when that guy was hassling me after we first moved here. I haven't talked to him since, but I have seen him around at the community center when I went over to play basketball after school."

"What do you mean he got arrested? What for?"

"I heard that he had a knife at school."

"A knife?" I screech. "Why didn't the school call me?" I demand. How could they not notify the parents?

"They sent out a text. Oliver's mom got one. I texted you, too."

I check my phone, then mentally kick myself when I realize it's because I'm out of minutes and didn't even realize it. *Tomorrow, I go get a real plan.* "I can't believe I missed it. You're okay?" I step forward and run my hands over his arms. I can see him, and he looks fine, but I need to hear it from him to steady my racing heart.

Danger. My son was in danger, and I didn't even know.

"Yeah, Mom, I'm fine." He laughs, brushing my hands away. "No one was hurt."

"Why did he have a knife?"

He shrugs. "No one is really sure. He hasn't even been to school for almost two weeks."

And then it hits me. Is that what Garrison was dealing

with? Did they call him because Kyle is a community center kid? *That explains the darkness in his gaze.* Garrison Holt strikes me as the type of man who takes a vested interest in everyone he tries to help. If Kyle was in trouble, that certainly seems like something the former SEAL would risk his health and safety for.

A tightness forms in my chest at the thought of a man who nearly died two weeks ago, risking going out because someone needed him. "I'm so glad you're okay." I pull him into my arms and squeeze him tightly.

"Kyle's not even in my class, Mom," Thomas says as he pulls away, then turns the TV off and yawns. "I'm headed to bed. I left dinner on warm in the crockpot. It was delicious. I love you!"

"Love you, too, sweetie. Um, I'm probably going to go run next door and make sure Mr. Holt is okay."

"Want help?"

"Nah, you get some sleep. I just want to make sure he was able to eat."

"Sounds good. Tell him I said hi. Love you. Goodnight."

"Goodnight, honey."

As Thomas heads down the hall toward his room, I move into the kitchen and unplug the crockpot holding the white chicken chili I'd set this afternoon before heading to the diner for my shift.

Carefully, I carry it out into the hall, then set it down to lock my door. With Garrison's keys in hand, I start to unlock his door, only to stop firmly when I realize he might be just getting out of the shower and still not dressed yet.

So, instead of unlocking the door, I step in front of it and knock, leaving my crockpot in front of mine just in case he doesn't answer.

Not ten seconds later, though, the door is pulling open, and my mouth is going completely dry.

Dark hair wet from his shower, Garrison stands in front of me in pajama pants and a grey tank top that looks *far* too good stretched over his muscled torso. Attraction burns through me, and the battle of letting my gaze run over him is one I lose before I even realize what it is I'm doing.

"I—sorry. I thought you might be hungry."

Garrison grins and leans against the doorjamb. "Fine. Four lasagnas."

"Lasagnas? Huh? No, it's—" And then I realize what he's doing. "Hah. No lasagnas necessary. I just want to be a good neighbor." Retreating toward my door and seriously asking myself whether or not I should do what I'm about to, I lift the crockpot, then carry it back over to where he's standing. "You didn't eat, and I have plenty." I start to hand it to him, then remember he shouldn't be carrying it. "I can bring it in and set it on the counter."

"Only if you'll eat with me. I'm assuming you didn't eat at the diner, and you definitely didn't have time to eat while I was in the shower."

"I-I can go home."

"Has Thomas eaten?"

I nod. "He's already headed to bed."

"You?"

"Not yet," I admit. *I should have set a bowl aside for myself so I could just leave this here. Why didn't I think this through?*

"Then will you come in and eat with me?"

Say no, say no. "Sure. I need to get back soon, though. My shift at the coffee shop is tomorrow morning at seven."

"Sounds good." He steps aside, and I move into the apartment. The scent of tea tree clings to the air, warming my blood in a way it really shouldn't.

God, help me, please. Why am I so drawn to this man?

"Bowls?" I question.

"Cabinet to the left of the stove."

I turn and stretch up to pull down two bowls, then set them on the counter. A warm body moves in behind me, and I freeze as Garrison passes by and opens a drawer to retrieve spoons. The heat of his body might as well be straight from a furnace.

Oh. Boy. Trouble. I'm in big trouble here.

"You go sit. I've got this," I scold, as much for my needing space as for his own safety.

Garrison chuckles. "I'm not good at being taken care of."

"So I see. Seriously, I don't mind. Sit."

He leaves his kitchen and takes a seat at a small round table big enough for two.

After searching for a ladle, I finally find one and scoop

white chicken chili into both bowls, then carry them to the table. When I set them down, I realize that I forgot the toppings. "I need to run next door for cheese."

"No need. Anastasia stocked my fridge. She knows my fondness for microwaved nachos, so there's plenty."

"Microwaved nachos?"

He laughs. "It's a particular favorite of mine."

I open the fridge and find three small bags of shredded cheese. After pulling one out, I return to the table and offer him the bag.

"My parents both died when I was young, and my aunt raised me," he explains. "She had a lot of medical problems, and we didn't have a lot of money, but she tried to make things special. Every year on my birthday, she'd microwave tortilla chips after topping them with cheese and whatever we had in the pantry or fridge at the time. It became a sort of comfort food for me."

My heart aches at the grief on his face. I know I don't have to ask because, from the way he's talking about her in past tense, he lost her.

"She passed a few months before I enlisted in the Navy."

"Is that why you went in?"

He nods. "There wasn't anything else for me. She was all I had, and I used every dime we had to bury her properly. Even took on some debt to do it."

I top my chili with some cheese, imagining a young Garrison standing alone beside a casket as it was lowered into the ground. Pain blooms in my chest, so I rub the heel of my palm against it. "She sounds like a great woman."

"She was." He smiles softly, then reaches out. "May I say grace?"

"Oh, yeah." Even as my fingers tremble, I slide them into his and bow my head.

"Heavenly Father, we thank You for this food. I want to thank You for this new friend sitting across from me. Please bless her and her son and be with them always. Please let this food nourish our bodies, and please be with the Hardings during this troubling time. In the name of Your Son, Jesus Christ, I pray. Amen."

"Amen." I pull my hand free, then take a bite of the food. The savory flavor is a welcome assault on my senses, and my stomach aches for more. "Thomas told me there was an incident at school today with Kyle Harding. Is that why you had to leave your apartment earlier?"

Something flashes over Garrison's expression.

"If you can't or don't want to talk about it, I understand."

He sighs. "This is delicious, by the way."

"Thanks. It's one of Thomas's favorites."

"I can see why." He takes a deep breath and swirls his spoon in his bowl. "Kyle is a good kid who did something he shouldn't have. He was afraid for his life and the lives of his mom and sister. He wasn't going to hurt anyone; the knife was because he wanted to protect his sister."

Pain for this poor boy makes my chest ache all over

again. "He stuck up for Thomas once. He was being bullied when we first moved here, and Kyle came to his defense."

Garrison nods, a haunted smile on his face. "Like I said, he's a good kid. Just makes poor choices. The school expelled him, but his mom is going to homeschool him through a charter school so he can still graduate next year. I'm going to spend some time with him, see if I can help him keep his nose clean until then."

Before we left the last town we lived in, Thomas was *really* struggling with his grades. His attitude was horrible, and he'd tried to run away twice, only to be brought back by the police. I can't even imagine being in the position Kyle's mom is in right now.

I don't know her, but I feel for her.

"His sister has a full-time caretaker, but he can't be trusted not to sneak out."

"A caretaker?"

"She suffers from seizures. They're trying some new medication to help her, but she's in and out of school because of it. Which is why Kyle was there today. She was having a good day and was able to go to class after over a week of being stuck at home."

"He went with her?"

Garrison nods, his expression tight. "He wanted to protect her."

"Oh, that poor family." My stomach twists just thinking about all that mother must be going through.

"It's definitely been rough, but Ursula—his mom—is

strong. She's fighting through it. Anyway, you may see him hanging around my apartment."

"That's really kind of you."

"I don't want this to be the setback that derails his future. Not when he's come as far as he has. So, I will be playing the distraction while I try to talk him through everything he's carrying."

"Why did he think he needed to protect his sister with a knife?" Garrison goes quiet again, and I worry that I've pushed too far. "You don't have to tell me. Sorry, I'm being nosy."

"No, it's okay. Uh, they don't want it to be public knowledge. And as his counselor—"

"Say no more; I completely understand. If anyone gets the need for privacy, it's me," I add quickly, then kick myself. *Watch what you say, Katelyn.*

He smiles appreciatively. "Things like this have a way of haunting a person, and Kyle has enough ghosts of his own. He's not a risk to anyone, though. I wouldn't allow him anywhere close to you or Thomas if he were."

The way he speaks those words sends my heart racing because there's no doubt in my mind that he means every single word.

This man doesn't know us, and we don't really know him, but there's this feeling in my gut, this understanding, that he'd protect us if we ever needed it. And there's a part of me relieved to know it. Especially with who I'm hiding from and what he's capable of.

"So, Navy SEAL to counselor. How did that happen?"

He laughs. "To be honest, I think God knew I needed that community center more than they needed me."

"Oh?"

He nods. "I was kind of just taking life day by day. I didn't see a future beyond active duty. So when the end came abruptly, I wasn't really sure what to do with my life. Pastor Reeves actually recommended me for the job. He put in a good word for me. I worked at the center alongside the previous counselor while I got my degree. Then, as soon as I was ready, he retired, and I've been running the place ever since."

"How long has that been?"

"Almost three years," he replies. "I've been working there for just over six, though."

"You have quite the reputation amongst the teenagers," I tell him with a smile. "Thomas and his friends talk about the infamous SEAL team all the time."

Garrison grins. "It definitely helped me earn the trust of some of the kids that came in. Since I come from a rough background myself—before my aunt took me in—it's easy for me to relate to them."

"It's really honorable. Helping out the way you do."

He shrugs. "It's not me. God led me here, and He's working in these kids' lives. I am just humbled to be a small part of it."

The way he speaks about God so candidly is a breath of fresh air. Thomas' father wasn't a believer. He'd mock me anytime I prayed. It got so bad that I would pray in silence, afraid of what he would do if he saw me.

Hiding that way is the first thing I repented for when I finally got the courage to leave. And it's something I've vowed never to do again.

"How about you? How is it you came to live in our small town?"

How much to tell him? "Uh, after Thomas' dad died, I needed a fresh start. We both did."

"I'm sorry to hear that."

"We weren't together anymore, but thanks. Life doesn't quite go the way we have planned sometimes, does it?" I glance up and immediately regret it when I find those dark eyes trained on me. As our gazes hold, I get the impression Garrison Holt sees far more than I want him to.

Far more than he should.

"No," he replies. "It doesn't. I can honestly say that I'm grateful God brought you here. I wouldn't be alive if He hadn't."

"Sure you would. Your other neighbor could have found you."

"Maybe." His gaze locks on me again. "But I'm glad it was you."

Heat spreads through me, beginning at my cheeks and spreading down my neck. *Danger. I'm in danger around this man.* Not the kind I'm running from, but the kind that could lead to my heart being absolutely shattered.

"Thanks again for this. I really do feel better." Garrison starts to stand, but I beat him to it and take his bowl.

"Sit. I've got it. And it's no trouble at all. I usually cook way too much for just Thomas and me."

"I meant what I said before. I want to make this up to you. You've been too kind."

"No need. I like helping."

"Do you have some kind of medical background?"

My muscles stiffen, but I force a smile. "What do you mean?"

"I was in and out of it when you found me after I'd been stabbed, but I do remember you were proficient in saving my life. Then, after the whole pepper-spray incident, you knew just what to do and how to answer the questions of the paramedics. So it just had me curious."

My pulse kicks up a notch, and my hands begin to tremble as the familiar panic sets in. *Breathe, Katelyn. He's just asking questions like you did.*

"Uh, I was a nurse for a bit when Thomas was little."

"I can see that," he says. I can hear the smile in his friendly tone, but can't bring myself to turn around just yet.

Not when the fear is likely plastered on my face.

"Why don't you work as a nurse anymore?"

"Just wasn't what I felt like doing when we moved." My tone is clipped, and with how intuitive he seems to be, I know Garrison picked up on it.

"Sorry, I didn't mean to pry."

Smile through it. Turning, I plaster what I hope is a

natural-looking smile on my face. "No apology necessary. I'm just tired. It's been a day."

Garrison nods. "Same here. Thanks again for dinner. I fully plan to return the favor as soon as I can." He pushes to his feet, his movements labored, given the soreness he's likely battling. That, coupled with his still-healing lungs, I imagine he's about ready to fall over.

"Can I do anything else for you?" I ask, fighting the urge to rush over and steady him when he places a hand on the wall.

"Nah, I can manage. Thanks, though. If you leave the crockpot, I can wash it and get it back to you. It's the least I can do."

"Nope. Not a chance, Mr. Holt." I lift it and head for the door. "If you need me, you know how to find me."

"I do," he replies as he follows me toward the door. I don't miss the way he lingers close to the wall, likely to reach out and steady himself should he need to. "Thank you, Katelyn. I seriously cannot tell you how much I appreciate everything."

"Stop thanking me. I am the reason for your healing setback after all."

He laughs softly. "If it meant getting to know you better, I'd let you pepper-spray me all over again."

I swallow hard, his words a punch of desire to my gut. Even though his tone and expression are light enough that he likely meant nothing by it.

"Yeah, well, let's not do that again. Have a good night, Garrison."

"You, too, Katelyn."

He lingers near the door even as I make my way over to mine. And when I set the crockpot down and unlock my door, I risk a glance over at him only to find him still watching.

Garrison raises a hand to wave, so I return the gesture before picking up the crockpot and heading into my apartment.

I set the small appliance down on my entry table and lock my door, then lean back against it and run both hands over my face as the image of Garrison, freshly showered, leaning against his door jamb, fills my mind.

Letting *anyone* close is a risk. Especially when that 'anyone' is an incredibly handsome, well-trained Navy SEAL who also happens to be a counselor. How many of my secrets could I accidentally spill if I got too comfortable around him?

Distance.

That's what I need to put between us.

Distance is safe.

Walls are good.

Otherwise, who knows what could happen?

Chapter 8

—

Garrison

One Month Later

"How does that look?" Kyle asks as he steps back and studies the bookshelf we just finished putting up in the church library.

"It looks good, kid." I clasp a hand on his shoulder, enjoying the absolute delight on his face when he grins at me. It's only been a month since his world fell apart when he took that knife to school, but the light is back in his eyes. The smile is back on his face.

"You do great work, Kyle," Pastor Reeves tells him. "Everyone is going to be thrilled to have more space for additional books. Though based on those boxes, we may be calling you for another one here soon."

We glance over at the four medium-sized moving boxes overflowing with books ready to be put in their new home.

"I would love to build you another one. And I can put those books up on the shelves if you'd like," Kyle offers.

"That would be great, thank you."

With a happy smile, Kyle sets the drill aside and crosses the room to grab books. Pastor Reeves nods toward the door, so I follow him out into the hall, just out of earshot of Kyle.

"He seems to be doing well," he comments.

"The first week was rough, but once I realized how much he enjoyed building stuff, he really opened up. We paid him to help repair the fence at the community center and then he fixed a chair over at the diner."

"The kid is gifted, that's for sure."

"He is," I agree. Aside from some basic help here and there, I purposely took a backseat. And not just because physically I'm still not quite where I need to be. He needed to feel accomplished. Especially since he was expelled from school where he was already sporting failing grades in every subject.

Grades that, according to the charter school that he's been meeting with three times a week, are actually climbing. Kid is coming back, and I'm so blessed to have a front row seat to it.

"How are you doing?"

I turn my attention to Pastor Reeves, surprised to see him watching me, a curious expression on his face. "I'm feeling better each day. There's still some pain." I leave out the nightmares. The mornings I wake drenched in sweat because I'm thrown back into the puddle of blood. Broken and dying.

Of all the situations I've been in, I've never felt so completely helpless as I was watching masked men drag Tessa away from me. I'd failed her, and I'd failed one of my best friends.

It doesn't help that Katelyn has been avoiding me. I haven't even been able to ask her why since, the few times I've run into her, she's been either rushing into her apartment or working at either the diner or coffee shop.

I'm not sure what changed, but she doesn't seem to want anything to do with me now, and I'm not one to press. Even though I crave conversations with her like a man in a desert craves water.

"I'm glad to hear it. Have you heard from Zane and Tessa?"

"Last I talked to them, they were spending some time in Greece. He said they'd be back by the fall."

"I think it's so great that they've come back together after all that time apart." He crosses his arms. "God works in such wonderful ways."

"That, He does," I agree and shift my attention toward the open patio doors overlooking the coastline. As I'm watching the waves, a woman wearing a maroon sweatshirt walks by.

My heart recognizes her before my mind registers that it's Katelyn standing beneath the bright sunshine.

"Can you keep an eye on him for a minute for me?"

Pastor Reeves follows my eyeline and laughs softly. "Absolutely. Go. We'll keep working on the books." He clasps me on the shoulder and heads back into the library, so I walk out onto the patio and take the stairs down to the beach as quickly as I can without looking too desperate.

"Katelyn!" I call out.

She turns toward me, and the sunlight catches strands of copper in her blonde hair. Her gaze is bright when she sees me, but that momentary joy is hidden beneath a mask she slips into place.

No matter what training I've had, what experience I've gained over the last few years, I can't seem to break through the walls she's placed around herself. I had a little glimpse that night last month in my kitchen, and now I'm desperate for more.

"You look like you're feeling better," she says when I reach her. Her cheeks flush with color. "I mean, you just look like you're moving easier."

I grin, unable to hide my own happiness that she seems to be at least a little attracted to me, since I'm so drawn to her. *At least it's not just me.* "I am. You look good, too."

She smiles, but it doesn't reach her eyes as she turns back toward the water. "I like coming out here sometimes. I had a break between shifts, so I wanted to get some fresh air."

"How are things? I haven't really seen you around."

"I've been busy. From what I've heard from Thomas, so are you. How is Kyle doing?"

"Really well." I point toward the church. "He just

finished a bookshelf for the church, and he's gotten his grades up at the charter school he's doing now."

"That's so good." She looks genuinely pleased. "His sister?"

"The medication they have her on seems to be working really well. She's been seizure-free for three weeks."

She looks genuinely relieved despite not having a close relationship with the Harding family. It's just another reason I'm drawn to her. She cares. Deeply. About everyone. Not a quality you find in a lot of people these days. "I'm happy to hear that."

I shove both hands into my pockets. "How's Thomas?"

"Good. Ready for baseball camp. He's counting down the days.

"And you?"

"Less excited that he'll be spending his spring break away from me, but I'm excited for him. I know he can't wait."

"Well, if you get bored while he's gone and want to hang out, we can do dinner or something. I do owe you a lasagna, remember?" The words are out of my mouth before I can stop them, and I mentally kick myself for choosing that particular verbiage to ask her out to dinner.

"I'll let you know. I'll probably be busy with work, though."

Ouch. "Sure." I run a hand over the back of my hair. *Just ask.* "Listen, did I do something?"

"What?" She turns toward me.

"To offend you. It's just, you've been kind of distant."

"What do you mean?"

"Well, I saw you around a lot, and now it's—"

"We lived next door to each other for months before we officially met. I'm just busy. You didn't do anything." She flashes me a guarded smile. As she starts to turn back toward the water, she freezes, her face paling.

I turn, trying to see what she's looking at.

A man dressed in black pants and a black sweatshirt is running toward us on the beach. He's too far away for me to recognize, but her body is stiff, her eyes wide as she watches him closely.

I move in closer, my system going on alert in response to her reaction.

"Katelyn, what is it?"

She doesn't answer as he grows closer, but her body language says it all—she's afraid. Her breathing is rapid, her hands trembling at her sides.

When the man gets closer, I realize it's Drew, one of the mechanics at Sawyer's shop. He offers us both a friendly smile and runs past us without so much as breaking stride. I don't know him well, but he seems like a good man. Married with two kids.

So why does she look at him like he's an unwanted shadow darkening her door?

I turn back to Katelyn. "Are you okay? Do you know him?"

She shakes her head. "No. I thought—sorry. I, uh, I

need to go. I have work." She forces a smile and turns away without waiting for my response.

Torn between my desire to rush after her and make sure she's okay and the understanding that sometimes people just need space, I remain rooted in my spot, watching her retreat until she's no longer in my line of sight.

It's only when I can't see her anymore that I trek back toward the church. Even though my thoughts are still on the beach.

***

"How are things working out with Katelyn?" I ask Anastasia as soon as I take my seat at the table in Linda's kitchen. The entire duplex smells absolutely delicious, thanks to the roast Linda prepared for dinner tonight.

"She's great. Super hard worker and really sweet. Why?" She wiggles her eyebrows. "Interested? I think she's single."

"Pepper spray is the first step of true love, I've heard," Sawyer adds, his tone dry.

Anastasia's boyfriend, Jack, laughs, which wipes the smile off of Sawyer's face. Over the past few weeks, he's made more of an effort to be here on weekends, and while I can honestly say I like the guy, Sawyer hasn't even tried to hide his disdain for the FBI agent.

Still, he's good to Anastasia, and she seems happy whenever he's around. So, until there's a reason not to, I remain neutral when it comes to Sawyer's issues with him. Especially since we both know he only dislikes the guy because of his own feelings for the woman sitting between them.

"Do *you* like her? Katelyn is a sweetheart!" Linda exclaims after taking a drink of water.

"I was just curious. I haven't really seen her around lately, so I wanted to know if things were working out. That's all." To avoid any further questioning, I shove a bite of Linda's delicious roast into my mouth.

"Yeah. Okay." Anastasia grins at me.

"How are things going with Kyle?" Ryker questions. He's been relatively quiet over dinner, as has Weston. Though that's not unusual for either of them. Especially since, more times than not, Weston is in a surly mood.

I finish chewing and swallow, then wash the bite down with some water. "He's a great kid. Just needed some direction."

"As long as you're not leaving your keys anywhere around," Weston growls.

"He was just trying to get help for his family," I defend.

"By getting my friend gutted? Nah. He'll need a better excuse than that," Weston says. "A poor choice is a poor choice despite one's reasoning."

"What charges did he end up getting for the school incident?" Jack questions, pulling my attention away from Weston. Which, in my current mood, is probably a good thing. His verbally attacking Kyle won't go over well, no matter his reasoning.

While I'm not overly thrilled that the FBI agent is involved in this particular conversation, I also appreciate Jack's moral compass. We kept the truth about his involvement in what happened to me a secret, so as long as Jack doesn't decide to shove his nose into it, that's how it will stay.

Hopefully.

"They dropped it to a misdemeanor," I say. "Kyle has community service, and he won't be allowed back at the school, but he's honestly thriving with the charter school route."

"That's good to hear." Jack takes a bite of his food, and Anastasia smiles over at him, adoration in her gaze.

I glance over at Sawyer, not at all missing the jealousy clinging to him like a second skin.

Not that I can exactly blame him.

I wouldn't handle it well if the woman I loved was in a serious relationship with another man, either. Though I'd like to think I wouldn't have sat on those feelings for six years like he has.

For some reason, Katelyn comes to mind.

Is she seeing anyone? I haven't caught wind of anyone in her life, but is that maybe why she's backed off from me? Or did it have something to do with what happened earlier on the beach? Is she afraid of relationships because of a previous one? My initial assessment was that she's been abused...how true is that?

"I, for one, am so glad that you're helping him," Linda says. "Sometimes people just need a nudge in the right direction." She gently elbows Weston, who grunts in response. He'd gotten into some trouble when he'd been a teenager, too, though none of his incidents involved anyone dying—or almost dying.

If I thought for a second that Kyle was an actual threat, or that he'd done what he'd done out of anything but desperation for his sister, I wouldn't have put my neck out the way I did. But he's a *good* kid who just needs a second chance. One I knew I needed to give. And the last month has done nothing but prove that.

"He's a good kid," I repeat, then continue eating.

Anastasia stands to carry her plate in, but Jack takes it from her and carries it into the kitchen. "I've got it, babe," he says.

"Thanks," she replies, then turns back toward the table. "What?"

I shift my gaze from her to Sawyer, noting the way he's staring at her.

"Nothing," he replies. "I think I need to get back to the shop. Do you still want me to take your car in?" he asks Linda.

"Only if you don't mind."

"Not at all. Happy to do it, Momma Knox." He stands and deposits his plate into the sink, then takes the keys to his truck out of his pocket and sets them on the small kitchen island before pocketing hers. "Just bring my truck by after your errands tomorrow, and I'll have your car ready to be picked up."

"You are wonderful. Thank you, honey. I don't know what I did to deserve such wonderful young men taking care of me."

"Least we can do for family," he replies, with a sideways glare at Jack, who is completely unbothered by the clear territory claim.

He even steps forward and rests a hand on Anastasia's shoulder. "Mrs. Knox, I was actually going to ask if you'd be up for grabbing lunch tomorrow, so I can take you wherever you need to go if you'd like. Then I can drop you by Sawyer's shop before I head to the airport."

The room falls completely silent, and my gaze levels on Sawyer. He closes his eyes and takes a deep breath to calm himself before opening his eyes again and plastering an uninterested expression on his face.

"Lunch would be good." She smiles, but I notice that it's not quite one of joy. *Interesting.* "I just need to run to the bank tomorrow."

"Happy to help." Jack grins, completely unaware that there's a man standing only a few yards from him who has the skills *and* desire to make him disappear without a trace. "I can pick you up about eleven tomorrow for lunch? Then we can head to the bank after that?"

"That sounds great," she replies, clearly taken aback by his offer. I wonder if she's thinking what the rest of us are.

That a one-on-one with Anastasia's only living parent might mean this relationship is moving a *lot* faster than anyone is prepared for.

"Fantastic. Should we get going?" he asks Anastasia. "I have a call in about thirty minutes, but that will give me time to drop you off and get back to my hotel."

"Sure. I—"

"I can take you home, Anastasia," Sawyer offers. "If you want to hang around."

"No, that's okay. I'm actually pretty wiped." She stands and kisses her mother on the cheek before taking Jack's offered hand. "Love you, Momma."

"Love you, too, sweetie. See you tomorrow, Jack."

"See you, Mrs. Knox. Good to see you guys," he adds to the four of us.

"You, too," I reply. Weston and Ryker say nothing but offer him nods, while Sawyer looks about ready to snap him in half.

The moment they're gone, Linda smacks Sawyer's arm. "You do *not* get to do that to her, Sawyer Maddox."

"Ow. Do what?" he asks, rubbing his arm.

"You know what." She glares at him pointedly.

"Seriously, Cable Guy," Weston adds, using the code name we have for Sawyer, "you had your chance to tell her how you felt, and you chickened out."

"I have no idea what any of you are talking about."

Linda simply shakes her head and smiles. "You wasted time, honey."

"He's not good for her. Do none of you see that?" Sawyer asks.

"He has a good job," Weston says. Which is only to torture Sawyer since he doesn't care too much for Jack and Anastasia's relationship either. Though his lack of support is for an entirely different reason than Sawyer's.

He just doesn't trust anyone. Not after his sister was murdered.

"Yeah, well, it's going to go sideways, and I'll be the first one to say I told you so," Sawyer replies.

"Maybe then you won't sit on your hands too long," Ryker offers as he stands, gathering his plate and the one holding the extra roast in the center. He carries it into the kitchen and gets to work washing the dishes.

Since Ryker and Weston have dish duty tonight, I stand and grab my jacket off the back of the chair. Sawyer does the same, but he heads into the kitchen to say his goodbyes to Weston and Ryker.

"Thanks for dinner tonight," I tell Linda.

"Anytime, honey." She lowers her voice and leans in. "If you have feelings for Katelyn, don't sit on them too long. Nothing like regret to break a heart." She smiles softly in Sawyer's direction.

"Isn't that the truth?" I pull her in for a hug. "Call if you need anything."

"You know I will." She returns my hug, then offers

Sawyer one, too. "You are a great man," she tells him. "You just need to work on your timing."

"Yeah. Thanks. I'll see you tomorrow." His tone is defeated, and I imagine he's wondering just what Jack has to say to her over lunch.

Will he fight for her if Anastasia says yes? Or will he give up and move on?

"Yes, you will." She pats his cheek, then heads into the kitchen to try to force Weston and Ryker into letting her help with cleanup. Something neither of them will allow.

Sawyer pulls the door open, and I follow him out onto the small porch. Overhead, the sky is already alive with whatever storm is coming this way. Lightning flashes in the distance, and the earthy scent of coming rain clings to the air.

It's one of my favorite times to be here in Stormwatch Landing. This calm before the storm always feels so *alive*.

"You good?" I ask Sawyer.

He shakes his head. "He's not good enough for her."

"Because you'd be better?"

He turns toward me. "Yeah. I would."

I clasp a hand on his shoulder. "At least you'll admit it to me. Now you just need to figure out how to tell her."

"Kind of like you need to figure out how to tell Katelyn you've got a thing for her? I have eyes, too, you know. And the knowledge that you've been swinging by for coffee every morning even though we both know you prefer to make yours at home."

"Can't a guy support his friend's shop?"

"Sure, but you've always done that by buying your coffee and supplies directly *from* Anastasia so you can make it at home."

Because I know that Sawyer won't let it go unless I admit it, I sigh. "I can't get a read on her, and it's driving me a little wild."

"A little?" He laughs. "I tell you what. How about I meet you there tomorrow morning and we can both daydream about what we want but can't have."

ead pounding, I open my eyes. The marble floor is cold beneath my cheek. What am I doing on the floor? But even as I think it, everything comes rushing back to me.

The screaming.

The profanity.

The fist.

A whimper leaves me as I sit up, my hands pressing against the cool stone as I pull myself up on the counter. I run my hand over my slightly swollen belly, panic pushing through the pain. What if this is the time that everything ends? What if—my son kicks. A fluttering in my belly that eases the fear.

He's okay.

Once again, Victor avoided the baby he hates.

With silent tears streaming down my cheeks, I study the

destruction. A vase that once held flowers is shattered all over the granite island, the red rosebuds that were Victor's last apology destroyed as well.

The glass he'd been drinking from last night has been shattered on the far wall, and the dinner I'd worked hard to prepare is cold and still sitting on top of the stove.

God, why me? Why is this happening to me? *I lean backward, the sobs shaking my shoulders as I cover my mouth and try to remain silent. It's doubtful Victor will wake anytime soon, but the fear sends tremors through my body.*

So with one hand to cover my mouth, the other cradling the life growing within me, I stand in my destroyed kitchen, wishing I were anywhere but here. A steady beeping from my cell phone alerts me to the time.

I have thirty minutes to clean this up before the staff gets here. Not that it will matter. They're all afraid, too. I could be bleeding to death on the floor, and I doubt that anyone would utter even a single word.

Not when the penalty for speaking up is them joining me in this hell.

The last thing I want is to put them in that predicament, so I'll do what I always do. I'll clean up, then go upstairs and use the fetal monitor to listen to the life I'm terrified he'll rob me of...just as he robbed me of mine.

The night air is cold on my face as I step out onto the balcony, a mug of tea in my hand. In the distance, lightning splits the sky even though the rain stopped about an hour ago. Wind sends my hair flying around my face, and a few strands stick to my still-wet cheeks, thanks to the tears I'd woken up crying.

It's always like that with one of my nightmares.

Each and every one is a reminder of what I escaped. What I'm still hiding from.

"You come out here often?"

I jump, the masculine voice a reminder of the screaming still fresh in my mind.

"Sorry, didn't mean to scare you." Garrison waves over at me from his balcony, a few feet away from mine and separated by a half wall.

"It's okay. I guess I'm not quite awake yet." I force a smile and press a hand to my heart. "What are you doing up?"

"Couldn't sleep." His expression is more serious than I've ever seen it.

"Are you okay? Kyle?"

"Everyone's fine. How about you? Are you always up this early?"

"Not usually. I guess I was just having trouble, too." I offer him a half-hearted smile, hoping that the shadows of the night will keep whatever remnants that remain of my nightmare hidden from view.

Still, when I meet his gaze, I can't help but feel

completely transparent. As though he can see down to the deepest, darkest pits of my soul.

Finally, he looks away, turning back to the sky as he grips the railing on his side with both hands. "Worried about baseball camp?"

I take a deep breath, so grateful he's not prying on any other level. "That would be a yes. I've never spent a night away from him."

"That's going to be hard."

"Understatement," I reply with a soft laugh. "He's my whole world."

Silence settles around us, and I take a moment to breathe deeply, inhaling the salty sea air just beyond our porches. Silvery moonlight shines down on the ocean, illuminating the waves as they gently crash into the shore.

There's a road between us and the ocean, but this view is one of the main reasons I chose this apartment. Because sitting here, looking out at it helps me realize that no matter how big my problems are—how vast the darkness may seem—it's nothing but a blip compared to the depth of the ocean.

A single tear in a seemingly endless depth.

"You're a great mom."

Those four words rip me from my thoughts, and I turn toward him, unsure how to respond. Aside from Thomas telling me from time to time how much he appreciates me, no one has ever told me I was a great mom.

I've heard all the ways I was failing from Victor in the

short month we stayed with him. How my son shouldn't need to cry and the only reason he did was because I wasn't providing for him in the way all other moms did. And I guess I never let anyone else close enough to see anything beyond the walls I've put up.

Yet standing here in the darkness with Garrison a few feet away from me, he manages to completely disarm me with four simple words.

"Th-thanks," I finally say once the silence has stretched enough to be awkward.

He smiles, and a small dimple appears at the corner of his mouth, barely visible through his beard. "I just thought you should know."

Heat flushes my cheeks. "I really appreciate you saying that."

With a shrug, Garrison turns his attention back to the view beyond the porch, and with his gaze turned away from me, I can finally draw a deep breath to steady myself against the pull I feel toward a man I barely know.

It has to be because I saved his life.

Right?

"What about you?" I question, hoping to shift the conversation back to him.

"Eh, just restless, I guess. I don't do well being cooped up."

"You don't look like a man who spends a lot of time inside." Heat climbs up the back of my neck. "I mean, you just have the build of someone physically active." *Oh, come on, Katelyn. You might as well have told him you thought he was hot.*

Garrison chuckles. "I don't tend to spend a lot of time inside."

"You do seem to be doing better, though."

"I am definitely getting back to normal, and I'm seriously hoping to be cleared completely tomorrow."

"Tomorrow? That seems soon."

"Doc Alex says I heal fast." He winks at me, and my knees go weak.

Ridiculous, the effect he has on me. Haven't I learned my lesson? Haven't I suffered enough to know better? I take a sip of my tea. "I'm glad to hear it. Well, I'd better get inside and try to grab another hour or so of sleep. Thanks for the late-night chat."

"Thank you," Garrison replies, his gaze locked on mine. "I hope you sleep well, Katelyn." The deep baritone of his voice warms me up from the inside.

"You, too." I force a smile, then step back behind the separator that will provide some privacy from Garrison Holt.

I open and close the door, but don't go inside. Instead, I settle back onto the patio chair and draw my knees up to my chest.

As the silent tears stream down my cheeks, I hear his door open and close softly. Will he go back to sleep? Or will he sit up the rest of the night, haunted by whatever ghosts he carries?

"You are so welcome, Mr. Jenkins. I hope you enjoy." After sliding my notepad into my pocket, I move back toward the counter of the diner. It's been a long few hours, but I'm nearly half-done with my shift.

"You doing okay?" Maddie, my boss and the owner of the diner, asks. Her grey hair is pulled back in a tight bun, her soft blue eyes full of concern.

"Yeah, why?"

"You just seem tired."

"I didn't sleep well."

"Ahh. Baseball camp. That's coming up fast."

"Yes." I turn toward where Thomas is sitting at a back booth, his homework open in front of him. "Seven days away."

"I wish I could tell you it gets easier the older they get. My Diana is twenty-six with kids of her own, and I still miss her every day."

Tears burn in the back of my throat as I turn back toward Maddie. "I am trying not to think about that."

Maddie laughs softly, then reaches forward and covers my hand with hers. "Getting to see how they handle what's thrown at them makes the journey worth the heartache."

The bell overhead dings, so I cover her hand with my other one and squeeze gently. "Remind me of that sometimes, will ya?"

"Anytime, darling girl." She pulls her hand back and winks, so I turn to greet the newest customer.

"Hey, Mr. Holt!" Thomas calls out.

I hate that my heart jumps in my chest at the mere mention of him. But it does. My treacherous body is delighted to know that he's so close even though my brain is screaming for distance. For safety.

Plastering a smile on my face, I hope doesn't look nearly as fake as it feels, I turn toward him. Only to find him settling into the booth across from my son. Those alarm bells turn even more frantic, a deafening screech that has the blood pumping in my ears.

On shaky legs, I make my way over toward him. Thomas's smile is wide as he talks to the man across from him, but I can't hear a single thing over my hammering pulse.

When I reach the edge of the table, my son and Garrison both turn toward me.

"Hey, Mom, I invited Mr. Holt to eat with me since he's alone."

"That's so sweet." I smile. "What about your homework?"

"I ran into an issue with algebra. But I'll figure it out."

"I'm actually pretty good with algebra. Can I see?" Garrison asks.

My heart leaps. "You don't have to do that."

"I don't mind. Math and science happen to be two of

my favorite subjects." He flashes a grin my way, and my stomach twists.

I want to pull Thomas away from him. Not because I'm worried about his safety with Garrison but because I'm worried about my own. About what will happen to my heart if I watch this man grow closer to the most important person in my life.

And what if we have to leave again? What if I have to pull Thomas away from someone else he's grown close to?

We're not moving, I remind myself of the promise I made when we first set foot into Stormwatch Landing.

Even if the fight finds me here, I will stand my ground. My son will graduate with his new friends. He will finish high school at *one* school. Not two, not three. One.

So, with that in mind, I take a deep breath and turn toward Garrison, who is already focused on the math book in front of him. "Can I get you something to eat or drink?"

He shifts that ridiculously gorgeous gaze my way. "Water and a burger with pepperjack cheese, onion rings, and a side of ranch, please."

"You've got it." I turn toward Thomas. "Did you decide what you wanted yet?"

"The same as Mr. Holt," he says. "Please." The grin on his face breaks my heart because I can see right through it.

He looks up to Garrison. And it only highlights the emptiness I have worried about since Thomas was young. I do my best, but I'm only one person, and I know he wishes he had a dad.

"Sure thing, honey." With tears gathering in the corners of my eyes, I turn away and move back toward the counter to turn the order in to Maddie's husband, who works the kitchen.

As I do, I hear Thomas's laughter ring out through the diner, followed closely by Garrison's, and the combined sound makes my heart ache in a way I'm not prepared for.

It makes me long for a future that feels completely out of reach.

Chapter 10

Garrison

"How you doing over there?" I glance up from my computer toward where Kyle is seated on the floor in front of the couch, a textbook open on the coffee table. He looks up at me, pencil hovering over the page of his notebook. He's been in that exact spot since we got back from lunch two hours ago.

"Good. Trying to decide what to do for my creative writing assignment."

"Oh? What's the topic?"

His brow furrows. "Anything I want it to be. That's part of the problem. I have no idea what to write about. It has to be three to five pages and have a plot twist."

"A plot twist, huh?" I push up from my chair and cross the room to take a seat on the couch beside him.

"I'm not a writer." He groans and sets his pencil down.

"I'm reading through my language arts textbook for inspiration."

"Well, there's your problem." I close the book and stand. "Come on, let's go for a walk."

"How is that going to help? This is due tomorrow."

"Well, procrastination is never a good thing." I reach down and tug him to his feet. "But sometimes the best remedy is fresh air. So, let's go get some."

With another groan, he opens the door and steps out with me right behind him. We move past the receptionist desk, and Suzie waves, her expression bright.

"Getting some fresh air?" she asks as she pushes her glasses back up onto the bridge of her nose.

"That's the plan," I tell her. "I have my cell, so call if anything comes up."

"Will do. If you happen to get fresh air by the coffee shop, I wouldn't complain about a caramel macchiato."

I laugh and nod. "You've got it." She doesn't even realize she's handed me the perfect opportunity to stop in on someone I haven't been able to stop thinking about.

We step out into the bright sunshine, and I breathe deeply, inhaling the cool spring air into my lungs. Man, I love this town. I had no idea what to expect when I moved here, yet I ended up getting what I didn't even realize I was asking for: a home.

"How exactly is this supposed to help?" Kyle asks as we step onto Main Street.

"Consider it a power cycle for your brain."

"Isn't that what sleep is?"

I laugh and shove my hands into my pockets. "I struggled with school, too, and anytime I'd get frustrated with an assignment, my aunt would make me go outside. Most of the time, we'd sit on the porch and just stare out at the back yard. We'd talk about everything *but* the assignment, and somehow doing that completely cleared my mind enough that I could actually focus."

"It really works?"

"It does. But only if we talk about something other than the assignment."

He smirks at me, something that's coming a lot easier to the boy weighed down with far more than his fair share of life. "So what should we talk about?"

"How about Pauline? How is she doing?"

"Much better." His shoulders relax, and the crease between his brow lessens. It's no wonder; the kid adores his little sister. She's his entire universe. "We went and saw a movie last night."

"Oh yeah?"

He nods. "She's doing so great, and I know she's starting to think that maybe she won't have any more issues, but..." He trails off, and his expression darkens. "I'm just waiting for the other shoe to drop."

"That's a stressful way to live, Kyle."

"We have to be prepared. What if it happens when she's walking to school? What if she falls and hits her head?"

I stop walking and turn him to face me, placing both hands on his shoulders. "That's where faith comes in."

"I don't know that I have much of that, Mr. Holt. I mean, I try, but why would God let these things happen? Why would He have made my dad who he is? Or made my sister sick?"

"God didn't make your dad who he is. Your dad's choices are what turned him into the man he is. As for your sister, God didn't make her sick, but He has given you everything you need to handle it."

"What's that?" He sniffles and looks up at me.

"Him. There is no storm we can't weather with the Lord in our boat. Having faith doesn't mean that everything is always going to work out okay, but it does mean that you go through nothing alone."

Kyle takes a deep breath and shifts his gaze away from me. I drop my hands from his shoulders and offer him the silence to process.

"I just don't know."

"That's okay. You can build on what you don't know."

"How's that?"

"The Bible."

"Mom has one of those. She and Pauline read it together every morning."

"And you?"

He shakes his head and starts walking again, so I fall into step beside him. "I usually try to be anywhere else."

"Then maybe that's where you start. Sit with them. You

don't have to talk or read, but you can listen. And that's a place to start." I pause just outside the coffee shop.

"That sounds way too easy."

I laugh. "Kid, it's going to be the hardest thing you've done, but it's the only thing that matters. Your past, your pain—none of that will exist in the eternity He has promised us. Your sister will be healed, and there will be no tears."

He shrugs and looks up at me. "That sounds nice, I guess."

I clasp a hand on his shoulder. "It's going to be perfect."

"I'll try. I can't promise anything, but I'll try."

"Good." I pull open the door to the coffee shop so he can move inside. When I follow him and take note of Anastasia working the cash register, I can't help but feel slightly disappointed that it's not Katelyn smiling at me.

"Hey there," Anastasia greets. Her smile is hollow, not at all reaching her eyes. My gaze momentarily falls to the large scar on her cheek. The bullet that left it nearly claimed her life almost two months ago. It makes my stomach churn to know how close we came to losing her. "The usual?" she asks.

"Hi, Miss Knox," Kyle greets. "Yes, please. For Miss Suzie." He's been coming here at least a few times a week, doing coffee runs for Suzie.

"And for you?"

"Just an iced tea, please."

"You've got it. Mr. Holt?" Anastasia asks.

"Just a regular coffee, please. Some cream and sugar." While she rings it up, I turn to Kyle. "Why don't you grab a seat?"

He nods and heads toward one in the far corner while I pay for the drinks.

"You okay?" I ask Anastasia, keeping my voice low so the other patrons seated around the café can't hear.

She lifts her gaze to mine, and her bottom lip quivers slightly. Anastasia has spent most of her life being strong, keeping her walls in place until she's alone and can safely let them down. But right now, that mask has fissures.

"I'll be fine."

"Anastasia," I say softly.

She closes her eyes, then nods toward the back where the entrance to her apartment is. I glance back at Kyle, who's playing a game on his phone, then follow her toward the back where no one can see.

"It's stupid," she says.

"I doubt that. What happened?"

"Sawyer just—" she clenches her hands into fists at her sides. "He won't let up about Jack, and we had a fight."

I arch a brow. "This have something to do with Jack's lunch with your mom the other day?"

"No. At least not completely." Anastasia closes her eyes. "Jack asked me if he should move here."

I arch a brow. "Oh?"

"Yeah."

"And what did you say?"

"That I didn't want him to change his entire life for me. That we were still new and I needed time to think about it."

"Ouch."

"He actually took it fine. It was Sawyer who made a big deal about it. Like he always does."

"How did he find out?"

"I made the stupid mistake of opening up to *my friend,* and he blew up on me." She crosses her arms and shakes her head. "I don't understand why it's such a big deal. He's never liked Jack, and I can't for the life of me figure out why."

I arch a brow. Surely, she's not serious. Still, I won't be the one to open that particular door. It has to be either her or Sawyer. And at this rate, they'll be dancing around each other until the end of time.

"Anyway. Sorry. I told you it was stupid. He told me that it was a mistake, that Jack isn't good enough for me and that, if I let him move here, then I will regret it."

"What do you think?"

She glares up at me. "Don't hit me with that counselor jargon."

I laugh. "I'm not. I'm asking as your friend."

She blows out a breath. "I'm not sure what I want. I mean, I care about Jack, but there's just something missing. I don't know. Maybe it is the distance causing it."

"Maybe," I say.

"Or?" she asks.

"I can't answer that question for you."

A bell over the door dings, so Anastasia glances past me, then grins. "Oooh look who's here."

I follow her gaze and have the air knocked from my lungs at the sight of Katelyn wearing a floral dress and a short jean jacket. Her hair is pulled halfway up, so the loose curls cascade down to her shoulders.

Speaking of unrequited feelings.

"Thanks for the talk, G-man. It actually helped." Anastasia gently smacks me on the shoulder, then steps past me to greet Katelyn.

"Hey! I thought you two were out taking the big city by storm."

Katelyn smiles. "I think we've got everything we need." Her gaze meets mine, and in it, I pretend that I see the same desire I know is reflected in mine.

Never, in my entire life, have I felt this way about someone.

This instant connection that might as well be a live wire waiting to ignite.

"Hey, Garrison." Katelyn's greeting rips me back to the present.

"Hey. Fun day?" I move back into the main room of the coffee shop. Thomas is sitting across from Kyle, the two teens chatting happily despite their age gap.

"It was." Katelyn's smile widens as she looks over at Thomas, but it fades slightly as she turns back to me. I can practically see those shields going back into place. It stings —a lot more than I care to admit. "We grabbed everything he needs for baseball camp. Thanks again for the afternoon off," she says to Anastasia, who waves her hand in dismissal.

"Please. No need to thank me. You want a coffee?"

"Yes, please. A vanilla latte with some lavender."

"And a hot cocoa for me, please!" Thomas calls out. "Hey, Mr. Holt!" He waves at me, so I return it, a smile on my face.

"Hey, Thomas. Getting excited?"

"Oh, more than. I seriously cannot wait."

Kyle says something I can't quite hear, but Thomas turns around, and the two start talking again.

"Here you go, Garrison." Anastasia offers me a tray with three drinks on it, then goes to work making Katelyn's coffee. Even though I have no interest in leaving, I take them, then turn to Katelyn.

"How are you doing?"

She sighs. "I'm managing. My boy will be safe and happy, and that's all I can ask for."

"If you need anything—"

"I'll be okay, but thanks." Her plastic mask slips into place. "See you later, Garrison."

"See ya. Thanks, Anastasia."

"Welcome! See you later, G-man."

"Kyle, you ready?"

"Yeah." He pushes up. "If I don't see you again before

you leave, good luck, Thomas. I hope you have a great time."

"Thanks so much, Kyle. Hoops when I get back?"

"Definitely." He offers Katelyn a smile and half wave. "See ya, Miss Ellis."

"See ya, Kyle." She offers me one final smile, then crosses over to where Thomas is still sitting.

What do I have to do to get her to open up?

Before I can press my luck by trying to engage her in another guarded conversation, I push open the door with my back and hold it so Kyle can walk outside.

"Thanks for bringing me out, Mr. Holt. I actually think I know what I want to write about."

"Oh yeah?"

"Yeah." His eyes light up. "I'm thinking a story about a soldier who comes home after service to find his entire town has been taken over by robots."

I snort. "That's a book I'd read."

"Yeah?" Kyle looks up at me, eyes wide and hopeful.

"Oh yeah, buddy. You're going to ace it." Overhead, the sky darkens, and the wind picks up. Two telltale signs that the nasty storm they've been tracking will be rolling in over the next few hours. "It might be time to get you home. Let's go get Suzie her coffee, and I'll give you a ride."

CHAPTER 11

KATELYN

By the time I've managed to finish cleaning up after dinner, I'm so exhausted I can barely see straight. I yawn and cover my mouth as thunder rattles the windows just outside. The news says this could be the worst storm we've seen all season, and I'd be lying to myself if I didn't admit that it's got me nervous.

Thomas can't be bothered, though, as he sits on the couch, playing his video game, a big smile spreading over his face when he scores a goal for his team.

I can't help but smile, too. He's *so* happy here. Of all the places we've lived over the course of his thirteen years, this has been the best place for him. He's made actual friends, joined the baseball team, and as of this week, his grades are finally where they are supposed to be.

As always, that sick churning in my stomach begins because, if I've learned anything over the last few years, it's that this peace won't last forever. Eventually, the ghosts of my past will catch up to us, and no matter what I've promised myself, I also know I won't remain somewhere he's not safe. I can't risk him—not even for his own happiness.

I'll be forced to rip him away from everything he loves here, all while coming up with some half-excuse as to why because the truth would absolutely wreck my sweet boy. And I can't do that.

Not now.

Eventually, he'll learn the truth. But right now, I want him to continue growing without that weight on his shoulders.

"I'm going to take the trash out; then we can do dessert. Sound good?" I say.

"I've got it." He tosses his controller down and jumps over the back of the couch. After planting a kiss on my cheek, he heads straight for the garbage can.

"Really? That easy?" I arch a brow playfully. Truth is, he's always been so incredibly helpful.

"I'll do anything for you, Mom, you know that. Besides —" He trails off and pulls the bag from the can. "This gives you more time to make the sundaes." He sticks out his tongue and heads for the door while I laugh behind him.

So happy.

Whole.

Why can't it stay like this forever?

As he runs the trash down the hall to the trash chute, I

pull out two bowls and the ice cream I grabbed on my way home today. After scooping some into a bowl, I start to top it with chocolate and whipped cream.

But the sound of a deep, muffled voice outside has my heart rate spiking. I toss the can to the side and sprint across the apartment.

No.

It can't be. We're safe here, right?

I rip the door open, ready for a fight, and the panic in my chest dies instantly, replaced by attraction as I meet the gaze of the handsome neighbor that I've been trying *really* hard to distance myself from. I'd been doing well, too, until yesterday when I ran into him at the beach.

Seeing him standing there before me, the golden sunlight bringing out the olive tones of his skin, is an image that's been with me ever since.

"Hey, Mom, look who I found," Thomas says with a smile. The trash is no longer in his hand. "He was just coming home, and I told him we had plenty of sundae stuff if he was interested."

Garrison's gaze never leaves mine as he steps into the doorway wearing the same dark jeans he had on earlier. His jacket is unzipped, revealing a blue button-down shirt that's open just enough to see a bit of dark chest hair.

My stomach twists, and heat spreads through my body. I swallow hard. "Yeah, we definitely do. Have plenty," I add.

"Are you sure? I don't want to impose," Garrison says.

His tone is neutral, but his expression is anything but. I just can't bring myself to look too closely at what's reflected in those dark, gorgeous depths.

"Not imposing at all," Thomas says, clearly oblivious to what's transpiring between me and this SEAL during this silent moment.

Why me? Why him? Why now? How can he affect me this way? How can he make me feel like the only woman alive, even as I *know* anything between us would be a major mistake? How can a simple look from him erase all of the fear I've carried at the mere thought of a relationship with any man after what I went through?

"Not at all," I agree, plastering a smile on my face. "Come on in." I hold the door open so he and Thomas can come inside.

"Are you sure?" he asks when he pauses near the door, his voice low and deep. "I really can just go home."

A shiver runs through me that has nothing to do with fear or cold, but a soul-deep attraction that has me desperate and terrified of being around him. He's the peace and the storm.

The calm and the chaos.

"Don't be silly," I reply. "It's just ice cream." I smile at him, hoping that he can't see past the mask I've so clearly slipped on.

The moment between us on the beach yesterday has my emotions toward him already charged. Especially since he had a front row seat to my momentary panic when that guy was running toward us on the beach.

Garrison offers me a curt nod, then moves into the apartment. I close the door behind him and head into the kitchen to prep another bowl, all while Thomas grabs a second controller and gets it set up to teach Garrison how to play.

Seeing them sitting side by side on the couch sends my pulse racing as the same fears I had seeing them together at the diner hit me full force.

What if he gets too close to Thomas?

What if my son gets hurt worse when we have to leave because he's attached to Garrison?

What if—*Calm your mind, Katelyn.*

Lord, please take these anxious thoughts. Please shield my heart and mind, God. I am spiraling, and I know You have a plan. Please help me focus on it. I pray this in the name of Jesus, amen.

I take a deep breath, then nearly jump out of my skin when Thomas lets loose a cheer loud enough to compete with the thunder just outside.

Get. It. Together.

After topping all three bowls with chocolate syrup, whipped cream, and a cherry, I carry them into the living room, balancing one of them on my upper arm just as I do when carrying plates at the diner.

"Dessert is served," I announce with a smile, then hand Thomas the first bowl before taking the one in my other hand and offering it to Garrison.

Our fingers brush, and warmth shoots through me. It's stupid—this reaction I'm having to him. Like I'm some foolish teenage girl unburdened by what's happened to me, simply excited about the cute boy next door.

Unfortunately, I know all too well what happened to kill that girl in me. It haunts me every time I close my eyes.

"Thank you so much for this," Garrison says as he takes a bite. "It's delicious."

"You're welcome, and thank you."

"Mom makes the best sundaes." Thomas sets his controller down and flips the TV channel to a show he's been watching for the last few weeks.

And as the three of us sit there, enjoying sundaes and watching a television show together, it takes *everything* in me to remain seated instead of grabbing my son and running as fast as I can.

"You excited for baseball camp?"

"Oh yeah." Thomas beams at Garrison. "I seriously cannot wait. Coach said how we perform at camp plays a huge part in the lineup for the fall season."

"Is this your first time playing?"

Thomas nods. "I wanted to play before, but I didn't get the chance." His joy dies down just a bit, and hearing that disappointment cements that promise I made to myself: I have to do whatever I can to keep us here in Stormwatch Landing. Even if it means facing down the darkness in my past. Who knows, maybe this place is just far enough off the map that it won't be able to find us.

"I played baseball in high school, too. Loved it."

"Really?" Thomas's eyes get so big it's almost comical.

"Yeah, I—" The power flickers and dies, plunging the apartment into darkness.

My heart catches in my throat, and the bowl in my now-trembling hand clatters to the floor. Logically, I know it's the storm.

Logically, I know I'm safe—especially with Garrison here.

But that fear slips in so quickly that I don't have any time for logic.

I'm thrown back into a dark closet. Pitch black with nothing but my own tears to keep me company while I waited for the inevitable fist.

"Oh man. Hang on." Someone shifts on the couch, and a light illuminates the room seconds later. "Katelyn?"

But my gaze is on the balcony—and the dark shadow standing just outside the closed patio doors.

I scramble to my feet, grabbing Thomas and pulling him up with me. I shove him behind me and back as far away as I can, the scream dying in my throat. No. He can't have him.

"Mom, what's going on?" Thomas' tone is terrified, but I'm locked on the shadow.

"Katelyn, what is it?" Garrison is right there in front of me, concern etched on his handsome face.

But with the next flash of lightning…the figure is gone.

"I—sorry, I was just caught off guard." But my voice is barely above a whisper, a tormented lie that seeps into my chest and remains there, a weight I can't shake off. "Thomas, can you grab the candles from your room?"

"Sure thing, Mom." Even he seems nervous as he pulls out his own phone and uses the flashlight to guide himself down the hall.

"What is it, Katelyn?" Garrison asks, keeping his tone low. "Something is wrong. Talk to me."

He doesn't touch me, and for that, I'm grateful. Because if he did, he'd be able to feel just how badly I'm shaking. I *saw* something…didn't I? Was it just a trick of my mind, or was someone really out there?

Has our time run out?

"Nothing. I just—it scared me, is all."

"Tell—"

"Got the candles!" Thomas announces as he strolls back into the living room. He sets them down, so I busy myself grabbing the lighter from on top of my TV stand, then light both candles.

Flickering flames dance off the walls of the living room.

Outside, the storm picks up as rain begins to fall in heavy sheets, battering the windows as wind sends it flying into the side of the building.

With the light, I can breathe a little easier, but that's

only if I force my attention away from the man watching my every move. He sees too much.

Way too much. What was I thinking, letting him in?

"Whoa. Crazy storm," Thomas says as he crosses over toward the patio doors.

"No! Get back!" I start toward him before I realize that my reaction was *not* normal, and both Thomas and Garrison know it. They turn to me.

"You okay, Mom? It's just a storm." Thomas questions.

Fake it 'til you make it. Deep breaths, Katelyn. "I know, honey. The wind is just strong. You should stay inside." I force a smile. "Besides, you should be getting ready for bed. Storm or not, you need sleep so you can get up and get ready for school. One week left until camp."

He rolls his eyes. "Ugh, fine. Thanks for coming and hanging with us, Mr. Holt."

"You're welcome." Garrison offers my son his hand to shake, then retrieves his bowl and carries it into the kitchen while I watch Thomas walk down toward the bedroom. There's no access to it—unless someone wants to climb the side of the building. Otherwise, I honestly don't think I would have let him leave my sight. Truthfully, it's safer in there than it is in here.

If someone was out there, they'd have to go through me first.

Breathe, Katelyn. You are safe. It was just a trick of your mind. There's no way someone is out there. Not in this weather.

"Are you sure you're okay?" Garrison asks. "I can stick around, sleep on the couch."

No, you can't, because that's where I sleep. "I'm okay. Thanks for the offer, though." To demonstrate just *how* "okay" I am with him leaving, I cross over and pull open the door. The hallway is pitch black aside from the faint glow of the EXIT sign over the stairwell.

Garrison pulls out his phone before stepping out and turning back to face me. The desperation on his face is clear as a sunny afternoon, even in the darkness of our current situation. "I'm here if you need me, Katelyn."

As he says it, the electricity flashes back on, fully illuminating the worry on his face.

"I know, thanks. See you later." With a smile, I gently close and lock the door, then lean back against it as I stare out at the patio.

Another flash of lightning illuminates it, reinforcing the idea that I imagined the shadowy figure I saw out there. Still, there's a gnawing in my gut that it wasn't my imagination and that this is just the beginning of what will inevitably be another relocation for Thomas and me, despite my earlier resolve to remain firmly planted right here.

CHAPTER 12

GARRISON

A piercing scream rips me from sleep. I shoot out of bed, adrenaline pumping through my system before my feet even hit the ground. I grab my gun and rush out into the living room, only to find it completely silent aside from the still-raging storm just outside.

Did I imagine it?

My breathing is heavy, my eyes still adjusting to the darkness, but—another scream.

Katelyn!

I yank my door open and run barefoot next door. "Katelyn!" I call out, my fist hammering against the door. "Katelyn! Thomas!"

I wait.

One heartbeat.

Two.

And then the door is pulled open by a wide-eyed Katelyn. She's frantic. Wind whips at her hair, partially shielding her face. The patio doors are wide open, and the storm is battering the inside of her apartment.

"Did someone break in?" I push past her with my weapon raised, determined to find the threat and eliminate it before it can hurt her or her son.

Wet carpet squishes beneath my feet, grounding me in the reality of what I'm really looking at. Her apartment is *wrecked.* The patio doors aren't open—they've been completely destroyed, and the harsh wind from the storm outside sends rain pouring into the apartment in thick sheets.

I lower my weapon and turn toward her. "What happened?"

"The windows just shattered. I think the patio table hit them." Her hands shake as she moves past me and goes to work, picking up the broken glass. All while wind scatters her mail and some of the lighter things that had been on her counter.

"Extra blankets?" I ask her.

"Hall closet."

"Grab them, and I'll be right back." Rushing back over to my apartment, I pull a t-shirt over my head, slip into some tennis shoes, return my firearm to the lockbox it stays in when I'm not carrying it, then retrieve my toolbox and a couple of the tarps I have left over from when I painted the kitchen.

By the time I get back, Thomas is coming down the hall with an armful of blankets. "Help me get these tarps up in place," I tell him as I set the stack down.

"Garrison, you don't have to—" Katelyn starts.

"Not a chance you're getting rid of me, Katelyn. Let me help." My tone is sharper than I meant, but she clearly needs help. Whatever walls she's put up can be reinforced tomorrow. But tonight, I'm going to insist on stepping in where I'm needed. Even if I'm not necessarily wanted.

Thomas pulls a chair into the kitchen and takes the corner of the first tarp. Even before I've managed to get a nail into the corner to hold it in place, I'm soaked. The storm is unrelenting as it sends rain soaring into the apartment, drenching the both of us.

I don't even want to think of the damage that will be done by the time it dies down.

With one tarp hung in place, we start on the second one. As soon as it's finished, I tie the two bottom corners together that I couldn't secure with nails, then start piling blankets at the bottom. They'll be absolutely soaked tomorrow—likely ruined—but hopefully they'll catch most of the water pouring in from the bottom.

Raindrops hammer into the tarp as the wind slams against it, billowing the paint-splattered blue plastic toward us.

I turn toward Katelyn, who is trying to gather as much broken glass as she can. Something that isn't going well, thanks to the water all over the tile.

"If we wait until tomorrow, some of the water will have dried," I tell her. "I can get a fan to dry the floor, then we can get all the glass up. Why don't you guys go pack some stuff and stay at my place?"

"No. We don't need to do that," Katelyn says, her tone shaky.

"Mom, this place is soaked. You don't have anywhere to sleep." He gestures toward the living room, and for the first time, I notice the pull-out couch with a thin blanket over the top.

Is this where she sleeps?

Her cheeks flush with color, so I wipe the shock from my face. "I have a spare room, and I can take the couch. You guys can have your own beds. I'll get help over here tomorrow, and you can call the landlord in the morning. I know Geoff will want to help, but he keeps his phone on silent at night."

"I can sleep in the tub," Katelyn says. "I've done it before."

My heart drops at her confession. The tub? She's slept in a bathtub?

"Come on, Mom. *All* of our blankets are on the floor. Please?"

She chews on her bottom lip but finally nods. "Okay. Thank you, Garrison."

"Yeah." Agitation laces my tone, but I can't figure out *why* she's so apprehensive around me. I haven't ever done anything to warrant it. The fear on her face when we'd been on that beach surfaces in my memory, reminding me that I have *no* idea what this woman has gone through. "I can help you grab some stuff if you want to make sure it stays safe."

"We'll just grab a set of clothes for tomorrow and his school stuff. We'll be over in a few."

"You don't need help?"

She shakes her head. "Give us just a few."

"Sure." I run a hand through my now-wet hair as she and Thomas head down the rain-soaked hallway. The carpet is saturated with it, and I imagine there will be damage not just to this apartment but the one below it, too.

Since I imagine her sending me home was her way of getting some space, I don't wait for them to get what they need before heading back toward my apartment. Quickly, I change into some dry clothes, then strip my bed, replacing my sheets with a clean set.

The bedding in the spare bedroom was changed after Zane's wife, Tessa, stayed in it before they were married. But I still pop in and make sure there's nothing out of place before tossing my sheets onto the couch for me to use.

I'm just about to head back over to Katelyn's when there's a knock on the door. I pull it open and step aside as she and Thomas come in. As soon as the door is closed, I engage the security alarm Elijah installed.

To be honest, I haven't actually used it yet, but with them here, it's not an option.

"This place is awesome." Thomas moves over toward

the pictures I have on the wall and points to one. "Is this from when you were in the Navy?"

I nod. "I was doing some training overseas, and those were the local kids. I still get letters from some of them."

"Really?" he asks.

I nod.

"That's so cool."

"They're great kids." With the adrenaline still coursing through my veins, I know I'm not going to be much for conversation, but I force a smile anyway. "I can show you guys the rooms if you'd like."

"Yes, please," Katelyn says. Her face is pale, eyes still wide from the shock of having her windows shattered. Her hair is soaked, and there's a bit of blood on her left cheek. Likely from a shard of glass hitting her.

Since it's not too bad, I don't bring any attention to it. The last thing I want to do is put her on edge.

"Whoa, is that where you—"

I glance back over my shoulder just in time to see Thomas point to the shadow of a stain on my floor.

"It is. Now come on. Bed." Katelyn gently tugs him farther down the hall, following me, all while he keeps trying to look back at it. I face forward again and push open the door to the spare room.

"This is the spare." I point inside, and Thomas goes in and sets his stuff down. "You can stay here," I tell Katelyn, pointing to the room across the small hall.

She leans in, then looks back at me. "I'll take the couch."

"Not a chance. I changed the sheets so they're clean. If either of you wants to shower, there's fresh towels in the cabinets and soap in both showers."

"I just need a bed." Thomas yawns and pulls back the sheets.

Katelyn moves into his room and pulls him into her arms. "Are you sure you're okay?" she asks.

"Yeah, Mom. I'm fine."

Feeling like an intruder in a private moment between mother and son, I head back into the kitchen. The adrenaline still hasn't fully left me, so I put some water in my electric kettle for tea. Maybe a mug of my aunt's Calm Down tea will help me settle.

Because between her scream waking me up, the chaos that is her apartment right now, and the fact that she's going to be staying here tonight—let's just say my mind is in overdrive.

"You have enough for two of those?"

My heart jumps in my chest at the mere sound of her voice. Will I ever come down from it? From this high I get just by being around her?

"Absolutely." Without turning to face her, I get a second mug and spoon some of my aunt's loose-leaf tea recipe into another teabag.

Katelyn takes a seat at the island and runs both hands

over her face before resting her elbows on the counter and remaining just like that. Expression guarded, shoulders slumped. How much of her life has she had to be on her own?

Is that why she's so against me? Because she's spent too many years relying on herself?

"Thanks for this. For letting us stay here."

I look away as soon as she starts to uncover her face so she doesn't catch me watching her.

"Of course."

"We'll be out of your hair tomorrow."

Based on that damage? I doubt it. "You're not in my hair. You guys can stay as long as you need." *Please stay. I never realized how lonely I was until I met you.*

"I appreciate that, but you're going to want your bed back," she replies with a soft laugh.

"The couch doesn't bother me," I tell her truthfully. "I've slept in a lot worse places. Believe me." *Even the bathtub of a safe house a time or two.* But, not wanting to pressure her, I keep that comment to myself.

"Yeah?"

My gaze locks with hers, and I can't bring myself to look away even when the kettle beeps. "Yeah."

Outside, the storm has slowed enough that the rain is barely audible through my patio doors, but the one within me? It's only picking up steam.

She clears her throat. "When you were in the Navy?"

After a moment, I tear my gaze away and pour water

into our mugs. "That and before. I told you that my aunt raised me?"

She nods.

"Well, after my parents overdosed, I was what the state called a 'flight risk.' I didn't know my aunt even existed because my mom had cut her out of our lives when I was a baby. Every group or foster home they stuck me in, I bolted from. I can't even count the nights I spent sleeping in alleys or on park benches."

"That's horrible," Katelyn breathes.

When I glance over at her, I see the pity in her gaze. "It wasn't a shining moment of my life, that's for sure. When they finally tracked down my aunt, she agreed to take me in without hesitation." I laugh. "To this day, I'm pretty sure she had no idea what she was getting into."

"I'm sure she loved every minute of raising you."

I laugh, then slide her mug over toward her. "I can recall more than a few moments where she struggled with me." Those moments still weigh on me. Even knowing how close we grew to be. "I was angry at my parents for putting me through what they did, only to die and leave me alone. And I was angry at myself for not being someone they were willing to change for." I take a seat across from her.

"I'm sorry, Garrison."

Wrapping both hands around my mug, I savor the heat. Even that's not enough to chase away the chill of my past. "If it weren't for my aunt, I can pretty much guarantee I wouldn't be sitting here. She was patient with me. Kind.

Everything I wished my parents would've been. And she loved me a whole lot more than I deserved."

"I'd say she loved you as much as you deserved," Katelyn replies.

My gaze lifts from the slowly darkening tea in my mug to the gorgeous woman sitting across from me. *Tell me your secrets, and I'll keep them safe.*

How can I get her to open up and trust me?

How can I convince her that, whatever she's hiding, it's not worth the weight she carries?

"What about you?" I pry. "Are you close with your parents?"

"It's just Thomas and me," she replies.

Which is not a direct answer.

"That must get hard. Raising him alone."

"You would think so," she replies with a soft smile. "But God blessed me with such a wonderful son. Don't get me wrong. There are moments where being a single mom *is* hard, but he makes it all worth it. Every single moment."

"He seems like a great kid."

She beams at me. The first real smile I've ever seen on her face…and it steals my breath. "He's my everything."

I can't look away from her.

I know I should.

That harboring any feelings at all for a woman who seems intent to keep me at arm's length is a risk.

But I can't help myself.

Still, if I'm not careful, I'll scare her away. So, even

though it pains me to do it, I shift my gaze back to my tea and take a drink. The heat scalds my tongue, but the pain grounds me in the present.

"I cannot believe my apartment flooded." She covers her face with both hands again.

"We'll get it fixed."

"It's okay. I can handle it. You've done enough already."

"I really don't mind. I help Geoff with maintenance sometimes. So, technically, it's kind of my job."

"You still shouldn't be doing anything overly physical."

"Actually, I was cleared completely. I may not look it, but I'm feeling stellar these days."

Katelyn laughs softly, filling my living room with the most beautiful melody. "I never doubted that there was anything about you that is less than stellar, Garrison Holt." Before I can even respond, her cheeks flush with color. "I just mean, you seem like you're in great shape."

I can't help the smirk on my face or the way my pulse kicks up a notch. *So she does feel this, too.* Whatever is building between us, Katelyn is not immune.

And that makes me far happier than it should.

CHAPTER 13

KATELYN

Even though he changed the sheets, Garrison's room smells just like him. A heady combination of tea tree and pine that seeps straight down into my bones. Before I've even opened my eyes for the day, I snuggle down closer beneath his blankets.

Here, in the privacy of his room, I can let my walls down.

I can let myself dream, pretending—even if for a moment—that this is my current reality. That Garrison Holt is the one I'm coming home to every night. That I spent a night wrapped in his strong arms, rather than sleeping alone in his room because my apartment was destroyed.

Oh no. What am I going to do?

The realization that my to-do list is a mile longer than even my busiest day has me opening my eyes and groaning.

First, get Thomas to school.

Then call Maddie and Anastasia. I'll need the day off so I can coordinate everything. Thankfully, I've already paid the bills for this month, and with the new job at the coffee shop, I was able to pay for Thomas' baseball camp and still put a little aside for a rainy-day fund. Which I will unfortunately have to use a lot sooner than I'd planned.

After taking a deep breath, I throw the blankets aside and swing my legs over the edge. As I do every morning, I bow my head and fold my hands.

Lord, thank You for this day. Thank You for being with us through the storm last night and for keeping both Thomas and me safe. And God, thank You for Garrison. Please walk with me today and guide me through the steps I will need to take to get everything taken care of. I'm struggling, God, and I know I can't do this without You. In Jesus' name I pray, amen.

Tears fill my eyes, but I don't have time to cry. So, I quickly wipe them away as I stand.

The room is still dark, so there should still be time to take care of everything I need to before getting Thomas to school. Without the ability to make breakfast, we'll need to swing by the diner, which will work out because then I can talk to Maddie directly rather than on the phone.

Maybe I can swing by the coffee shop on my way home.

I grip the handle of the door and pull it open, only to be assaulted by bright sunlight. As my eyes adjust, I note the open door across from me. The bed has been made, and Thomas is nowhere to be seen.

Pulse kicking up a notch, I rush down the hall.

Garrison is seated at his table, a Bible open in front of him, a steaming mug of coffee beside him.

But I don't see Thomas. My palms begin to sweat, and I continue forward. Surely he's here somewhere. He has to be.

Garrison turns toward me and smiles. "Hey. Want some coffee?"

"Where's Thomas? What time is it?" I demand, my tone sharp.

"He's at school," Garrison replies. A line forms between his brows as his smile falls slightly. "It's almost nine."

"Nine?" I screech. I missed getting him off to school *and* the start of my shift at Anastasia's!

"Relax, I walked Thomas to school this morning and let Anastasia know what happened. She said to take the day."

"You walked my son to school?" I stare at him as he stands, trying to understand *why* this is happening. Why would he walk my son to school? Why did I take him up on his offer last night? I should have stayed in my apartment. Should have insisted on it.

"I did. He said that sometimes he walks himself, but since you were asleep, I didn't want to wake you up and ask to confirm." Garrison moves into the kitchen and points to a sticky note on the counter. "We even left you a note just in case."

"That's not your job."

Garrison turns toward me, and something passes over his features. It's quick enough that, had I not been so in tune with the body language of others, I likely would have missed it. "I never said it was. He needed to get to school, and you needed sleep. I figured it would be fine, but I am sorry if I overstepped; that wasn't my intention."

Of course it wasn't. Because Garrison Holt is not the type of man to overstep. Which is why he *insisted* on helping me last night and pushed me into staying here when I could have been perfectly comfortable sleeping in my tub.

I've done it before. I could have done it again.

Sudden anger surges through me. It doesn't matter that I recognize it as irrational; it's there. Burning hot and fast before I can stop it.

"I don't need you to take care of me. I've been doing just fine on my own for the last thirteen years."

"Katelyn, I'm not trying to take care of you. I'm trying to help."

"Why? Why do you care enough to help?"

I expect anger from him. I expect that mask he surely wears to slip away, revealing the monster beneath. What I don't expect, in any way, shape, or form, is the kindness that remains on his face.

Or the way his shoulders slump forward ever so slightly. "Because you're a great mom and Thomas is a great kid. Because you're two people who deserved a dry, safe place to sleep last night. Or, maybe it's because I genuinely care about what happens to the woman who saved my life and cared enough to bring me trays of food so I wouldn't go hungry." He comes around the kitchen island, each step bringing him closer to me.

A part of me wants to run.

To flee so the anger that surely simmers beneath the surface of his cool façade doesn't explode on me.

But there's a stronger voice cutting through the fear. And this one assures me that Garrison will never hurt me. Not on purpose, at least. So I remain rooted in my spot as he comes to a stop right in front of me.

"Take your pick, Katelyn," he says softly. "But if you want the truth, it's all three."

I stare up at him, my gaze locking on his while I try to understand *why* he seems to care. Especially since I happen to be the reason he wound up back in the hospital that second time. Sure, I tried to make up for it by doing something nice, but standing here in his living room, looking into his kind, dark gaze, I get the impression it has nothing to do with what I did and everything to do with who he is.

A man who wants to do good in a world riddled with darkness.

"Thank you," I reply. Every ounce of my anger deflates like an old balloon. "And I'm sorry."

"You don't need to apologize," Garrison says. He reaches toward me, and I flinch out of habit.

Embarrassment floods me as Garrison drops his hand and his expression shifts to one of understanding.

"I do need to apologize because I was rude." I take a step back, needing distance before I do something stupid and lean in so he'll do exactly what it was he was thinking about when he raised that hand. Was he going to run his fingertips over my cheek? Brush hair behind my ear?

"You woke up and found your son gone. That's not rude. Can I get you some coffee?"

"I could definitely use some." I smile. "Thanks."

"Not a problem at all." As he starts making my coffee, using an impressive-looking espresso machine on his counter, I am helpless to look away. The strong muscles of his arms shift with each movement.

Victor was a quarterback, and his lithe runner's body gave him the speed he needed to weave through the other team's defense. My stomach churns as the memories assault me. The handsome quarterback with a bright future. A real-life Prince Charming...or so everyone thought.

They had no idea what happened when the doors closed.

Or the truth of the nightmare that led me to be on the arm of the sport world's most eligible bachelor. No one but his brother...who is even more of a monster than Victor ever was.

Victor may not have been a muscular man, but his hands were violent.

Garrison, on the other hand, is built like a fighter, yet I know, without a doubt, his touch would be tender.

In another life.

Back before my innocence was ripped away. Before I was forced to live a life of lies until I was finally strong enough to fight back.

Before I had to run.

That's the lifetime when something between Garrison Holt and me could have been possible. And as I sit here in the kitchen, watching him, I let myself imagine what that might have been like.

With the addition, of course, of my sweet boy. Because, no matter what I had to go through, I'd suffer through it all over again for Thomas.

Where would Garrison and I have met?

What would we have done on our first date?

Would I have fallen deeply in love with him? Somehow, I think I already know the answer to that. Probably because, as much as I'm trying to deny it, the feelings I already have for him are very, *very* real.

Garrison slides the mug over toward me. "Here you go."

"Thanks." I shutter my fantasy, burying it deep down, and take a sip of coffee. As the gingerbread spice dances on my tongue, I nearly groan in absolute delight. "Anastasia should have hired you. This is amazing. Where did you get gingerbread syrup in the spring?"

He laughs then winks at me. "I have my ways. And I'm

glad you like it." After rinsing everything he used, Garrison lifts his own mug and turns to face me. I find myself captivated once again by those gorgeous eyes and the way they seem to bore straight through me.

Is that why he's so good at his job? Why he's able to connect with the teenagers no one else can reach?

I've spent a lot of years living in the shadows. Choosing to remain hidden was about survival. But standing here, feeling *seen* by this man—it's the safest I've felt in a long, long time. There's a voice in the back of my mind, though. A warning that, even though I feel safe, I'm at risk of losing something I vowed never to offer up: my heart.

"So, I'll give Geoff a call today and see if he can get someone over to help with my apartment. We'll be out of your hair this afternoon."

"You don't need to rush out. I'd be surprised if they don't have to completely gut the apartment. The carpet needs to be replaced, and the patio doors are destroyed. I was actually going to head over there here in just a bit so I can get them properly boarded up for you."

"You don't need to do that. You've already done enough." I gesture toward the apartment. "I'd say we're more than even." I laugh awkwardly, unsure how to handle the intensity of the expression on his face.

"I want to help."

"Because you care what happens to us," I reply, repeating what he'd said only a few minutes ago. "Though

I still can't figure out why. I mean, until I found you on your floor, we'd never spoken."

"What is it you said to me? Kindness doesn't need familiarity." He grins, and I might as well have been reduced to a puddle on the floor.

I smile at him. "Fair enough, Mr. Holt."

He leans in, gaze sparkling with something I'd rather not look too closely at. "I'm glad you think so, Miss Ellis."

"I still can't believe my doors broke. I mean, why mine and not yours?"

"Did you chain down your patio furniture?"

I stare at him, half-expecting it to be a joke. "Was I supposed to?"

He arches a brow. "Around here, the wind can get pretty strong."

Embarrassment and frustration quickly push aside everything else, and I run both hands over my face. "This is going to be an expensive fix."

"Nah, it'll be fine."

"It's my fault they broke."

"And we can fix it. Seriously, Katelyn, don't worry about it."

Throat burning, I try so hard not to wear my emotions on my sleeve. How am I supposed to afford it? Will my renters' insurance be enough to cover it?

"Katelyn."

I open my eyes, mortified that they're full of tears.

He steps around the counter and stops in front of me,

but he doesn't reach out. What does it say about me that I want him to?

"I'm sorry. I just—"

"We're going to get it fixed."

But at what cost?

"I know. Everything will be fine. It's just a lot."

"I'm here for you. Whatever you need. Let me help."

"You've already helped enough." I wipe my cheeks and look up at him. The emotions swirling in his dark gaze are enough to have my breath catching in my throat.

Oh, this is a mistake.

There's a sharp knock on the door that breaks the moment between us. Garrison heads toward the door, and I watch him pause just on the other side as he checks the peephole before pulling it open.

"Hey, Mr. Holt. Sorry, I know I'm a little early." The voice reaches me before I can see who's there, cutting a conversation short that was getting far too intimate. Especially since Garrison has this ability to make me forget every reason we won't work.

"No problem at all, Kyle, come on in." Garrison steps aside as a boy who looks to be only a few years older than Thomas walks in, wearing dark jeans and a black hoodie sweatshirt. He removes his hat once inside and toys with it when he sees me. "Kyle, you remember Ms. Ellis. I'm going to go change, and I'll be right back."

"Nice to see you again, Ms. Ellis," Kyle says. His gaze darts away from me quickly, though, almost as if I make him nervous. My heart aches for this boy who has clearly seen a bit too much of the darkness in this world.

"It's nice to see you again, too," I reply with a smile. "Thomas has always spoken highly of you. He said that you came to his rescue when some bullies cornered him shortly after we'd moved to town."

"Thomas is cool. Always nice to everyone."

I smile. "That makes me very grateful to hear. So, are you working with Garri—Mr. Holt today?"

He nods. "He's about the only one who hasn't given up on me completely. I've made some mistakes."

Like bringing a knife to school? Even though that weapon could have posed a risk to Thomas, I can't find any anger at the boy trying to protect his sister. "He definitely seems like a good man."

"Yeah. I don't deserve the chance he's giving me, but I appreciate it anyhow."

I smile at him, appreciating his candidness. "What are you guys going to be doing today?"

"Uh, I think we're boarding up windows."

"My windows?" I ask, honestly surprised. Has Garrison already made official plans to start working on my apartment?

"I think so. Thomas said you lived next to Mr. Holt. So, if so, then yes." He smiles at me, and a bit of the darkness slips away. "I'm happy to help. More than, really."

"Well, I really appreciate it." I return his smile. "Will you excuse me for just a second?"

"Of course. Yeah."

"Thanks." I push off the stool and head down the hall. Garrison's door is cracked, so I gently push it open…only to have the air knocked from my lungs when I see him standing partially in his closet, his shirt in hand. "Sorry, I—"

He turns toward me, revealing the still-healing scar on his side, along with quite an assortment of others on his chest and abdomen. Heat spreads through me like a wildfire as attraction burns heavy in my gut.

Oh boy.

I'd seen him shirtless before, but then he'd been covered in his own blood and barely clinging to life.

Now, every inch of a hair-dusted, muscled chest is on full display.

DANGER. The word echoes through my mind like a battle cry.

"Sorry, hang on." Moving quickly, he shrugs into a long-sleeved shirt. "Sorry, Kyle's a good kid, but I wasn't sure how comfortable you would be being left alone with him, so I kept the door cracked just in case. Everything okay?"

"Yeah, I—" *Get it together, Katelyn. Why am I in here again?*

"Katelyn?"

"I can't date you." I blurt the words out without thinking, then immediately wish I could take them back. "Sorry.

I don't know if that's what you're trying to do, but if it is, then you need to know that I—"

"I would absolutely love to date you," he interrupts. "But that's not why I'm helping."

I stare at him, taken aback by his candid response and my *very* potent reaction to it. "I—then why are you helping me?"

Garrison cocks his head to the side. "I thought we covered this earlier? With your own words, might I add."

"I just… You don't even know me. Not really. And this is a whole lot more than some frozen food."

"So, not really knowing someone should keep us from helping?" He crosses his arms. "Do you know the parable of the Good Samaritan?" When I continue staring back at him while I try to recall the story, Garrison continues. "A man traveling to Jericho was attacked by robbers. They stole his clothes and beat him. By the time they were done with him, he was half dead. A priest and a Levite both traveled down that road, and even though they saw him, they left him there to die. But when a Samaritan happened upon him, he took pity on the injured man and bandaged his wounds. He then took the man from where he was on the side of the road to an inn to take care of him. When it was time for him to leave, he paid the innkeeper out of his own pocket and promised to return and reimburse him for any additional expenses as the innkeeper cared for the injured man."

"I'm hardly a beaten man on the side of the road," I reply, though it's not entirely far from the truth, when you take into consideration what's happened to me in my past.

Garrison leans in, close enough I can make out flecks of copper in his dark eyes. "God calls on us to love our neighbors. To care for others. I'm helping you because it's the right thing to do. And because the thought of anything happening to you or Thomas is unthinkable."

Tears threaten, stinging the corners of my eyes. It's been years since I've had anyone to look out for me. Since I let anyone close enough to do just that. Truth be told, if Thomas weren't so happy in this town, I likely would have already left this place behind me.

But for the first time, I want to stay.

I want to fight for my place here.

And I'd be a liar if I didn't at least admit to myself that part of the reason has to do with the man standing in front of me.

Garrison clears his throat and steps back, then offers me his hand. "So what do you say, Katelyn Ellis? Want to be my friend? No strings attached? No romantic relationship on the horizon?"

I study his large hand, knowing that I would love to be so much more than that. But with secrets like mine, it's just not possible. So I take his hand, letting the large, calloused palm envelop mine. "Friends."

Garrison beams. "Then this friend is going to go get

started boarding up your windows. If you have time, you should come get some of your belongings and bring them over here so you have them."

CHAPTER 14

———

GARRISON

"So you boarded up her windows." Sawyer shakes his head and bounces on the balls of his feet. Across from him, Weston sets up for another round.

Boxing is a favorite pastime of ours these days, though it'll still be a while until I'm in the ring. I was cleared by Alex to go back to my normal routine—with minor limitations. Boxing being one of those. Though right now, I could seriously use the physical exertion. It's been nearly a week since Katelyn and Thomas started staying with me, and I'm slowly losing it. She's right there—so close but still out of reach.

"They broke."

"And you were right there, ready to lend a hand. Tell me, where has she and her kid been staying the past few days?" Sawyer dodges when Weston charges. The two men differ in size, with Sawyer being more on the lean side and Weston carrying a bulk of muscle built by a lifetime working on a ranch. "Missed me, Cowboy," he taunts.

Weston glares at him and takes his stance again. Hand-to-hand, he has Sawyer beat hands-down. That is if he can catch him.

"What was I supposed to do? Let her handle it? Let them sleep in a flooded apartment? The entire thing had to be emptied so the carpet could be replaced."

"I'm sure that's not what Mr. Manners is trying to say," Anastasia says as she strolls toward us from the back of the gym, a tray of coffees in her hand. "Besides, taking life or relationship advice from Sawyer is a poor choice."

The distraction is just enough that Weston manages to clock Sawyer, knocking him down to the mat with a grunt. I can't help the laughter that bubbles out of my chest as Sawyer glares up at Weston.

"Eyes forward, Cable Guy," Weston taunts.

"That was a cheap shot, Cowboy, and you know it." Sawyer takes Weston's outstretched hand and lets him pull him to his feet.

"How is Katelyn doing?" Anastasia asks as she offers me a coffee.

"Fine, I think. She and Thomas are at the batting cages. He leaves for baseball camp tomorrow."

"Really?" Sawyer arches a brow and tugs off his gloves, then takes a cup from Anastasia's tray. "And just where is Ms. Ellis staying while her son is away?"

And then it hits me. With Thomas away, it'll be just the two of us in my apartment. Which, given my current promise of just maintaining a friendship with her, shouldn't be too hard.

Except…it's going to be impossible.

As it stands now, I had to turn down Thomas's offer for me to go with them to the batting cages out of sheer desperation for space. Katelyn insisted on helping Kyle and me with her apartment, so I spent the last few days working in close proximity to her.

It's been torture.

Her subtle perfume haunts me like an old memory.

"Maybe you two need a chaperone," Sawyer offers.

I shake my head. "Katelyn has made it clear she just wants to be friends. I will respect those wishes."

"Sure. It's all easy sailing until she starts making those googly eyes back at you," Sawyer replies.

"Googly eyes?" Anastasia laughs. "How old are you?"

"Old enough to know that Garrison here is playing with fire. I've seen the way you look at her."

"But like he said, she's not looking back. Besides, Garrison is a good man. He will keep his distance." Anastasia wraps an arm around me and squeezes.

"Such a good boy," Weston quips.

I roll my eyes. "As much as I appreciate your concern, Katelyn's privacy is perfectly safe with me. I'm just giving her a place to stay until her apartment is back in order."

"An apartment that *you're* fixing for her. That's awfully

close to relationship rules," Sawyer says. "Back me up, Cowboy."

Weston shakes his head. "Not getting involved."

"I'd have offered her my spare room except it's currently full of baskets for the spring auction." Anastasia grimaces. "And I mean *full.* We're talking top to bottom. Remind me again why I volunteered to help put them together?"

"Because you have a heart of gold." Sawyer bows, then grins up at her. "And because you haven't figured out how to tell Pastor Reeves' wife *no.*"

Anastasia glares at him. "Yeah, yeah. Well, see if I bring you coffee next time." She takes a deep breath and turns to me. "Let me know if anything changes. I can try to get that spare room cleaned out."

"I'll be fine. But thanks. If she decides she's uncomfortable, I'll probably just give her my place and crash with Sawyer."

"Did Sawyer agree to this?" Sawyer asks. When I don't respond, he downs the rest of his coffee and groans. "Fine. But I am *not* braiding your hair."

"I bet he does," Anastasia whispers loudly. "Anyway, I'm headed out. Errands to run, baskets to prep."

"I'll walk you out," I offer. "See you guys later. Try not to mess up his face," I tell Weston. "It really is his only redeeming quality."

"You're just jealous of the fact that I have charm, wit,

and good looks!" Sawyer calls back at me as I follow Anastasia out.

Once we're on the sidewalk, she turns to me. "You doing okay?"

"I am. Taking things day by day."

"And Kyle?" Anastasia used to babysit Kyle back when he was little more than a toddler. While she lost touch with Ursula over the years, I know she's been particularly upset with everything that's happened with the family recently.

"He's doing good. Grades are up, and he's been working hard."

She nods. "I keep meaning to call Ursula, but it's been so long, and I don't want her to think I'm pressing her for information after what happened with you. She knows we're close."

"I don't think she'd think that," I reply. "Honestly, the support would be nice."

"Okay." Anastasia looks honestly relieved as she tips her face up toward me. "I'll call her then."

"Good. And since we're on the subject of calling people, how are things with you and Jack?"

Anastasia snorts. "Great segue, Garrison."

"I thought so. You make any life-changing decisions lately?"

She starts walking toward her car, so I follow. "Not yet. Things are okay. He's great—really."

"But?"

"I don't know. Like I said, there just seems to be something missing." She glances back at the gym, and I follow her gaze through the glass to where Sawyer and Weston are squared up on the mat.

"Someone missing?" I question.

She turns toward me, and her cheeks turn a deep pink. "What? Oh, no. Sorry, spacing out, I guess. Things are good. I'm looking forward to seeing where they end up." She unlocks the door to her car and climbs in. "Call if you need me. Tell Katelyn the same."

"Will do. See ya, Anastasia."

"See ya." She shuts her door and turns on the engine, then pulls away from the curb. Shoving both hands into my pockets, I stand there and watch her taillights fade, my thoughts focused entirely on Katelyn Ellis and how hard being "just friends" is going to be.

***

"And he is asleep." Katelyn jokes as she comes to sit on the opposite end of the couch. I glance up from where I was reading through Romans and have to take a moment just to catch my breath.

Hair wet from the shower, it falls in sodden strands down past her shoulders. She's wearing a grey crew-neck sweatshirt with *UCLA* on the front and a pair of plaid pajama pants.

She's gorgeous.

"I'm surprised. Anytime it was the night before something I was excited about, I couldn't seem to get to sleep, no matter how hard I tried."

Katelyn laughs. "Same here." Things have been easier between us since our conversation at the beginning of the week. Almost like, since we agreed to just be friends, she doesn't see me as a threat anymore. I can't decide if that's a good thing or a bad thing, considering how desperately I want to be more than what I promised her I could be.

"I'm glad the batting cages were a hit. I go there sometimes when I need to blow off steam."

"You should have come with us tonight. Thomas would have enjoyed having you there. I know absolutely nothing about baseball except you hit the ball with a bat and run in a circle."

I snort. "There is a lot more to it than that."

"See, you should have come."

"I appreciate that. Maybe next time." I close my Bible and set it on the table.

"Do you read it every night?" she asks.

"My Bible?" I question when I see her gesture toward it.

"Yeah."

"I do. Even if it's just a random verse, I try to begin and end my day with God's Word."

"I love that."

"You?"

"I don't actually have a Bible anymore."

"Really? Why?"

Her gaze darkens. "I don't like to talk a lot about my past. It's not a great story."

"You don't have to tell me anything."

"I know. Maybe that's why I want to." She laughs softly, but there's no humor in it. "Uh, he was not a man of faith. He didn't like being told what to do or how he should live his life, so following God just wasn't something he was interested in doing." She closes her eyes. I want to know more, but pressing only gets people to lock up, so I remain silent as she opens her eyes and stares down at her hands. "Anyway, anytime I would pray, he'd make some rude comment or mock me. It eventually got so bad that..." She trails off, and her eyes fill.

"You don't have to tell me, Katelyn. But I am here if you want to."

She smiles at me and wipes her eyes. "I'm ashamed that I let him bully me into hiding my faith."

I try to keep a level head as I imagine just what that "bullying" might have looked like. Did he physically hurt her, too? What damage did he inflict on this beautiful woman before she was finally able to leave?

"You shouldn't be ashamed."

"I asked for the Lord's forgiveness for it."

"Then that's all you needed to do."

She purses her lips together in a tight smile. "When I left, I didn't take anything. No spare clothes, no supplies, no Bible. To be honest, I didn't even know I was going to leave. I went out to take Thomas to his one-month checkup, and when the appointment was over, I just couldn't bring myself to go back. I sat in that parking lot for three hours while my son napped and I tried to decide what to do. In the end, I took what I had on me, and I ran. As far and as fast as I could."

Which explains why she stopped working in nursing. With a new baby to raise on her own and no money for child care, she'd have been forced to take whatever job she could that fit her circumstances.

"It sounds to me like you made a brave choice for the both of you."

She nods. "I don't regret leaving. You don't even know the half of what he put me through." Anger pushes through her tone now, and it mixes with that same emotion building in my chest.

I want to hunt him down and make him pay for the pain he caused her. For the pain he caused Thomas by not being a decent enough human being to be there for his son.

"I do feel bad for Thomas, though. Not having a dad hasn't been easy on him."

"You've done an amazing job with him, Katelyn, and I'm not just saying that. I work with teenagers all day long, and Thomas is exceptional."

She smiles at me, an unguarded expression of pure delight, and that line she drew between us begins to blur. "Thanks for that."

"It's the truth." I look away. Because if I don't, I'm

going to do something stupid. "You said his dad isn't alive anymore?"

She nods. "He died when Thomas was three."

The way her voice softens, I sense there's a lot more to that story. Still, I don't press.

"I miss reading my Bible. And going to church. I was really active in mine growing up. Right up until—well—I met Victor."

"You haven't been to the church here?"

She shakes her head. "Most of the time, I'm working on Sundays. Or getting ready for work."

But there's more to it than that. I can see it written all over her face.

"Want to come with me this Sunday? I usually go every week, but since I was in the hospital, it's been a little while for me."

"I don't know. I—" But she stops. "You know what. Yes. I would love to come with you."

The joy that spreads through me is more than I expected. "Great. My team and I usually do brunch afterward at Momma Knox's. You up for that?"

"Linda's? Most definitely. She's delightful." Her smile is bright and honest. An absolute ray of sunshine in the dim light of my apartment.

"I think so, too." I grin at her, and our gazes hold. As they do, something shifts in the air around us. Something that has me thinking maybe being friends with Katelyn won't be so impossible.

After all, it's definitely better than being nothing at all.

CHAPTER 15

KATELYN

"You packed your uniform? Cleats? What about sandals for the shower?" I ask as I stand in front of Thomas. The sky is still dark overhead, but despite the early hour, my boy's eyes are wide and bright.

At least two dozen other teenage boys are also standing here in front of the school bus, saying goodbye to parents who are likely far less neurotic than I am.

I can't help it. This is the first time since he was born that Thomas will be away from me for longer than a few hours. Six nights and five full days.

How am I going to survive? *Lord, please protect him.*

"Yes, Mom," he replies with a laugh. "I triple checked everything."

"Okay." My stomach is a pit of rocks, and I'm doing everything I can not to let the tears fall. Not until he is on that bus and out of sight of me. As soon as I'm alone, all bets are off. "I got you something." Reaching into my purse, I withdraw the cell phone I'd bought for him as a surprise when he'd been at school on Friday. "On an actual plan, no hours needed."

"Seriously?" His eyes widen, and he takes it from me, pressing the power button on the side. The screen illuminates, and he stares down at it like I just handed him the keys to the city.

"I thought it was time. Especially with this trip. But, you'd better promise me you remember everything from our internet safety talk. No social media and absolutely no photographs shared anywhere or to anyone, deal? You use it to call and text me or play games. That's it."

"Yes, ma'am," he replies and pockets it, then withdraws the simple flip phone I'd purchased at a gas station last year. After handing it to me, he pulls me in for a big hug. Even at thirteen, he's nearly as tall as I am. Another few months and he'll likely pass me completely.

My sweet boy is growing up, and I have to be okay with that.

Grateful for it, even.

So why does my chest ache?

"Thanks so much, Mom."

"You're welcome." My treacherous eyes fill, and I quickly blink the tears away.

"Are you going to be okay?" he asks as he pulls back.

"Oh yeah." I force a smile. "I'm going to be just fine. You go and have the best time."

"Mom, I can sta—"

"Don't you dare finish that sentence." I grip either side of his face, my thumbs stroking his cheeks. I don't care that his friends can see; this is *my* boy. My wonderful, smart, strong son. "You go and have fun, Thomas Ellis. Do you hear me?"

He grins at me again. "Yes, ma'am."

"Good." I plant a kiss on his forehead, then release him.

Thomas hoists his duffel bag up and steps away. "See ya, Mr. Holt!" he calls out, waving at someone behind me.

Garrison? What is he doing here?

"See ya. Have a great time, Thomas," he replies.

Garrison's voice shouldn't have brought me comfort.

It shouldn't have made me feel less alone as I say goodbye to my only child.

Yet, it does, and it did.

I band one arm around my waist, then wave to Thomas as he climbs onto the bus. He takes a seat near one of the windows, already chatting happily with the other boys on the bus.

Swallowing back tears that are searing my throat, I close my eyes.

Lord, please watch over my boy. Please keep him safe, guide him to make good choices, and bring him home to me safe. God, please. In Jesus' name I pray, amen.

I open my eyes just in time to see the bus pull away. Thomas waves at me, his bright smile beaming. I wave back, and as soon as I see nothing but tail lights, I wipe my wet cheeks and turn toward Garrison. He's seated on the short brick fence in front of the school, with an understanding smile on his face.

"Sorry, I didn't want to intrude, but I also knew this was going to be hard. Friends are there for each other, right?"

I laugh, appreciating his playful tone more than I'd like to admit. "Yes. That is true. And thanks, if you weren't here, I'd probably be sitting on the curb, rocking and bawling my eyes out."

Garrison flashes me a smile. "Glad I can be of service." His expression softens. "Are you okay?"

"Not really," I reply. It doesn't help that my night was riddled with nightmares, thanks to the way I'd opened up to the man in front of me. I'd gotten hardly any sleep then said goodbye to the one constant in my life.

It might only be a week, but it feels like forever.

"Then come with me."

I arch a brow. "And where are we going?"

"It's a surprise," he replies with a smile. "Come on. Don't you trust me?"

More than I should. Even though the voice in my head is screaming that I'm about to enter uncharted waters, trying to be friends with a man like Garrison Holt, I take that first step anyway.

After driving for nearly twenty minutes, Garrison guides his truck off the main road and onto a dirt side road. My heart jumps in my chest, not out of fear but out of anticipation for what's to come. He hasn't given anything away, but with each mile we drive, I find the excitement building.

With the sun just beginning to creep over the horizon, the world has a glow to it. Rays of color paint the sky, and as always with a sunrise, I sit in awe of the world God created for us.

The pain of letting Thomas get on that bus has eased just enough, thanks to the distraction and the fact that he's already texted me half a dozen times, thanking me and telling me he was already having so much fun.

We round a corner, and an olive-green truck comes into view. Three brightly colored kayaks are resting beside it, a man standing in front of them. I recognize Sawyer instantly, and my excitement turns into pure delight.

How did Garrison know kayaking is on my bucket list?

I've never told anyone.

Garrison parks the truck and turns to me. "You up for an adventure, Katelyn Ellis?"

His grin ignites another wave of attraction in me, and I can't help but smile back. "Absolutely."

We sit there a moment too long, our gazes holding, until Sawyer knocks on Garrison's window. With a laugh, Garrison opens his door and climbs out.

"Oh good, I thought you drove out here to just sit in your truck." Sawyer turns to me. "Hey, Pepper."

I snort at the nickname. "Hey, Sawyer."

"You ever been kayaking before?" he asks.

"I can safely say I have not," I reply.

"Really?" Garrison questions, seemingly surprised at my confession.

"Really. I never had the chance before Thomas, and—well—after, I just didn't have the time."

Garrison's expression darkens a bit in understanding. There's not a lot of time for adventure when you're a single mom.

"Look at that! We got a newbie with us!" Sawyer exclaims. "I tried to get Anastasia out here today, but she's a party pooper. Come on, let's get you in a life jacket, then let's get on the water."

As he walks away, we follow. Sawyer offers us each a life jacket, then slips into his. I've just finished buckling mine in the front when Garrison turns to me.

"Good?" he asks.

"I think so." I check my buckles. "First-timer all the way around here."

Garrison laughs, low and deep, and the sound echoes through me like the richest type of dessert. The kind that you *know* is bad for you, yet you can't seem to stop eating. "Here, let me help."

He grabs the front of my straps and tightens them, cinching down so the brightly colored life jacket sits snug against my body. And then he looks down at me, his dark gaze locking on mine, his hands still on the straps of my jacket.

We're mere inches away, and the tension between us grows with every beat of my heart.

Oh boy.

"You guys ready to go?" Sawyer calls out.

His voice cuts through the moment, and Garrison pulls away.

I take a second to breathe, drawing in the fresh air as my heart rate begins to slow.

Just friends with Garrison? It should be easy, right?

As soon as I can trust myself to walk, I move toward the edge of the water, where Garrison and Sawyer are both prepping the kayaks.

"This is for your phone," Garrison says as he hands me a waterproof bag on a lanyard. "I figured you wouldn't want to leave it in the truck just in case Thomas needs you."

Swoon. Thoughtful too? Fantastic.

"Thanks so much. You would be right." I slip my phone inside, seal it up, then slip it around my neck. "He's going to be so jealous when he hears that I did this."

"Well, we'll have to bring the kid with us next time, won't we?" Sawyer says with a grin. "That is if you enjoy it enough to want to go again."

I stare out at the water. Tall grass sprouts through the top, breaking the glassy surface. There are no loud sounds, no hustle or bustle, just—life. Beautiful, peaceful life. Which is something I haven't felt in a long, long time.

"I have a feeling I'm going to love it," I reply, my gaze landing on Garrison. *Yeah, I have a feeling about you, too.*

"Good. Let's get out there then." Sawyer claps his hands together.

"The most important thing about kayaking is to keep your balance," Garrison explains. "It can tip if you lean too far from one side to the other. Aside from that, you alternate sides as you row." He lifts a paddle and demonstrates. "We won't hit any rough water, so you're good there. Any questions?"

"I've always been a learn by doing kind of person," I reply with a grin in his direction.

Garrison returns my smile. "I knew there was a reason we were friends."

Friends. There's that word again. I asked for it— insisted even. So why am I starting to wish we could be so much more?

CHAPTER 16

GARRISON

Warm sunlight shines down as Sawyer, Katelyn, and I guide our kayaks through the tall spartina grass along one of South Carolina's hidden waterways. It's a true gem, only half an hour outside of Stormwatch Landing, yet very few ever come this far.

Most people prefer the beaches. But there's something deeply serene about being out here. The still water. The way the grass bends with the breeze, swaying without breaking. To me, it feels more alive than any stretch of sand.

The air hums with energy. And on quiet days like this, we might even catch sight of dolphins exploring the waterway that winds toward the ocean miles away.

We never experience the same day twice.

Each one is new.

A surprise.

And then there's today.

My gaze lands on Katelyn just ahead of me, tucked between Sawyer and me. Sunlight pulls amber from her hair, and she's smiled more in the last hour than I've seen in all the time we've spent together. And I mean *really* smiled. It's the first time I've seen unguarded happiness from her.

I knew today was going to be hard on her. I almost let fear stop me.

But seeing her smile—even once—was worth every nervous second I spent wondering if she'd say no. As if she can feel my thoughts on her, Katelyn turns and smiles at me.

"Having fun?" I blurt. *Does she know I was staring?*

"I am. This is gorgeous."

I couldn't agree more. "Definitely. Sawyer and I try to come out at least once a month."

"I can see why. Out here, everything feels so simple. So calm." She closes her eyes for a moment, then opens and grins at me. "I can feel the life all around us, yet, at the same time, it's almost as if we're completely alone."

"There are few places in this world that calm my mind. This is one of them."

"It definitely—" She squeals and shifts in her seat as her kayak rocks.

"Easy!" I call out, paddling a bit faster to get to her. I'm about two feet away when I see a dolphin break the surface of the water. Another comes up beside it before slipping back beneath the surface.

"Was that a dolphin?" she squeals and leans over the edge of the kayak.

"Yes, but be careful because—" But I'm too late. Her kayak tips, and Katelyn falls into the water with a loud splash. "Katelyn!" I call out and tip my own kayak over to get to her. Just as I hit the water, Katelyn surfaces and starts laughing so hard that tears slip down her face.

"I can't *believe* I did that! But it was a dolphin! Did you see it? It was right there!"

I swim toward her, stopping only when I'm close enough to grab her should anything happen. "Are you okay?"

Her gaze locks on mine, and the air around us charges.

Her laughter dies, and her expression shifts to something else—something so similar to the desire coursing through my veins that I *almost* pull her into my arms right here in the water.

Would she pull away? Or lean into what I'm offering?

"Yeah, I—sorry." Her cheeks turn pink. "I should have been more careful."

"It's nothing I haven't done before," I tell her.

"I've never seen one so close. It caught me off guard."

"Yeah. I know something about that." I move a bit closer. *You caught me off guard.* I want so badly to confess that to her. Sure, I admitted that I'd love to date her. But what I feel is so much more than that.

So much more than anything I ever thought I'd find.

I reach up and push some of the wet hair from her face.

She looks up at me through thick lashes.

My gaze drops to her mouth.

Her lips part. An invitation maybe? Does she want this as badly as I do?

And then—Sawyer clears his throat. "You two going to swim the rest of the way?"

I glare up at him, and based on the grin he's sporting, he knows *exactly* what he just did.

"Thanks so much for this," Katelyn says as she drops down on the log beside me. In front of us, flames crackle in the fire ring of the campground. Sawyer sits across from us, shooting a glare at where Anastasia and Jack sit, all while Cowboy and Tank try their best to distract him so he doesn't do something stupid.

It shouldn't make me happy that Sawyer is frustrated, but after what he interrupted earlier—well, let's just say I'm taking a bit of satisfaction from his irritation.

"Of course. I'm glad you had fun." I pop a fry in my mouth and offer her one from what's left of the dinner Anastasia and Jack brought out for all of us just before sunset. We'd spent the rest of the afternoon finishing our kayak adventure—wet clothes and all. By the time we were taking off our life vests, the sun had dried us.

Katelyn takes a fry. "I really did."

"How's Thomas doing?" I gesture to where she set her phone between us.

She smiles brightly. "He's doing fantastic. Which only added to my joy over the day. This is the first time he's done anything like this, and he's just—he's having the time of his life." Her smile fades slightly. "It makes me wish we would have done this sooner."

"Baseball camp?"

She finishes chewing the fry she put in her mouth. "Settled in."

"What kept you from settling?"

Silence carries between us even as the conversations around the fire continue on. There's a heaviness settled on her shoulders that wasn't there just a few seconds ago. "Just never found someplace that felt like home, I guess."

But it's not the truth. Not the whole truth, anyway. Still, I don't press.

"I'm glad you found your way to Stormwatch Landing."

Katelyn's gaze levels on mine, and she smiles softly, firelight illuminating her features. "Me, too."

Once more, that thick tension settles in the air around us until Anastasia claps her hands. "All right. It's time."

"Time for what?" Sawyer asks.

Anastasia stands. "Be right back."

"So, Katelyn, how long have you lived here?" Jack questions.

"Uh, a few months." She smiles, but it's awkward. Uncomfortable. My guess is that it has something to do with his occupation. Did she have a bad interaction with the police before? Maybe filed charges on her ex-husband and had things go sideways?

"You like it?"

"I do. It's a great place."

"Yeah, I'd have to agree with you there." He glances behind him. "I'm thinking about moving here myself."

Sawyer starts coughing uncontrollably, sucking in air like he just completed a competition dive. "Swallowed wrong," he chokes out. Ryker fights a grin as he pats him on the back.

"Sure you did," Ryker replies, earning a glare from Sawyer and a chuckle from Weston.

"Well, it's a great place full of great people." Katelyn glances my way before she looks back at Jack.

The fact that she looked at me at all brings me more joy than I've had in a long, long time. Those walls she's had up nearly every day are gone, and I can only hope they stay that way.

"Okay, back!" Anastasia announces as she steps into the light, a violin case in her hand. *Because, of course, she brought it.*

"You have got to be kidding me," I groan as Anastasia hands it to me.

"It's been so long. Besides, it's tradition. Campfire equals music."

"So get Weston's guitar."

"I don't have a key to Weston's house."

"And you never will," Weston retorts.

Anastasia sticks her tongue out at him, then turns to me.

"You play violin?" Katelyn asks me.

"I do. It was my aunt's favorite instrument. I learned it for her birthday one year."

"Yeah, yeah, Demo's a great guy. Super talented. Now play," Sawyer says.

"Come on, Garrison, please?" Anastasia asks as she takes her seat beside Jack, who puts his arm around her shoulders and presses a kiss to her temple.

I look at Katelyn, feeling the heat building on the back of my neck. "All right. Fine. But I'm hiding this better in the future." After unzipping the instrument case, I lift the violin and bow. As I settle it beneath my jaw, the weight is familiar and steady.

The smooth curve of the chinrest fits the hollow of my throat. My left hand slides up the neck, finding the strings. As I draw the bow, slow and careful, I work to adjust the tuning of the instrument.

The fire crackles softly as I draw the bow more intentionally now. The violin answers, and "Amazing Grace" drifts into the night, the melody carrying a story of the Lord's mercy and redemption.

And then she starts singing.

My eyes fly open.

Katelyn's eyes are closed, her voice steady and clear as

it fills the space around us. My heart hammers in my chest as I keep playing, though I barely hear the instrument anymore.

For all I know, I miss every note. It doesn't matter. With her singing, my attention narrows until she's all that exists.

The others join in—everyone except Weston—but their voices fade beneath hers.

She's all I hear.

All I see.

CHAPTER 17

KATELYN

"I cannot believe you can sing like that and you held out on me," Garrison says as we climb the stairs toward our floor.

Feeling lighter than I have in years, I laugh. "I could say the same to you. Violin is not a common instrument."

He shrugs and opens the door for me. It's such a simple action, but it absolutely thrills me. "Like I said, it was my aunt's favorite instrument, so I learned it for her birthday."

"Like I told you the other day, she was lucky to have you."

Garrison smiles down at me, his gaze holding mine. Logically, I know I should look away. Staring up at him like this will do nothing but put me exactly where I've been determined not to go.

But would it really be so bad to be loved by a man like Garrison Holt? To be held in kindness?

Garrison clears his throat and starts down the hallway toward his apartment, a bag of dirty clothes in his hand. I was beyond grateful Anastasia brought us a change when she came out because, while they were dry, the clothes had stiffened thanks to the saltwater.

"Thanks for today. It was—" I sigh. "The first time in thirteen years I did anything for myself."

He unlocks his door, then pushes it open and turns toward me. "I know I've said it before, but it deserves saying again: You're a great mom, Katelyn."

"I try." I smile, feeling a bit guilty that this was one of the best days I've had in a long time, and my son wasn't here to enjoy it. "We'll have to take Thomas out when he comes back. That is if you don't mind."

"Not at all. I'd love to take you guys out again. I had more fun today than I have in a long time."

I swallow hard.

I'd love to date you.

Oh how those words are ringing through my mind right now, right along with my response. I'm pretty sure, with my refusal of those few words, I managed to break my own heart before I'd even had the chance to give it to Garrison.

"Well, I need to get cleaned up." I move into his apartment, and when he closes the door behind me, realization sets in. Along with the understanding of just how much trouble I'm in.

My heart begins to pound.

I'm alone with him.

The last time I was alone with a man—I shake my head. Garrison is *not* Victor. Not now. Not ever.

We've been alone together before. A few times over the last week. When Thomas was at school or out with friends. This is no different.

"I'll get our clothes in the wash. You want some tea?" he questions as he moves away from me and into the kitchen.

"Yeah. Tea would be good." I watch him, that bit of fear dissipating with each passing moment until my entire body relaxes. He has that ability, this man I tried so hard not to get to know. No one in this world can bring me the peace that Garrison Holt offers just by being present. "Hey, Garrison?"

"Yeah?" He glances back at me, dark hair a mess on top of his head. So very handsome.

"Thanks for everything," I tell him. "You've quickly become one of two people in this world I trust. And I don't think you know just how important that is."

"I'll do everything in my power to never break that trust, Katelyn," he replies, tone low and deep.

I smile and take a deep breath despite the emotion burning in my throat. It's the closest I've come to telling him how I feel. To confessing that, though I was once worried about my son getting too close to him, now I *know* leaving him would shatter the remaining pieces of my own heart. "I know you will. See you in a few."

Leaving him behind, I move into the bathroom. After

turning the water on to warm up, I strip out of my clothes and set them in a pile to carry into my room later. Then, I turn toward the mirror—instantly regretting when I do.

There are a lot of things from my past that I try to avoid. Triggers that spark memories better left as dead and buried as my ex.

The jagged scar that runs the length of my side is one of those triggers. A horrible reminder of the pain I suffered at his hands. I gently touch the puckered skin, the memory flooding back plain as day.

Victor got angry and threw me into a pane of glass that separated the dining room from the living room. It shattered, slicing into me. I know, even without seeing them, that there are at least a dozen more of these on my back.

Then he'd tossed a towel down onto me and told me to stop the bleeding and to keep my mouth shut. That it was my fault.

No one at the hospital ever suspected a thing. They all truly believed the story that I'd tripped and fallen into the glass.

And why wouldn't they?

There were no other marks on me.

And Victor was the best actor.

I swallow hard, throat burning as I turn away from the mirror and back toward the shower. Thomas had been two weeks old. They'd blamed my clumsiness on my exhaustion as a new mother.

After all, who would suspect the charming quarterback?

"That smells really good." Freshly showered, I step into the kitchen. My mood may have been soured by the unwanted memory, but my stomach growls in response to the scents coming out of the kitchen.

Garrison looks up from where he's standing in the kitchen. "I know I said just tea, but I was hungry. Falling out of a boat will do that to a person." He flashes me a smile to let me know he's not the least bit annoyed with our unplanned swim.

"Yeah, I guess it will." I force a smile and take a seat on one of his barstools to watch him cook what looks like taco meat.

"You feel up for nachos?"

"Always."

His adorable crooked grin thaws a bit of the ice my memory of Victor placed around me. But when he turns to fully face me, head cocked to the side, I know that once again—he's seeing too much.

Too much of me.

Of my past.

How am I supposed to keep things hidden if he makes me want to spill every single memory weighing me down? Would he protect my secrets? Would he hold me as I unloaded everything I've been carrying for far too long?

"What is it?" he asks.

I could tell him. I know, without a doubt, I can trust

him. But I just can't bear to see him look at me differently. "I'm just tired."

Garrison nods, but I can see that he doesn't believe me. It's written all over his face. "You know you can talk to me, right?"

"I know."

"Then I'll take your excuse." He winks and turns back toward the stove. "You hear any more from Thomas?"

A bit of my resolve dissipates. I want so badly to have someone to talk to, but the last person I confided in—I shake my head. *No.* I will not go there. "Not since he went to sleep. He's on cloud nine. So beyond excited about baseball camp. I doubt he'll want to come home."

"Nah, he will. He'll miss you too much."

More of that ice melts. "Thanks for saying that."

"It's the truth."

Silence wraps around us, both a comfort and a weight I desperately want to shed. When it's too quiet, the darkness hiding in the recesses of my mind escapes. Little by little, it taunts me.

I clear my throat. "So, why did Sawyer call you Demo earlier?"

Garrison lets out a laugh as he begins shredding cheese. "It was my code name."

"Code name?"

He nods. "We all had them. Zane—you haven't met him yet—is Cap, Sawyer is Cable Guy, Weston is Cowboy, and Ryker is Tank."

I snort. "I can definitely see the last two. But Sawyer as Cable Guy? Like the movie?"

"Nah. Sawyer's specialty is—was—communications."

"Is it hard? Transitioning from the military to being a civilian?"

He piles some chips onto a plate, then spoons some taco meat over the top. "It is. We actually worked off-books for six years, which made the transition even harder if I'm honest. There was no final day for us. We worked, and then one day, they didn't need us anymore."

"That is hard."

He shrugs. "I have the community center, Sawyer has his shop, Weston has the ranch, Zane's got Tessa now, and Ryker's been talking about becoming a cop."

I can see his pain, though. The grief he must feel over such a rapid life change. "Still, when you get the rug pulled out from under you, sometimes it's hard to get back on your feet."

He glances over at me. "You'd know something about that."

"Yeah, I guess I would." I think of how happy I was when I graduated nursing school. It was all I wanted to do. Help people. Then, before I even had the chance to finish my first year, Victor happened. I was thrown into a gilded cage after that, only let up for air when it suited him. When I had a part to play.

"Here you go." Garrison slides a large plate between us.

A heaping pile of chips, meat, cheese, beans, sour cream, and a side of jalapenos.

Even though I ate what Anastasia and Jack brought out to the campsite earlier, my stomach growls.

"Can I?" He reaches out a hand, so I slide mine into his, trying to ignore the way his touch ignites a flame long gone cold. "Lord, we thank You for this meal. Please let it nourish our bodies, amen."

"Amen."

He releases my hand and starts eating.

"So, what does Demo stand for then?"

"Oh, sorry. I forgot you asked." He laughs. "Demolition."

"Demolition, as in blowing things up?" I stop, chip halfway to my mouth, and stare at him. Of all the words I would use to describe him, Demolition wouldn't even come close to making the list.

"Yeah. The guys like to joke because I'm good at putting out fuses here, but in the field, I'm all about lighting them."

"So you, like, actually blow stuff up?"

He nods. "Strategically, but yes."

I finish chewing and swallow, then shake my head in awe. "Just know that, if Thomas finds out, he will pepper you with questions until you can't take it anymore."

Garrison laughs. "I can take a lot."

I imagine there's not much that rattles you. "I'm honestly surprised."

"Why?"

"You don't strike me as the kind of guy who likes to destroy things."

"I don't think of it as destruction." He leans in, resting his forearms on the counter so he's eye-level with me. "More like removing an obstacle so what's really important stays standing." He stands. "For example, our last mission had Zane, Sawyer, and Ryker trapped behind enemy lines. They'd gone in to rescue a teenage girl, and we had significantly underestimated the number of hostiles. I came in and strategically placed charges so I could drop the floor above where they were being held."

"And the girl?" I question, hanging on his every word.

"She survived."

I let out a breath, so grateful for the life of a girl I've never met and likely never will. "How many missions like that did you go on?"

"I honestly have no clue. We received orders, and we went."

"Simple as that?"

"Simple as that," he replies. "Water?" But his tone suggests there was a lot more to it than simply following orders. And if I weren't so afraid of him tugging my secrets loose, I might have tried to press further.

"Yes, please."

Garrison turns away and retrieves two water bottles from the kitchen. He opens one before offering it to me, then opens his own.

Another simple gesture, just like the door, and yet—"You're not like anyone I've ever met," I blurt.

"Don't meet many demolition experts in your day-to-day?"

I snort. "No, that's not what I meant. You're just—" I trail off, trying to choose my words carefully so I don't end up telling him *exactly* how hard I'm falling for him. Sweet gesture by sweet gesture, he's repairing the damage Victor inflicted. "Sweet. Most men would have already tried something, and you're making me nachos."

A hint of a smile plays at his mouth. "You told me you wanted to be friends. So this is me, making my friend something to eat. I also plan to make my friend tea once I've showered." He straightens and pushes the plate toward me. "Which I'm going to go do right now. Need anything before I go?"

Just you. "No, I'm okay." I lift another chip from the plate. "Thanks, Garrison. For everything."

"Anytime, Katelyn." He moves past me and into his room, then closes the door behind him. Moments later, I hear the shower turn on, and I stare at the door, half-hoping he'll come rushing out and tell me that he doesn't want to be just friends.

That it's not enough anymore.

And I'm also half terrified that he will do just that.

CHAPTER 18

GARRISON

The sermon hit home after another night riddled with terrifying nightmares that had me up in a cold sweat more than once. I was sitting on a boat in the middle of a furious ocean. Each angry wave that slammed into the boat brought about a memory.

Of the times my parents were so high they forgot I existed.

Or worse, when they remembered.

Of the night I found them, wide-eyed and pale, cold as the tile they were lying on.

Of my first time in combat.

Of my last.

One after the other, they hit me, harsh reminders of all I've lived through.

But just as it always does, dawn broke.

The sun rose.

And God is still good.

Beside me, Katelyn wears a beautiful blue dress that shows off her curves and incredibly long legs. She's styled her hair in loose waves and dusted some color across her eyelids.

She's stunning, and the battle to keep my gaze off her has been a fight that I keep losing. What am I supposed to do from here? Because remaining just friends feels like a mission I'm going to fail. Will I lose her when I do?

"May God's peace be with you all," Pastor Daniel Reeves announces as he smiles out at us.

Where moments ago, the church was silent, now it's full of chatter. Happy voices as people get to their feet and make their way toward the exit. I stand, reaching down to offer Katelyn a hand as I do.

Since, thanks to my sleepless night, we were nearly late this morning, we're seated toward the back of the church.

"That was excellent," Katelyn says as she beams up at me. "I can't believe I haven't made an effort to get here before today." She closes her eyes and draws a deep breath before opening them again. "I feel so full right now."

"Me, too." I smile down at her, and for a moment, the rest of the world fades away. *Lord, what am I doing here?*

"Garrison, Katelyn! It is so good to see you."

We both turn at Linda's greeting. She pulls Katelyn in for a hug first.

"It's so good to see you, too, Mrs. Knox."

"Please, honey, call me Momma Knox. This is my

friend Marlene." She smiles kindly as she tugs an older woman up to her side.

Marlene's brown eyes crinkle at the corners when she takes Katelyn's hand. "It is so good to meet you. Linda speaks very highly of you and your son." She glances up curiously at me. "I have to say, I'm quite impressed you managed to catch this one. He's been dodging my set-up attempts for years now."

Even as heat spreads along the back of my neck, embarrassment coloring my cheeks, I force a smile and try to play it off. "You mean all those blind dates you keep trying to set me up on? I told you, Marlene, you should have just asked me yourself." I wink at her, and she throws her head back, a throaty laugh erupting from her.

"Please, we all know I am not afraid to put myself out there." Someone calls her name, so she glances over, then returns her attention to us. "I need to catch her before she leaves. It was great meeting you, Katelyn. Garrison," she adds with a purr and a wink, then walks off laughing.

"You just made her day," Linda tells me.

"Good. She's a nice lady."

"The nicest," she replies.

"Nah, Momma Knox, I think you take that one," I tell her.

Linda's cheeks flush with color. "You, sir, are a smooth talker." She turns to Katelyn. "Will I see you at lunch?"

"Yes, if that's okay. Garrison invited me."

"Sweetie, it is *more* than okay. In fact, I insist. I'll see you both there in an hour."

"That sounds great." Katelyn slings her purse over her shoulder as Linda waves at someone off to her right, then rushes off to greet them, too.

When I glance over to ask Katelyn if she's ready to go, I see that she's checking her phone.

"Anything?"

She smiles sheepishly up at me. "Not since this morning. I think he's just having too much fun."

"I bet he is."

She slides her phone back into her pocket. "Well, we have almost an hour. That should give me time to get another load of laundry washed before lunch." She starts toward the door.

"Or—" I start.

"Or?" she glances up at me as I hold the door open for her to move through it.

"We could go for a walk. Weather is good."

Katelyn's answering smile is *everything*. "A walk would be good."

"Great." Relief rushes through me in a tidal wave as I change course and head for the beach steps rather than the parking lot. Katelyn stops at the bottom of the steps and removes her shoes, so I take time to do the same, then roll up my pant legs enough that the water won't saturate them.

I may prefer the waterway where we kayaked yesterday, but the beach certainly has its charm. The moment my bare feet touch the sand, a peace washes over me. A calmness that likely also has a lot to do with the woman beside me.

"So how did you like the service today?" I ask as we start walking toward the ocean. Wind pulls at my clothes and flutters her thick curls.

"I loved it." She takes a deep breath. "You know, I've lived in a lot of places, Garrison, and nowhere has ever felt as much like home as Stormwatch Landing."

"Good."

She glances over at me, eyebrow raised.

"I wouldn't want you to have settled down anywhere else."

She laughs. "You didn't know me then."

"I would have known something was missing," I respond instantly. For a moment, her expression darkens like the sky right before a storm.

Did I say too much?

But before I can counter to try and lessen the weight of my words, Katelyn faces forward again.

"So that woman—Marlene, she set you up a lot?"

"I only let it happen once."

"That bad?" She laughs.

"It was horrible."

Katelyn laughs again. "Really?"

"Really."

Cool water rushes around our ankles as a wave comes in.

"How bad?"

I grin down at her, so happy to see that she's looking up at me, too. "You're not going to let this go, are you?"

"Not a chance, *Demo.*"

"Fine," I reply with a soft laugh. "Well, since it was a blind date, we met at the restaurant."

"Naturally."

"I opted for Steel & Salt."

"The steakhouse?"

I nod. "She agreed to it, so I assumed everything was fine. When I showed up, she was wearing dark jeans with red paint splashed on them and a t-shirt that said 'Your steak had a face'."

Katelyn stops in her tracks and gapes up at me. "*No, she didn't.*"

The wind picks up, grabbing a loose curl and wrapping it across her face. Without thinking, I reach out and brush it behind her ear.

Katelyn shivers.

I force my treacherous hand back down at my side and clear my throat. "Oh, she did. She made it her personal mission to protest everything on the menu—loudly. When the waiter came by to take our order, she asked for 'something that didn't cry when it was murdered'."

Katelyn laughs. "Oh no!"

"Oh yes. And it got even worse."

"How could that get any worse?"

"Well, I ordered a steak."

She sucks in a breath, and I risk a look at her, delighted to see her stifling a laugh. "I'm sure she loved that."

"She made mooing sounds under her breath every time I took a bite. All while she picked at her salad."

"Why in the world wouldn't she just have said she wanted to go somewhere else?"

Shrugging, I start walking again. "I would have happily taken her anywhere else. The last thing I would have wanted was to offend her, but she was just so rude. Start to finish."

"Why didn't you just get up and leave?"

"Have you been to Steel & Salt? Their steaks are epic. I wasn't about to let her chase me away from it. After that last bite, I paid, tipped the waiter generously, then left. She started crying hysterically and telling me that she was just passionate, but I'd had enough."

"Uhhh, there's being passionate about something; then there's being downright obnoxious. She was definitely the latter."

I snort. "Yeah, I stopped letting Marlene set me up after that."

"Can't say I blame you there." She shakes her head in disbelief, then pauses and turns toward the ocean.

"How about you? Any horrible dates?" I question after a beat of silence.

"Dates? No. I mean, I had my cute teenager dates. Dinner and movies, things like that. But they were normal and awkward. Then I—" She trails off, and darkness clouds her expression. "Well, I didn't get the chance to date much."

The heaviness of her tone settles on my heart like thick chains. I want to reach out and pull her into my arms. Want to assure her that she'll never suffer another day so long as I'm around.

I want to tell her that I'm falling helplessly in love with her even though I promised the both of us that I wouldn't. But doing so could ruin what we have, and nothing is worth that risk. And just like that, I understand Sawyer's predicament with Anastasia. I would laugh at the irony if it weren't so frustrating.

"I'm sorry."

She shrugs and turns toward me. "It is what it is. Or, as Thomas says, 'It do be what it do be.'"

I snort at the teenage slang, but my smile dies almost immediately when I see the hurt reflected in her eyes. "You deserved better. You both did."

She swallows hard and nods. "I've always known that Thomas did, but it took me a long time to realize that I did, too."

My chest aches with the pressure of all I'm holding in.

"I knew better than to stay, though. But I did because I was afraid."

"Of him?"

"That," she nods. "And of what others would think of me."

"What do you mean?"

We start walking again, and Katelyn falls silent. Instead of pushing for more or changing the subject, I simply keep cadence beside her, grateful for her company.

"I didn't—" She stops and turns toward me. "I've only ever told one person this before."

"Your secrets are safe with me, Katelyn, but if you don't want to talk, that's okay, too."

"I don't remember the night that I—" She closes her eyes. "That Thomas was conceived."

Anger, hot and fast, flashes through me at the implications of what she's saying. Was she raped? I bite back the questions and shove my free hand into my pocket so she can't see how white my knuckles are.

"I don't drink. My grandfather was an alcoholic, so it was just not something I ever wanted to touch. My college roommate had gone to this party, but I'd stayed in to study. She called me about one in the morning and asked to be picked up, so I went." Katelyn's eyes shimmer with tears. "When I got there, she was laughing and talking to this guy I'd seen around but never met. He was a football player, I was a nerd, so our paths just didn't cross."

Even as I can see where this story is going, I seriously hope I'm wrong.

"Anyway, we got to talking, and he seemed sweet. Charming. Brought me a soda when I told him I didn't drink. That's all I remember until the next morning. I woke up, naked, in a bed I didn't recognize."

That anger turns to blinding fury, and it's all I can do not to lose it right here on the beach. The desire to hunt him down—dead or not—is so strong I literally dig my toes further into the sand, hoping it will hold me here.

"The guy—Victor—was lying beside me, still passed out. Before I could leave, the door opened, and his older brother came in. He accused me of being a tramp and threw my clothes at me." She closes her eyes, and tears stream down her cheeks. "I still don't know how I managed to get dressed—I was shaking so bad."

I force my hand out of my pocket and gently brush the tears from her cheek.

"I told my roommate. She apologized profusely for making me go and told me that I needed to report it. So that afternoon, I went to do just that. Before I got the chance, though, I found out she'd been killed on her way to work. A car accident. The next morning, Victor's brother showed up with him and told me that we needed to talk."

"You never got the chance to get help?"

"I could have," she says, eyes full of tears. "But after our "talk," I was so afraid. Who was going to believe me? There were no witnesses, and Victor's family was very well known. It would have been a massive media firestorm, and I would have been caught in the middle. My family would have found out what—" She trails off. "My silence is something I've had to live with."

"Katelyn, you didn't do anything wrong."

She nods, jaw tight. "I know that now. Victor told me he didn't remember what happened either. That he didn't slip me anything. His brother showed me a lab report showing high levels of some drug—I can't remember the name of it now—in Victor's bloodstream. He said we'd both been drugged, and then one thing led to another. He convinced me it was one horrible turn of events that we'd both been caught in. A way to derail Victor's budding career. I should have known better, but—"

"You were grieving the loss of your friend. And reeling over being assaulted." My tone is sharp, anger barely leashed beneath the surface.

"I should have known better," she repeats. "And by the time I realized what was happening, our engagement had been announced in the papers, and there was nowhere for me to run."

She'd been bullied into a marriage to the man who raped her.

Who took what wasn't his to take.

Who spent the time they were together, causing her nothing but pain.

My fury is only matched by the heartbreak I feel for the woman standing in front of me.

"Katelyn." What else can I say? How can I put into words how furious I am that she suffered? How badly I want to hunt Victor's brother down and inflict on him the pain he and his brother put on this beautiful woman?

"I have spent the last thirteen years trying to hide the truth from everyone because I am so terrified that Thomas will find out someday. That he will know who his father truly was."

I take a step closer and drop my shoes so I can cup her face in my hands. "The only thing Thomas will ever know is that his mother is the strongest woman in the world. And she sacrificed unbelievably to give him everything."

Katelyn's lashes flutter against her cheeks as shimmering tears fall freely. "I was such a fool."

"You are a survivor, Katelyn. A fighter."

She looks up at me. "Do you understand now? Why I can't—why I said—"

"You don't have to explain anything to me. Not now, not ever. I will *always* be here for you. Even if it's only as a friend."

"What if—" She tips her face up to look at me, those hazel depths so full of pain that it breaks me. Even still, amidst the pain is something else—longing? "Is that all you want?" she whispers.

"I want whatever you're willing to give." It's the truth. If all Katelyn wants to be is friends, then I will bury what I feel for her so far down it'll never surface. Even if I have to cut myself to the bone to do it.

I will *never* push this woman into something she's not comfortable with. Anything she wants from me, she'll have to ask. It's up to her to set the pace.

"What if I'm not sure?"

Her face in my hands, I lean down and rest my forehead against hers. Eyes closed, I can feel her breath fanning against my face. Our noses are touching. Our mouths a mere breath apart. "I'll be right here when you are."

Chapter 19

Katelyn

My evening shift at the diner went by at the speed of molasses in January even though it only lasted five hours. After our walk on the beach, Garrison and I had joined the others at Linda's for a delicious lunch, then he drove me back here and made coffee while I got dressed for my shift.

We didn't talk much. But a lot was said in those quiet moments.

I'd confided in him about my greatest secret. One I've kept heavily guarded since that day that Yasmin died. I thought that I'd feel embarrassed, mortified by the truth. But to be honest? I feel lighter.

As if I'm one step closer to being able to move on.

"I'll be right here when you are."

I can still feel his breath fanning across my face. His thumbs stroking my cheeks. I'd wanted so badly to feel his lips on mine. To accept a kiss because *I* wanted it. Not because it's what was expected of me.

But the heaviness of what is between us kept me from lifting my face and closing the distance. I want to make absolutely sure that, when we do take that step, I'm ready. Otherwise, I'm terrified that I'll run scared the moment we do and ruin what we have.

And he's far too important to me to do that.

I push open the door to our apartment building, then check my inbox. The elevator doors open, and a man steps off. I've never seen him before, but the hairs on the back of my neck go on end. I start to back toward the stairwell, putting distance between us as he makes his way toward the front door.

"Evening," he greets as he passes by.

There's nothing overly imposing about him, but my stomach twists into a knot, and I reach for my phone before I step into the stairwell. As my hand closes around it, he steps out onto the street and pulls the hood of his black sweatshirt up over his head.

He keeps walking without looking back.

Breathe, Katelyn. You're just nervous because of the bandage you ripped open earlier.

After taking a deep breath, I push into the stairwell. My desire to get upstairs where I'm safe, with the man who makes me feel safe, is so great that I take the steps at a near-run, trying to reach the top as quickly as I can.

It's not until I've pushed the door to our floor open and

made my way down the hall that the fear finally slips away. As I reach the front door of my apartment, I note that it's partially open. Curious, I shove it the rest of the way.

Garrison is inside, wearing tattered jeans and a white tank top stretched over his muscled torso. A baseball cap sits backward on top of his head, and he has a paintbrush in one hand, a can of paint in the other.

He cautiously paints the new patio doors, the fresh panes taped off with blue painters' tape. With each stroke of the brush, more of the wood is covered in crisp white, erasing the damage done to them just last week.

The floor is still bare, but the carpet is supposed to be going down in the next day or so; then we get to move my furniture back in—what wasn't damaged, at least.

And then—a sudden wave of sadness hits me.

Then that will be it. Thomas and I will move home, and we'll go back to merely being Garrison's neighbors.

No morning coffee.

Or late-night tea.

Garrison turns and jumps when he sees me watching, then lets out a laugh. "Sorry, I didn't hear you come in. What do you think?"

I just keep staring at him. How can I not? This man has been more gentle with me than anyone ever has.

He's made me feel seen.

Cherished.

My eyes fill.

"Katelyn, what is it?" Garrison sets the paint and brush

down, then wipes both hands on his jeans as he crosses toward me. "Did something happen?"

"I'm ready," I blurt because I'm honestly afraid that if I stand here and think about it too long, I'll chicken out.

He stops in his tracks and stares at me. "For what?"

My heart begins to pound, and I close the distance between us, tilting my face up to look at him. I'm so close, I can see the bronze flakes in his otherwise dark eyes. "To find out what this is."

Garrison's lips twitch at the corners, but I still see hesitation in his gorgeous gaze. "Are you sure—"

I stretch up and press my lips to his.

The connection is instant.

A rush of electricity.

Garrison stills for a moment, and I pull away, panicked. *Did I cross a line?* Heat creeps up the back of my neck as I open my eyes. But the moment my gaze locks with his, I know—he feels it, too.

He snakes a hand around the back of my neck and pulls me in, slamming his mouth to mine. It's rough and tender at the same time. Patient yet frenzied. He devours every single fear I had, demolishes every barrier I'd put between us with the mere contact of his lips on mine.

It's not until my back presses against the wall that I realize he's moved us clear across the room. His chest is hard against me, his touch tender, though I can feel the barely leashed hunger simmering beneath the surface.

Love.

Is that what this is?

Did I stumble into friendship only to fall head over heels in love with the Navy SEAL next door?

Garrison pulls away, then kisses me again, this time a quick meeting of the lips.

Breathless, he rests his forehead against mine and releases me to plant both hands against the wall of my living room. "I had no idea what I was missing," he says. "Until you."

I smile at him, then reach up to run the tips of my fingers along his stubbled jaw. "I feel the same." *Please be gentle with me,* I want to say. *Please don't break me.*

"You and me?" he says. "It's all I want. And I will do whatever I can to prove to you that I will *never* hurt you, Katelyn. You're safe with me. You both are."

The kiss is still on my mind first thing this morning.

Even as I roll out of bed, I have a smile on my face. My cell rings, so I reach for it. Thomas' picture flashes across the screen, only increasing my good mood. "Hey, baby!" I greet when I answer the FaceTime call.

"Morning, Mom!" His beaming smile lifts my mood even more. Sweat already beads on his forehead, and his t-shirt is smeared with red dirt.

"How is your day so far?" I ask as I settle back down onto the bed.

"Good. We ran laps and practiced our slides. I slid into home three times!"

His joy permeates the air around me. "That is wonderful, baby."

"How about you?"

"Not too much to report here. I worked last night. Oh! We should have our apartment back by the time you get home! I imagine you're ready to be home."

His smile falters just a bit. "I kinda like hanging with Mr. Holt. Think he'll still want to when we move out?"

The kiss flashes back into my mind. "Oh, I think so," I reply with a beaming smile of my own.

Someone calls Thomas' name, and he glances off toward the right. "Oh, sorry, Mom! I have to go. I'll call you later. Love you so much!"

"I love you, too, baby!" The call ends way too soon, leaving me with a slight emptiness. Man, I miss my kid. Four nights and three days to go.

Even though I know it'll be a while before I hear from him again, I still take my phone with me as I leave the room. After brushing my teeth and untangling my unruly hair, I step into the kitchen.

Garrison is sitting at the table, wearing basketball shorts and a t-shirt. His back is to me, but I know he'll have his Bible in front of him. As I move farther into the room, he turns and grins at me in a way that sets my insides on fire.

How did I ever think I could be just friends with this man?

"Morning."

"Morning," I reply. "Do you need a refill on coffee?"

"No, I'm okay. But thanks. Here, sit. Let me get you some." He starts to stand, but I shake my head.

"I've got it."

Garrison gets up anyway and follows me into the kitchen. Where most men would have moved in closer, he gives me space, letting me make the choice to step into those strong arms.

As I do, he wraps one around me, then cups my cheek and tips my face up to plant a quick kiss on my lips. "Good morning," he says again.

"You already said that."

"But now I've said it after a kiss. Which is what I really wanted to do all along."

I grin up at him, feeling more hopeful than I have in longer than I can remember. "Well then, good morning." I wind both arms around his neck and kiss him again.

He deepens the moment, the hair of his beard scraping delicately across my face. Oh boy, could I stay here forever?

Garrison ends the kiss, then releases me so I can get a fresh cup of coffee. As soon as I'm done adding cream and sugar, I turn toward him.

"So, listen, your carpet will be in today."

"Really? I thought it would be another day."

"Well, it would have been. I pulled some strings and got Harry to agree to laying it today."

I arch a brow. "Ready to get rid of me?" Even as desperate as I was to get back to my routine, it stings.

"Not at all." He takes a step closer. "But with what's happening with us, I think it's better if we have more than a hall between us."

My stomach twists.

"Look, I have no intention of taking that step until I'm married, and I would *never* push you into anything, but it was hard enough to keep away from you before, and now that we've decided to move beyond friendship, it just feels responsible."

My heart warms toward him, the love I already carry deepening. I take a step closer and place my free hand on his chest. The beat of his heart is steady beneath my palm. "I understand, and I appreciate your candor."

His larger hand covers mine. "It's not an easy thing for me to admit because I love having you close, Katelyn. Being able to get up in the morning and see both you and Thomas has been nothing short of a gift."

I smile up at him. "I feel the same. And Thomas just asked me this morning if you'd still want to 'hang out' with us after we move home."

"Nothing in this world can keep me from doing just that," he replies, leaning down to press a quick kiss to my lips before pulling his hand away.

We walk into the dining room together, and Garrison pulls a chair out for me before taking a seat back behind his Bible.

"What are your plans for today?" I ask, seriously hoping those plans include seeing me. I have a packed day, though, so the likelihood of our paths crossing is low.

"This morning I'm headed to the gym. I can't quite hit the mat yet, but I'm hoping to work up a sweat."

"The mat?"

"Boxing," he replies.

Concern for him erases the smile from my face. "Should you be doing that? I mean, I know it's been a couple of weeks, but—"

"I'm only going to use the heavy bag. Doc says I need to work up to getting back on the mat."

"I didn't realize you boxed."

"Not professionally, but it is a nice way to keep my reflexes sharp."

The image of him slick with sweat, dodging a fist, has me shifting in my seat. *Is it getting hotter in here?*

"After that, I'll be back here to work on getting your apartment ready for you." He grins at me, easing some of my discomfort at the idea of him getting hurt.

"I feel so bad that you're doing that without me."

"Don't. I don't mind in the least. Kyle's coming by to help, and it gives him something to do, too."

I reach over and cover his hand with mine. Touching him is far easier than I thought it would be. Especially after spending thirteen years avoiding all physical contact from men. "Thank you so much."

"Anything for you," he replies, then finishes off his coffee. "How about you?"

"I have my shift at the coffee shop in an hour. Then an hour to come back and change for my shift at the diner."

"You amaze me."

I arch a brow and study him. "How so?"

"You work harder than anyone I've ever met."

"It keeps me busy."

"Because being a single mom isn't busy enough?"

I laugh. "Fair point."

Taking a sip of my coffee, I let my gaze lift to his patio doors. They're closed, but the curtains are open, giving me a clear view of the ocean.

"So, there's actually something I've wanted to talk to you about, but I wasn't sure how to bring it up."

"Color me intrigued." Crossing my arms, I study him, trying to figure out what's got this soldier so nervous.

"I noticed that you only have one bedroom."

"Yes. There weren't any two-bedrooms available when I moved here." *Not that I could have afforded it even if there was.*

"Well, as you know, I have one more than I need."

Realization dawns on me, and I shake my head. "I am not taking your apartment."

"Please? Look, rent-wise it'll stay the same."

"How is that?" Embarrassment heats my cheeks even though I know he's only trying to help.

"Every apartment in the building is the same price."

"That can't be true."

"Call Geoff and ask him. When I rented this place, there were no single-bedrooms left. Otherwise, I would have taken one."

"So I'm doing you a favor by swapping apartments with you?"

"Katelyn, please? I've been trying to figure out how to approach this all week; the last thing I want to do is offend you."

I take a deep breath because I know he's telling the truth. His offer is beyond sweet, but I can't put him out. Not anymore than I already have.

"Garrison, the single bedroom works fine for us."

"But a two-bedroom would work better. Look, you don't have to give me an answer. Just think about it, okay?" He pushes up from the seat and slides the chair in. "I've got to go. Please think about it?" he asks again.

I look up at him and nod. "Sure."

He flashes me a quick grin and presses a kiss to the top of my head. "Great. Thanks. I'll see you later."

"Bye." I wave at him as he leaves, closing and locking the door behind him.

Sitting in the silence of his apartment, I look around. A two-bedroom would certainly give me the privacy I've been missing. And having Thomas across the hall puts him closer to me than he is now.

But I can't make Garrison move out.

I can't take his space from him, no matter what he says. It's too big an ask.

"Just think about it, okay?"

"Okay, Garrison," I say aloud to the apartment. "I'll think about it."

CHAPTER 20

GARRISON

"Well, look at that. Garrison managed to move out of the friend zone. Maybe you can give Sawyer some tips," Ryker jokes as he holds the heavy bag that I've spent the last hour taking out every bit of anger I've buried since Katelyn told me what she suffered through.

"Ha-ha. Very funny." Sawyer rolls his eyes and racks the bar he was using. Then, he sits up and glares our way. "I'm happy in the friend zone."

"Not a single person believes you," Ryker retorts. "But go ahead and keep lying to yourself."

I slam my fist into the bag. Every muscle in my body is warm, my skin slick with sweat. While I confessed we'd actually taken a step forward, I kept everything else a secret. Katelyn trusted me, and I won't break that trust, even though I feel like I'm going to explode beneath the weight of the anger it caused.

How could that happen to her?

How could someone do that to another person?

"Man, that bag say something nasty to you?" Sawyer asks, likely to move the attention off of him and onto me.

"Just glad to be back in the gym," I say. It might not be the entire truth, but it is the truth. I've missed being in here. There's something about working your muscles to exhaustion. Pushing your body to the absolute brink of what it can handle—and then going over that line and starting again.

But even today, it's not exhausting me. I'd been up all night, taunted by images of a young Katelyn bullied into submission. Of feeling like a failure for not being able to protect her, even though I know that's in no way a logical feeling.

"Seriously, man, you good?" Ryker questions.

"Not really," I admit. "But I'll manage."

"What's going on?" Sawyer crosses over to grab a bottle of water from the small refrigerator. At this time of day, we're the only ones here, but I still won't divulge Katelyn's secrets. Not even to these men who I know will hold it like a vault.

"Can't get into it."

"Are things okay with Katelyn?" Ryker asks.

"She's fine. Thomas is having a blast at baseball camp."

"But?" Sawyer presses.

"Can't get into it," I repeat. "So, how about you hold

the bag and let me just work through it?" I ask Ryker with a forced grin that I hope diffuses the concerned curiosity written all over his face.

He obliges with a single nod, then takes his stance behind the bag, stabilizing it while I work my body into complete and utter exhaustion.

By the time I'm done, there's not a muscle in my body that doesn't ache. There's a pain in my side that wasn't there before, and the knuckles of my hands are bruised despite the tape I'd used on them. But I do feel a bit better.

What happened to Katelyn was horrific. A nightmare. But it's in the past, and I can't imagine she wants to relive it by rehashing it over and over again. So, as I wave goodbye to Ryker and Sawyer and step out onto the side-walk, I decide not to bring it up again. Not unless she wants to talk.

Until then, it'll remain buried.

Main Street is quiet this morning, so I slip into the bookstore and offer Marie a wave. She was close friends with Anastasia for years, but it seems like the two of them have drifted apart over the past few months. Likely because Anastasia spends most of her free time with Jack.

"Hey, Garrison, how's it going?" she questions.

"Not too bad. Um, any chance you can show me where the Bibles are?"

"Sure can." She smiles at me as she moves around the counter, leading me toward a shelf near the side of the store. "They're organized by translation."

"Great, thanks." I reach down and lift one adorned with pink flowers on the front, then follow her back toward the front of the shop. Zane bought Tessa a Bible here when she was struggling with her faith.

Katelyn isn't struggling, or at least I don't think she is, but she'd talked about wanting one. Is it too much to get her one? Especially since I'm already trying to get her to take my apartment?

"Garrison?"

"Huh?" I look up at Marie.

"You want me to scan that?" she asks, amused, her hand outstretched for the Bible in mine.

"Oh yeah, sorry. My mind is elsewhere, apparently."

Marie chuckles. "I totally get it." After scanning it, she wraps the Bible in tissue paper and slips it into a plain brown bag.

I insert my card into the reader, then shove it back into my pocket.

"How are things going with the Community Center? You guys start planning for your summer extravaganza yet?"

Smiling, I shake my head. "It's on the to-do list." The summer barbecue cook-off is our largest fundraising event of the year. What we earn that day typically funds most of our activities throughout the rest of the year. Normally, I'd have already started the planning, but getting stabbed and pepper-sprayed really seemed to put a damper on it.

Or, at least I'm telling myself that's what's got me distracted, and not the gorgeous neighbor I am falling head over heels in love with.

"Well, let me know if I can help." She smiles at me as she offers me the bag.

"Thanks, Marie. Will do. See ya." After offering her a wave, I step out onto the street and head toward Anastasia's coffee shop. I really should be getting back; Kyle will be at my apartment in less than an hour to help work on Katelyn's, but the pull I feel toward her is too strong to ignore.

So, I make my way down the street anyway.

The coffee shop is busy this morning, with patrons coming in and out of the brightly colored door even as I make my way toward it. I count no less than six people who have exited just since I've been in view.

But one person pulls my interest.

A man, dressed in dark jeans and a black hoodie, is standing just out front. He has his phone up to his ear, so it's likely he just stepped out to talk, but something about him has awareness tingling through my body.

He glances up and makes eye contact with me, then offers a slight nod and turns his back to me, returning to his call. It's a move that should have confirmed he's not a threat—but I can't shake the feeling in my gut.

And then a woman strolls out of the shop on three-inch heels, wearing a black pencil skirt and a white button-down blouse. She taps him on the shoulder, hands him a coffee, and the two of them take off down the street.

Maybe I'm just on edge.

With a deep breath, I head up the steps and into Anastasia's coffee shop. The place is packed this morning with spring break tourists and locals alike gathered at the tables around the small café. Katelyn is taking orders while Anastasia fills them, bustling around behind the counter with far more energy than I think I've ever had.

"Hey, Garrison!" she greets happily when she catches sight of me standing just inside the door.

Katelyn's gaze sweeps over to me, and her smile falters just a bit. Did I really set her off with the apartment question? Or is it something else?

"Hey, there, Demo," she greets playfully.

"Hey, yourself."

"Eww, you two are so cute it's nauseating," Anastasia says as she makes a face.

"Ignore her," Katelyn replies. "You want a coffee?"

"Please." I hand her my card and wait as she finishes ringing me up, then offers me my card back. My gaze travels toward the large windows at the front, and I scan the area for that man or the woman who came out to greet him.

Nothing.

So why am I so bothered?

"You okay?" she asks.

Turning back toward her, I flash a smile. After seeing her reaction to the runner on the beach the other day, the last thing I want to do is worry her about something that, more than likely, is merely me overreacting. "Better now."

Color dusts her cheeks. "How was the gym?"

"Eh. I'll feel it tomorrow, but it was worth it."

The look of concern she gives me is as appreciated as it is adorable.

"Here you go, G-man," Anastasia says as she hands me my cup.

"Thanks."

"You're welcome." Her smile widens as she looks between Katelyn and me. "You know, there's no line; you could take a quick break."

Katelyn looks hopeful. "You sure?"

"Yeah, go for it."

"Okay. Be back in ten." Katelyn hangs her apron on the hook, then comes around the counter. "Feel like taking my break with me?"

I grin at her, overjoyed at the fact that I clearly didn't make her so angry this morning that she second-guessed what's between us. "Lead the way."

She turns and heads toward the back of the house that Anastasia had converted into her shop. Just past the stairs that lead up to Anastasia's apartment is what used to be the original kitchen. It's now been turned into a break room, outfitted with a plush couch, a set of lockers, and a bathroom.

Katelyn takes a seat on the couch and pulls out her phone. "Look what Thomas sent me today." Her grin would have knocked me off my feet if I weren't already on my way to sitting.

I drop next to her on the couch, trying to leave enough distance so she's comfortable, but she completely eliminates it by scooting so close that her thigh brushes against mine.

Heat radiates up through my body, but I beat it back down.

Something that becomes a whole lot easier as she distracts me from our close contact with photos of the baseball field and Thomas with his friends.

"He looks like he's having so much fun, doesn't he?" she asks, turning to face me.

"Absolutely."

She hugs the phone to her chest for a moment, then sets it aside. "I'm really glad I let him go. I was so nervous about it, but it's been really good for him."

"I think so, too." I take a sip of my coffee.

"Look, about this morning," Katelyn starts. "I'm sorry I got so defensive. It's just—Garrison, that is your apartment."

"It's just a couple of rooms and a kitchen," I tell her.

"It's your home."

"My home has never been a place," I tell her.

She sighs. "It feels selfish of me."

"I offered."

"I know, but…" she trails off. "Okay."

"Okay?" Absolutely delighted, I set my coffee aside and take her hands in mine.

"Okay, but I want to talk to Geoff first and confirm what you said about the rent. I refuse to let you keep paying the two-bedroom rates if you're staying in my apartment."

"Go right on ahead and call him." I grin at her, glad I already made that phone call first. Geoff confirmed that he hadn't changed prices and that he had no intention of doing so. Since he inherited the building from his late mother, his only goal is to make sure it doesn't get sold to a builder who will tear it down and turn it into condos or a multi-purpose structure.

"You're sure?"

"Positive." I lean in and press my lips to hers. "I think we should go out tonight and celebrate your new apartment."

"Go out?"

"Why not? Dinner, maybe some dancing? If you're up for it."

She stares at me. "Like a date?"

"I never got the chance to date." Those words are a kick in the gut. "Exactly. So, Katelyn Ellis, would you care to go on a date with me? I promise to be nothing but a gentleman."

She continues staring at me for so long, I'm genuinely not sure she'll say yes. And then, she smiles. "I would love nothing more, Garrison Holt."

"Good."

"Oh, but I have to work tonight."

"We can go out late. When do you get off?"

"Eight."

"Then when you get back home, you can get changed, and we'll head out."

"Really?"

"Really." Reaching forward, I cup her face, then draw her in for a kiss. It's slow, a reverent meeting of our lips, but it stirs a hurricane within me. I pull away before I completely lose myself in it. "So, are you interested in a good steak for dinner?"

She arches a brow. "What do you have in mind?"

"Well, all that talk about Steel & Salt the other day made me hungry."

"That sounds wonderful. And I promise not to make any mooing sounds at you."

I laugh, then stand and pull her to her feet. "That would be much appreciated."

CHAPTER 21

KATELYN

"Thank you so much," I tell Mr. Rodney, one of the usuals at the diner, when he hands me a twenty as a tip. "You really don't need to do this."

"Nonsense. I heard about what happened at your apartment last week. Such a shame. If you need anything else, don't hesitate to ask, girl. We take care of our own 'round here." He smiles at me, his cheeks pink, and I have to actively fight the tears in my eyes.

All week, I've had people casually offering me their help should I need clothes, shoes, or other household items now that my apartment will be finished tonight.

Apparently, word has spread, courtesy of my landlord, Geoff. A man whom I still have never met in person, but who has always been beyond kind whenever we're on the phone. It all adds up to one more reason why I really don't want to leave this town. It's the closest thing I've had to family since walking away from mine.

As it always does, the thought of my parents results in a stabbing pain in my chest. The grief still hasn't dissipated. Likely because, if I were brave enough, I could reach out to them. They would welcome me with open arms, even despite everything I've done.

They would welcome Thomas.

Keep it together, Katelyn.

I swallow down the pain and shove the twenty into my pocket. "Thanks again, Mr. Rodney. Can I get you some more coffee?"

"Nope, I'm plenty caffeinated." He beams at me. "See you around, Miss Katelyn."

"See you," I reply as the older man gets up from the barstool he's been occupying for the last hour and heads out into the night. As I do every time I get a break, I check my phone for a message from Thomas. There haven't been any since this afternoon, but I know one will be coming in soon. He always texts or calls right before dinner.

The days that have passed haven't made it any easier to cope with him being away for the first time, but I am so happy I let him go. If I hadn't, he wouldn't be having the amazing time he is.

And I likely wouldn't be where I am with Garrison.

I smile to myself, then shove my phone back into my apron and clear the dirty dishes from the counter. Thoughts of Garrison occupy my mind. Our first kiss, and every one since. Soft promises of letting me set the pace. Of understanding that I need to move slow, given everything I've been through.

Lord, how did I get so lucky?

"I know that smile," Maddie says, pulling me from my thoughts of a handsome Navy SEAL and how excited I am for our date tonight.

My first real one ever.

"I don't know what you're talking about," I reply, but my smile only widens.

Maddie arches a brow. "This have anything to do with that handsome neighbor of yours? You know, the one who was in here earlier and couldn't take his eyes off of you?"

The smile on my face widens so much that it actually makes my cheeks ache. "Maybe."

"Girl, it's about time!"

"What does that mean?"

"Do you know how many times since you started working here, he's done just that? Of course, it was never so obvious. He'd sit with the others and glance over whenever you weren't looking."

It's news to me, but honestly, it makes me even happier. "Really?"

"Really. The guy has had it bad for you for a while now."

"I guess the timing is finally right." I take a deep breath. "He makes me feel so—"

"Alive?" she asks.

"Yes. And beautiful. He looks at me like I'm the only one in the world."

"That's how a good man *should* look at you."

I laugh and glance back at her husband, who is currently cleaning off the grill as we get closer to closing time. "You'd know all about that. How many years has it been?"

"Twenty-seven," she replies with a wink. "And there's not a single moment of it I would trade for anything in the world."

"I love that." Will I have that, too? Will what's between Garrison and me continue to grow? Or will we drift apart? The thought of anything changing darkens my mood just a bit. Is it possible that we're only as close as we are now because I'm staying in his guest room?

"Whatever you're thinking now—stop," Maddie instructs. "You'll damage what you have before it even has a chance to begin."

"Am I that obvious?"

"Girl, you've had walls up since the moment I met you. This is the first time I've seen you truly happy. Let it be. Don't overthink it." She pats my shoulder, then turns back to the register, where she's been going through the credit card receipts.

I continue cleaning off the counter, then wipe it down with a cloth. As I straighten, movement just outside the large bay window catches my eye. I narrow my gaze, the darkness outside making it hard to see at first.

But then I see him. A hooded figure standing just across the street. Just like the one I saw on my balcony the night of the storm. Only this time, he's directly beneath a street light—unmistakable.

My heart leaps into my chest as I take a quick step back. *No.* But when I blink—he's gone. *Did I imagine it?*

"You okay, Katelyn?"

Heart still racing, I turn toward Maddie. She's still standing at the register, a few feet away from me, eyes narrowed in concern.

I look back outside, but there's no one there. "Yeah, I thought I saw—never mind."

"What is it?" She follows my gaze out the window, but there's nothing there.

No one.

Just a trick of my tired mind. Despite my happiness during the day, the nightmares have been in full force ever since I told Garrison about the night my life changed forever. I should have known opening that box would have repercussions, and still I'd do it again. Because letting even some of it out made me feel a bit lighter.

"I'm just tired, that's all." I force a smile. "It was a good night."

"It was." She returns my smile, but there's still that layer of concern on her aging face. "Why don't I have Ed drive you home?"

"Nah. I enjoy the walk." Garrison had offered to come get me, too, but I insisted on walking. It's only a mile, and to be honest, I need it so I can unwind from the day. Then I'll be able to go into the evening unburdened.

Just the thought of it brings me a giddy excitement.

"Honey, it's no trouble," she insists.

"I know, but I'm fine—truly." I gather the dishes I'd collected from Mr. Rodney's spot, then carry them into the kitchen where Maddie's husband, Ed, has transitioned from cleaning the grill to washing what's left. "Here's the last of it."

"Rodney?" he questions, arching a brow.

I laugh. "You know it."

"That man would close down a twenty-four-hour place," he replies. His tone lacks all annoyance, though, since I know he and Mr. Rodney are best friends who play cards together every Sunday after church.

"So true. Do you need any help?"

"Nope. You go home to your neighbor." He wiggles his eyebrows.

I roll my eyes and laugh. "Thanks. See you tomorrow."

"See you then." He begins whistling as he washes dishes, so I step back out into the main room of the diner, where Maddie is putting chairs on top of clean tables.

"You go ahead and go home, honey. Get some sleep," Maddie tells me.

"No, I can stay and help."

"You already refilled all the salt and pepper shakers, rolled silverware, and prepped the menus for tomorrow.

You're good. Go. Home." She grips both of my arms gently, then pulls me in for a hug.

"Only if you're sure."

"I am." Her expression darkens slightly. "Are you sure you won't take me up on the offer to have Ed drive you home?"

"Positive. I'll send you a text when I get home." With a smile, I retrieve my purse and head for the door. "See you tomorrow," I call back.

"See you then."

She locks the door behind me as I step onto the dark street, and I remain where I am, illuminated by the light coming through the windows, until I'm absolutely sure that I'm alone.

Even now, as I make the walk home, though, I can feel eyes on me. The late-night settles around me like a thick blanket, shielding me as I move along the empty street, but the awareness is there.

A tingling in my veins.

"Hey, Pepper!"

I glance over at the nickname, just in time to see Sawyer jog toward me. He's wearing a pair of baggy shorts and a tank top, his skin slick with sweat. The sight of a familiar face removes the rest of my nerves.

"Hey, Sawyer. Late-night run?"

He smiles and stops running to fall into step beside me. "I needed to wind down from the day."

Jack was here this afternoon, arriving at the coffee shop

while Sawyer had been there visiting with Anastasia. My guess is that's what led to this late-night burn-off. Poor guy. I genuinely feel bad for him.

"You know, you should just tell her," I say.

"Tell who what?" But the grin on his face tells me he knows *exactly* who I'm talking about. "I don't want to ruin what she has for something that is probably just better left to the imagination."

"You think a relationship with her is better left to the imagination? Because of her or you?"

He snorts. "Me, obviously. Anastasia is perfect."

Laughing softly, I shake my head. "You have it so bad."

"Eh, I—" but he's cut off when a pair of bright headlights blind the both of us. "Hey, man! Ever heard of low beams!" Sawyer yells into the darkness. Right before the tires squeal to a stop. Every ounce of Sawyer's mood shifts, his body tensing. It's like I'm watching him transform from man to soldier in the blink of an eye. "Run, Katelyn!" he bellows, turning to shield me as he shoves me back toward the diner.

I take off, my legs pumping.

But I don't make it far.

A heavy body slams into me, taking me to the pavement. I'm flipped over onto my stomach before I can so much as scream. A hand clamps over my mouth, and my gaze finds Sawyer in the headlights, fighting off two masked men. He drops one to the ground, but a third rushes up, something in his hand.

The muffled sound of a gunshot fills my ears, and Sawyer stiffens—sinking to his knees.

"No! Help! Sawyer!" I try to scream, but the hand over my mouth is firm. One of the men rushes toward me, blocking my view of my new friend. I thrash, adrenaline pumping through my veins as my hands are zip-tied behind my back and a gag is shoved into my mouth.

Still, I continue to fight even as I'm ripped to my feet and thrown over a shoulder.

"We have to hurry! Someone could have heard that!" one of the men orders as I'm rushed toward what I now see is a white, windowless van.

Sawyer is thrown in first, blood saturating the front of his shirt. Then I'm tossed in next, landing right beside him. He groans, his breathing ragged.

The doors are shut, and a soft light illuminates the inside of the cabin. One of the men removes his mask and grins down at me, one of his front teeth missing. There's a large scar on his face, somehow making him look even more menacing.

"Hey there, pretty," he says, then reaches forward to run a finger over my face.

"Touch her, and I'll cut that off," Sawyer snarls.

The guy grins at him. "You're in no position to make demands, are you?"

I fight against the gag as the van starts moving.

"You got something to say, pretty?" he reaches forward and tugs the gag free.

"You have to let me get pressure on his injury, or he'll die."

"What's that to me?" the man asks, tone uninterested.

"Cut her loose so she can tend to him," another man who still has his mask on says.

"Why? We weren't here for him."

"Boss might say otherwise. Now, cut. Her. Loose." The order is clipped, frustrated.

With a muttered protest, the man with the scar leans forward. "Turn around, pretty. I can't cut you free if you're facing me."

The idea of showing my back to this man, of being vulnerable in any way, makes my skin crawl. But Sawyer's life depends on it, so I swallow hard…and turn.

He rips me back against his body, a move meant to intimidate. Instead of letting it work, though, I close my eyes and focus on the place I created in my mind where no one—not even Victor—could ever touch me.

The moment my hands are cut free, I shed my jacket and apply it to the wound in Sawyer's side. He looks up at me. "I'm sorry," he says. "I should have been able to help."

"It's not your fault." Tears in my eyes, I keep pressure as the van barrels down the road, going who knows where. "This is my fault."

He narrows his gaze on my face.

"They're here for me, and you got caught in the cross-fire. I'm so sorry, Sawyer. You should have kept running. Then you'd be okay."

"But you'd be alone," he whispers. "And don't worry." He looks past me, so I follow his gaze where the man who'd cut me free is sitting at the back of the van beside the man who'd ordered him to do it. They're engaged in a low conversation, so I lean down closer. "The others will come," he says. "It's kind of what we do."

I swallow hard, hoping that he's right, but also not wanting to point out one very harsh truth: Will we be alive when they do?

CHAPTER 22

GARRISON

I check my watch for the tenth time in as many minutes. Katelyn should have been back already, right? Unless she got caught up at the diner? Even though it's only been about ten seconds, I check my watch again.

Something's not right.

My cell rings, so I retrieve it from the counter, honestly expecting her name to be on the screen. Instead, Thomas' name flashes. That feeling of unease in my gut turns volatile. "Hey, bud."

"Hey, are you with my mom?"

"Not right now. Why? Is everything okay?" I try to keep my tone steady. Calm. Even though inside I'm anything but.

"I mean, I think so. But she didn't answer when I called her."

"She had a shift at the diner tonight, so maybe she got caught up. I'll run over and check on her."

"Thanks, Mr. Holt."

"Of course." I grab my keys and rush out the door. "I'll let her know you called as soon as I get there, okay?"

"Okay. Sounds good." I can hear the shift in his tone. The normally happy boy is worried, and why wouldn't he be? Katelyn may have missed my call earlier, but Thomas? She'd answer even if she was elbows deep in something. "Talk soon, Mr. Holt."

"Talk soon, Thomas." I end the call, then shove the phone into my pocket as I press the elevator button. Standing still when my heart is pounding is impossible, though, so I abandon the elevator and sprint toward the stairs.

I rush down them as fast as I can, then sprint toward my truck in the parking lot.

But I don't make it even halfway there when I see the red and blue lights in the distance.

No. God, please no.

My entire body trembles as I shift course and race down the street. The diner is only a mile away. One mile. Nothing bad can happen in a mile, right? Heart in my throat, I reach the scene right after the police do. They've already blocked off the area, but I push through it.

"What happened?"

Deputy Phillips, a new officer, holds his hand up to stop me.

"You can't be here. This is a crime scene."

I scan the area. No bodies. That's good, right? "Leopold!" I yell as soon as I see the familiar police captain in the distance.

He turns toward me, then offers a wave for me to enter the scene. Without waiting for the deputy to grant permission, I shove past him and run toward Alan.

"What happened?" I demand again.

"We're not sure." He shakes his head and turns toward a dark shadow on the pavement. Even without the work lights set up, I know what it is: blood.

"Is there a body?" Bile burns the back of my throat with even the thought of Katelyn lying somewhere, covered in a white sheet. How will I tell Thomas? *Easy, Holt, you don't even know if it's her.*

"No body. There's a trail of blood that leads from there over toward the street, then it vanishes."

"An abduction?"

He nods.

"Any witnesses?"

He shakes his head. "Someone heard tires screeching and what sounded like fighting, but when they got to the window to look outside, all they saw was a pair of taillights racing out of town."

I scan the area. We're right across the street from the marina entrance, and the only cameras there are pointed at the boats—not the street. Dread twists my insides. "Katelyn was supposed to be home." I turn toward him. "She never arrived."

Leopold's mouth flattens into a tight line. "Okay. Where was she coming from?"

"The diner."

He looks past me. "Phillips!"

"Yes, Captain?" he asks as he runs toward us.

"Go talk to Maddie and Ed. Find out if Katelyn Ellis is still at the diner. If she's not, get me the time she left."

"You've got it." He turns and rushes down the street toward the diner while my gaze narrows on the blood.

It's not so much that I worry she already bled out, but that doesn't mean it's not a life-threatening injury. It's entirely possible whoever took her moved fast.

"Easy, Holt. We don't know that it's her."

"We don't know that it's not," I reply.

"Let's get the facts first, okay?"

He turns to talk to a woman wearing a black windbreaker with the words STORMWATCH CRIME SCENE INVESTIGATOR printed in bold letters on the back. All while my world crumbles.

It's her.

I know it in my gut.

So when Deputy Phillips comes back toward the scene, a grim look on his face, I don't need his answer.

"When?" I ask. "When did she leave?"

"Twenty minutes ago. A few minutes before the call came in."

Twenty minutes.

One mile.

This shouldn't have happened.

"Captain, we found this." Another officer rushes forward with a purse in his hand. Katelyn's purse.

Leopold opens it and pulls out a cell phone and wallet. He checks the ID, then slides both back into the bag before giving it back to the officer.

Everything moves in slow motion as the realization sets in: Katelyn is gone.

Taken.

"Garrison," Leopold says softly. "Where is her son?"

"Baseball camp."

"Okay. Do you know if she had any local family? Someone who can go pick him up?"

I shake my head, the shock settling over me like concrete. "No family. I, uh, I can get him. He knows me."

"You should do that," he says, then clasps a hand on my shoulder. "We'll find her, okay?"

I turn toward him, my own resolve filling me with one single purpose. There is not a place in this world I won't go to get her back. "I know we will."

"Here you go." Anastasia brings me a cup of coffee. I barely taste it as I sip from the paper cup, my mind already formulating a plan. Who could have taken her? Why? Was it random? Or does it have something to do with why she's here in the first place?

I consider her evasive answers. The way she and Thomas have moved around constantly since he was a baby.

Add that up, and it's proof that she's running from someone.

But who?

Thomas's dad is dead.

The front door opens, and both Weston and Ryker move into the small house.

"Sawyer's not answering the door," Weston says, crossing his arms.

"He didn't answer my call either," Anastasia offers. Her eyes are red and swollen from crying, her jaw set. "But a lot of times, he'll go for a run after work. He usually calls me back by ten."

I check my watch. "That's in an hour. We can't wait."

"I left my brother a message, but I don't know when they'll get it." Anastasia sniffles. "Do you think she's—"

"We'll find her, Anastasia," Ryker assures her.

She nods. "I'll make more coffee."

"Any idea who might have taken her and why?" Ryker asks.

"Random abduction?" Weston offers.

"That's what Leopold is leaning toward."

"But you think something different," Weston says to

me. It's no surprise; the guy is great at reading people. The only member of our team who's better is Zane.

How much do I tell them? I don't want to betray Katelyn, but if something happens to her because they don't have all the pieces— "Katelyn's ex-husband was abusive. She left him when Thomas was a year old."

"You think it was him?"

I shake my head. "According to her, he's dead."

"We need to look into that," Ryker says. He withdraws his cell and taps on the screen before putting it up to his ear. "Come on, Sawyer." When there's no answer, he shoves it into his pocket.

"Call Elijah Breeth and Tucker Hunt. See if they can both dig into her past."

"On it." Ryker steps away and taps on the screen again.

"What do you want me to do?" Weston questions.

I turn toward him. "I'm going to pick up Thomas from camp. He needs to be protected."

"I'll keep him safe. He can stay on the ranch."

Nodding, I check that off my mental task list. Next, I need to find out exactly where that van went. I turn toward Ryker, who places his phone on speaker.

"I've got Elijah and Tucker on a call," he says.

"What can we do?" Elijah asks through the speaker.

"I need to know everything you can find about Katelyn, her ex-husband, and her former brother-in-law."

"Brother-in-law?" Ryker asks.

"She mentioned that he was just as bad as her ex-husband."

"I can look into that," Elijah offers.

"I also need to know where the van went after it took her. Tucker, can you check the security cameras?"

"On it," he says. In the background, I can hear keystrokes as he types on the keyboard.

"Let me know when you guys have something. And thanks."

"Anytime," Elijah replies.

"Call with any updates," Tucker adds.

"Thanks, guys." Ryker ends the call and slips his phone into his pocket.

The intel portion of a mission is always the hardest. Gathering all of the pieces together before acting. But it's so much worse now. So much harder knowing that Katelyn is out there somewhere, injured.

What if I can't find her in time?

What am I supposed to tell Thomas?

"Keep me updated. I'm going to go grab Thomas."

"I'll come," Weston offers. "Give me time to get to know the kid so he's more comfortable around me."

"Sounds good, thanks." I turn toward Ryker. "Keep a pulse on the police. Let me know if they find out anything."

"Will do." He heads for the door and slips outside.

"What can I do?" Anastasia asks. Her arms are wrapped around herself, her eyes full of tears.

"Keep trying Sawyer. And call Jack. We may need his resources."

CHAPTER 23

KATELYN

The van comes to a stop, and my heart begins to pound all over again. Sawyer's complexion is pale and clammy, his skin slick with sweat. He's not doing well. And if he doesn't get medical attention soon, he's not going to make it.

Tears prick the corners of my eyes. *Please, God, no.*

Sawyer reaches up and covers my hand with his where I'm still applying pressure to his wound. He squeezes gently in an attempt to calm me. But I'm nowhere near calm.

Not even close.

Because I know what's waiting on the other side of those doors. Or rather, who. And he's so much worse than Victor.

The double doors open. Earnest Marks is not an overly

imposing man. Dressed in a black suit, his dark hair silver at the temples, he looks like any other businessman. Only, this man makes deals that destroy people.

"Katelyn, been a long time," he says.

"Earnest Marks." Sawyer scoots up the side of the van so he's sitting. I don't tell him to remain still or risk bleeding to death because I imagine he knows the risk and doesn't care.

"Do we know each other?" he asks. "This the counselor she's been bedding down with?"

"No," the man who took his mask off replies. "Just some guy she was walking with."

"Hmm," he replies, then turns back to me. "Been talking about me, Katelyn? I thought we had an agreement."

"She hasn't said a word to me. But your ugly mug isn't one I'd forget. Owner of the West Coast Wranglers—the sorriest excuse for a football team in the league."

The man with the scar snarls and reaches for Sawyer, but Earnest clicks his tongue.

"Easy, Leo. No need to let him taunt you into a temper. Who shot him?"

"I did," a man comes around the side of the van, his mask removed. Dark hair, a crooked nose, and eyes so cold they might as well be inhuman. *Bradley Jenkins.* The fear I already felt increases tenfold.

Because the only reason Bradley didn't force himself

on me before was because of who I was to Victor, though he tried plenty of times.

What will he do now?

He grins at me. "Hey there, beautiful. Long time."

"Keep your hands off her," Earnest orders. "For now at least," he adds with a glare in my direction.

"Whatever you're going to do to me, fine, but let Sawyer go. He has nothing to do with this."

"You're not exactly in a position to make demands, are you?" Earnest asks.

Sawyer shoves my hands off of him and tries to stand, using the wall of the van for support, but he falls back, too weak from blood loss.

"I'm so sorry," I tell him.

"As you should be. You do seem to have a habit of getting good men killed." Earnest props one foot up on the back of the van. "Now, where is my dear nephew?"

Fear slices to the bone, even as hope surges through me. If he doesn't know, then Thomas is safe—for now. But who will keep him that way? Who will pick him up from camp and make sure my boy remains protected?

Garrison. That one name echoes through my mind and eases every question I have.

Thomas will be okay because Garrison will make sure of it.

"I will *never* tell you."

"No?" he looks back at a man standing behind him.

"Call the doc and have this one stitched up. We may need him. Katelyn is easily persuaded when someone else is suffering for her."

"No. Please don't." Panic thrums in my veins, and I release pressure long enough to put myself between Sawyer and the man coming for him. "Let him go. Please."

"You've misbehaved for quite some time now, Katelyn. I think it's well past time you learn your lesson. Grab him."

The man Earnest had called Leo rushes forward and yanks me out of the truck. I scream and thrash in his hold, my only goal getting back to Sawyer, who is already trying to get to his feet.

"Go ahead and scream, Katelyn. There's no one here to hear you. There never was," Earnest calls out with a laugh.

Still, I fight. Even though I know it's a useless endeavor. These guys are professional football players. Bruisers with a reputation for being ruthless on and off the field.

"It's going to be okay!" Sawyer yells. He tries to get up again, but stumbles back, tank top saturated in blood.

"I'm so sorry!" I scream as I'm dragged away. "I'm so sorry!"

A door closes in my face, cutting off my view of Sawyer as I'm carried down a long hallway. I fall still, conserving whatever energy I have left for my first opportunity at an escape. I'll get help, then find Sawyer.

We'll get out.

We have to.

A door creaks open, and I'm shoved forward, nearly falling on my face before a massive hand steadies me. He spins me around to face him, then shoves me down onto a chair. My head cracks back against something hard, and a burst of white-hot pain explodes behind my eyes. I suck in a shaky breath, fighting for my calm.

If I've learned anything, it's that panicking won't do anything but make men like this rougher. They love to see their prey afraid. I won't show him that—not again.

"Get comfortable, Pretty," Leo snarls. "You're going to be here awhile. Now, be a good girl, and give me your wrists."

I glare up at him.

A hand cracks across my cheek. "Boss never said you had to keep looking pretty. If I were you, I'd listen."

Body trembling, jaw set, I put my wrists onto the armrests.

But when he moves forward, I drive my leg up into his groin. He grunts and falls to his knees. I don't waste any time as I sprint toward the door and rip it open. The hall is long, but I race down toward where I last saw Sawyer. If I can see where they take him—the door at the end opens, and Bradley strolls in, Earnest at his side.

Earnest clicks his tongue. "Well, well, Katelyn. Seems you have a bit more fight in you than before. That's okay, we'll break you of it. After all, we've got all the time in the world."

Something slams into the back of my head, and I fall forward, hitting the ground. It's cool beneath my cheek, but before I can even try to push up, the world goes dark, and I slip away—my last thought a prayer.

Lord, please protect my son. Please save Sawyer.

CHAPTER 24

GARRISON

"What do you have for me?" I ask when I answer Tucker's call on Bluetooth.

"Nothing good," he replies. "Are you in a place where you can see something?"

I guide my truck off to the shoulder of the highway and put it in park. "I am now." After retrieving my phone from the cupholder, I open up a message from Tucker Hunt and turn it so Weston can see as well.

"What am I looking at?"

"The security camera from outside the hardware store. I was able to remotely access it, but it's the last camera before the dead zone where she was grabbed."

As he says it, Katelyn comes into view. The picture is grainy and dark, but she's unmistakable. Her purse hangs up on her shoulder, her hair pulled back in a ponytail. Just seeing her is a knife to my chest, knowing that it may be the last time I do.

"Did you see who grabbed her?"

"No. But she wasn't alone." Tucker's voice is strained, his tone serious.

Katelyn pauses and glances off to the right as a man jogs toward her in running shorts and a tank top. *Sawyer.* Dread fills me, saturating every part of me from my head to my toes, because I now know without a doubt that the blood wasn't Katelyn's.

It's Sawyer's. If he were with her, then he likely fought back.

Anger and grief permeate the cab of my truck as Weston watches Katelyn and Sawyer start walking again, disappearing off-screen.

The video ends.

"Sawyer was with her," Weston snarls. He reaches into his pocket and pulls out his phone.

"I'm sorry, I don't have anything else. I'm still combing security cameras out of town, but so far, nothing."

"Thanks, Tucker. Please let me know if you find anything." I end the call.

"You heard from Sawyer yet?" Weston asks into his phone. "Thanks." He ends the call. "Anastasia hasn't gotten hold of him. She went by the shop, and he's not there. His phone is on the counter." He slams his fist into the dash and mutters something under his breath. "They took him, too."

The realization twists into my gut, giving me a new

level of appreciation for my friend, even as my fear just doubled. "He tried to save her."

"The blood is his," Weston says.

"It has to be. That's the only way they would have gotten her. He wouldn't have gone down without a fight." *Oh, God, please don't let me lose either of them.*

"Garrison, if they didn't come for him—" Weston starts.

I already know where he's going, and it makes my stomach churn. "Then they have no reason to keep him alive."

It's just past two in the morning when I make it to the camp. I pull up in front of the main cabin and put my truck in park, my heart heavier than it's ever been. How am I supposed to deliver this news?

How do I tell a young boy that his mom is missing and I'm not sure she'll ever come home?

There has been no news from Elijah or Tucker since Tucker's call an hour ago, and I can't help but worry the next call I get will be from Leopold, telling me they found Sawyer's discarded body.

The woman I love and my best friend. Both ripped from me on the same night.

How is this fair?

Because I'm not sure what else I can do, I close my

eyes and bow my head, reaching for the only One who can stop this storm from leveling my entire life.

God, I can't do this. Please help me. Please guide me so I can bring them both home safely. Please, Lord. In Jesus' name I pray, amen.

"You ready?" Weston asks as soon as I've opened my eyes and raised my head.

I take a deep breath. "No. But let's go anyway." As I'm shoving open my door, the cabin opens, and Coach Jesse Rivers steps out, his expression grim. I'd called him on my way here and let him know what was going on.

He assured me that Thomas wouldn't be notified until I got here and, after getting Leopold's permission, agreed to release the teen into my care. *My care.* He should be with his mom. It should be her picking him up from the school after an amazing week with his friends.

"Any update?" Jesse asks.

I shake my head. "We've got people looking into every possible lead."

He nods. "I haven't said anything to him, but I did have his counselor go get him when I saw your truck coming down the drive."

"Good." But is it? How can it be when Katelyn and Sawyer's lives hang in the balance?

"Mr. Holt?" Thomas' voice cracks what little restraint I've had over my own emotions ever since seeing those red and blue lights.

"Hey, Thomas."

His eyes go wide and fill with tears. "Where's my mom?" he stammers, voice cracking. "Where is she? Is she okay?" He rushes forward, and I reach up to place both hands on his trembling shoulders.

"We don't know where she is, but we're going to find her, okay?"

His bottom lip begins to tremble, and he throws himself into my arms. I wrap both of them around him and hold on. *Lord, please let her be okay. Please bring her home to him. Please God, don't make this boy bury his mother.*

"We're going to take you back to town, okay?"

He nods and pulls away, wiping his cheeks. "I want to help."

"I know you do. Let's go get your stuff."

"Got it," an older boy—likely the counselor who ran to get him—holds up a duffel bag.

Weston crosses over and takes it from him, then carries it back and tosses it into the truck.

"Come on, Thomas." With an arm around his shoulders, I guide him back toward the truck.

"Let us know if we can do anything," Jesse calls out.

"Will do, thanks."

"Thanks, Coach," Thomas manages.

"Anytime, kid. You're not alone, okay?"

He nods. "I know." But his voice is barely above a whisper.

Does he know that? Does he know that I'll die before I let anything happen to him?

That I'd gladly trade my life for Katelyn's?

"Can you think of anyone who might want to hurt your mom?" Leopold asks Thomas. I'm sitting next to him, across the desk from the police captain, where we've been for the better part of half an hour since we returned home.

He shakes his head. "My mom never hurt anybody."

"But you moved around a lot. Any idea why?"

He closes his eyes, the questioning taking its toll on his already damaged heart. "She never said anything. But I always suspected she didn't want someone to find us."

"Who?"

"I don't know. I don't remember." He drops his head and puts both hands on his cheeks.

"I think we need to call it," I say and stand. "Come on, Thomas. Let's get some food."

"I'm not hungry. I don't want to eat. I want to find my mom," he cries.

"I know," I tell him. "And we will. I promise. Can you go wait with Weston so I can talk to Captain Leopold?"

Thomas hesitates for a moment but finally nods and heads out into the hall. Through the glass, I see him stop beside Weston and Ryker.

"Any update on the blood?" I question.

"We can't tell whether or not it's his, but—"

"You can get a DNA profile."

He nods. "It's not hers," he says.

Sawyer.

"Thanks." I reach for the door handle.

"Holt."

I turn back toward him.

"We both know you're not going to let this go, and I'm in no place to tell you to drop it. But I do expect to be kept in the loop. You let me know if you find anything else, and I'll do the same."

"Yes, sir."

Chapter 25

Katelyn

The door opens, and Sawyer is shoved inside. He stumbles, the momentum nearly taking him to the ground, but he recovers quickly. Both of his hands are bound in front of him, and he's shirtless, but his injury has been tended to, a crisp white bandage over his side.

Which means, they want him alive…for now.

Relief rushes through me at the sight of him. *Thank You, Lord!*

"Easy, bud, I require a more tender touch," he says to Leo.

"Shut up." He shoves Sawyer down into a chair beside me, then secures his feet at the ankles with zip ties.

Sawyer glances over at me. "Come here often?"

How he's joking right now, I have no idea, but his uplifted spirits are a good thing, right? Doesn't that mean

he feels okay? Does he know how we're going to get out of
here?

"Are you okay?" I ask.

"Eh, I've had worse."

Leo zip ties one wrist to the chair, then cuts the one that
is binding both of his wrists together and secures his right
wrist to the other side of the chair. "Don't go anywhere,"
Leo says, then throws a wink at me.

"Not planning on it." Sawyer winks right back.

Leo snarls and mutters obscenities as he leaves the
room and slams the door behind him.

Sawyer turns to me, the humor from just seconds ago
leaving his face. His gaze drifts over my body as if he's
checking me for injuries. "Are you okay?"

"I'm not the one who was shot," I reply.

"I'll be fine." He's quiet for a moment, nostrils flaring.
"Did they touch you—"

I shake my head, already knowing he's about to ask
whether or not they assaulted me. "I'm okay." My gaze
fills. "But I'm so sorry, Sawyer. I'm so sorry that you got
dragged into this."

"Hey, it's not your fault. Besides, this isn't even the first
time I've been tied to a chair this year. But I do need you to
tell me what's going on so I know what we're dealing
with." Sawyer glances around the room, then nods toward a
camera mounted in the top right. "Watch your words,
though. We have an audience," he says, tone low.

I'd noticed it earlier, too. "Earnest is my brother-in-law," I tell him. As much as I hate to rehash this again, the time for secrets is past. If there is anything I know that can help, I'll say it.

"Victor Marks is your ex-husband?"

"Technically, my late husband. We never officially divorced," I tell him. "I ran and was too afraid to send him divorce papers, just in case he could use them to track me."

"He was abusive?"

I nod. "Among other things."

"You said late husband. He's dead?"

"He died when Thomas was three."

"That why big brother is after you? What does he want with Thomas?"

Tears burn in the corners of my eyes, and my stomach twists. "He has been trying to kill Thomas since Victor died."

Sawyer's gaze turns downright murderous. "He wants to *kill* the kid?"

I nod. "He blames me for Victor's death and—"

"Because you murdered him," Earnest announces as he pushes into the room.

"I didn't kill him! He had a heart attack!"

"Brought on by you." He takes off his coat and sets it aside, then rolls up his sleeves. Bradley and Leo come in behind him, though they remain near the door. "Go ahead, Katelyn, finish the story. Might as well tell your buddy here who he's dying for."

I don't want to speak, though. Don't want to relive that horrific moment.

"Go on," Earnest orders. "Tell him how you drove my brother to complete madness. How you tortured him into his death."

"I didn't do that! He found me! He tracked me!" I scream, tears blurring my vision. "He could have just left us alone!"

"Breathe, Katelyn. You're okay," Sawyer says.

I close my eyes, drawing in breath after breath and trying to calm myself.

"I suppose the why doesn't really matter anymore since I buried him," Earnest snaps. "It certainly doesn't change the outcome, does it?" He closes the distance and stops right in front of Sawyer. "Where is Thomas?" he asks me.

"Somewhere you'll never touch him," I growl. No matter what he does to me, I won't tell him.

Earnest smirks, rears his fist back, and slams it into Sawyer's face. His head whips back, and as he leans forward again, he moves his jaw from side to side.

"No! Stop!" I stare in horror as he shakes his fist. Sawyer spits some blood out, and it splatters to the tile floor.

"You're going to have to do better than that," Sawyer quips. "Maybe let muscles over there have a turn. He looks like he enjoys having a good time. Don't ya, big guy?"

"You've got a big mouth," Earnest snaps.

"I've been told it's one of my best features." Sawyer

grins. "Just know that whatever damage you do to me will be done to you—tenfold when Garrison gets here."

Earnest laughs. "You think I'm afraid of your friend? I looked him up. Guy is a counselor for kids. I think I'll take my chances." He turns to me. "Let's try this again, Katelyn. Where is Thomas?"

Sawyer smiles widely, then laughs, blood trickling down the corner of his mouth. "You really have no idea what you've done, do you?"

Earnest, almost bored, turns to Sawyer. "And what exactly have I done?"

"Do you even know who we are?" When Earnest doesn't respond, Sawyer shifts forward in his seat, movements slowed by pain. Still, his expression remains neutral. Unbothered.

"I know you used to be in the military," Earnest says. "Navy, right? Again, not worried."

Sawyer laughs. "You should be."

"And why is that? You're no longer enlisted. My contact said your file isn't even all that impressive."

"It's because it's so impressive that you have to have the highest of clearances to even access the real records."

Earnest glances over his shoulder. "Guy has an ego on him, doesn't he?"

"I can fix it, boss. Just let me know," Leo offers.

But Sawyer hasn't shifted his gaze from Earnest. "You want to know why I'm not worried, Katelyn? That's because everyone on our team has their own special skill. You know, like a team of superheroes." His grin spreads as he glances over at me, then turns back to Earnest. "Tank can tear you apart with his bare hands. Cowboy can stop your heart before you even realize you're at risk. Cap?" Sawyer glances over at me, "You haven't met him yet, but I imagine you'll be meeting him soon." He looks back at Earnest, who has crossed his arms. "Cap has a gift for making people tell the truth—even when they swear they won't." He leans forward now, just slightly, his eyes never straying from Earnest's face.

"Me? I notice things. I listen. I remember. Information is power after all. Kind of like how I know your pal there has a weak knee. Left side, right?" he asks. "One hit and —" Sawyer clicks his tongue. "Boss man here has so many weak spots he's basically a liability with a pulse."

Earnest scoffs. "That supposed to scare me?"

Sawyer exhales on a quiet laugh. "No. Not me. After all, I'm a bit tied up at the moment. But do you want to know what your biggest mistake was?"

"I imagine you're going to tell me." Earnest deadpans.

"You made up your mind on who Garrison is when you have *no* idea."

My stomach tightens, bile burning the back of my throat. Sawyer is here because of me. He's going to die because of me. The idea that anyone else is going to plunge headfirst into my nightmare makes my skin crawl.

"Oooh, I'm shaking." He turns away from Sawyer, his

tone mocking. Both Leo and Bradley laugh obnoxiously in response.

"Demo is the last resort," Sawyer says evenly as soon as the room has quieted again. "For a reason."

He pauses, letting his words sink in. And based on Earnest's hesitation as he reaches for the door handle? They're doing just that.

"Demo's specialty is destruction. Buildings. People. He will destroy *everything* around his target. Brick by brick, he dismantles until there is nothing left standing."

Earnest turns back toward us, his face a bit paler than it was. *Is Sawyer getting to him?* "By the time he finds either of you, you'll be dead. There will be no rescue."

Sawyer's smile doesn't fade. It deepens. And somehow, his confidence builds my own. As he said, they're a team. That means, if anyone is going to come for us, who better than a team of Navy SEALs?

That moment on the stairs with Thomas all those weeks ago swims to the front of my memory: *"I heard he can kill a guy with just his pinky finger," Thomas says, wiggling his own in demonstration. "That he and the others once went into a fully armed compound."*

Are they coming for us?

Can they survive it?

"By now, our rescue isn't his mission anymore."

Silence stretches. "Oh?"

"No." Sawyer leans back in his chair. "Now it's you."

"Then I guess I'd better get what I can out of you

before I kill you both." He turns and looks back at Leo. "Give me your knife."

"No. Please, let him go. You can do whatever you want to me—" I insist, that slice of relief I felt dissipating at the idea of anything happening to Sawyer.

"Oh, I plan to," Earnest interrupts. "But first, I want to know where Thomas is. For every word out of your mouth that isn't what I want to hear, I'm going to take out my frustrations on your overly confident friend here. Until he's either dead or you've told me what I want to know. Either way, you should know better. I'm not a man who doesn't get what he wants."

"You think you're the first one who's tried to get information out of me? Do your worst," Sawyer replies. "Neither one of us is letting you lay a finger on that kid."

The door opens, and a man I don't recognize comes in. He leans forward and whispers something to Earnest. Something that has a chilling smile spreading across his face. He offers the knife back to Leo, then turns to me.

No, please, God no.

"Looks like we won't be needing playtime after all. Seems dear sweet Thomas was just brought into the police station to be notified that his mother is missing. How convenient."

"Don't you dare touch him!" I scream as I thrash against the bindings. "Don't touch him!" My throat burns as I fight against the hold. "Please, Earnest! Please leave him alone!"

Earnest kneels in front of me. "You're going to be doing a lot of begging before this is over, Katelyn. Don't wear yourself out just yet. Don't worry, I'll let you see your boy one last time."

"Good luck," Sawyer says, his tone lacking all humor now. "You're going to need it."

Earnest collects his jacket. "You may have your team, Navy man, but so do I. And mine doesn't play by any rules." Without waiting for a response, he, Bradley, and Leo leave the room.

"Mine neither," Sawyer replies softly, then turns to me. "We don't have a lot of time."

"He's going to kill him, Sawyer. He's going to kill my son." Tears stream down my cheeks, my heart racing. I can't just sit here. I can't just wait for him to march Thomas in here.

"No," Sawyer replies. "Because Garrison won't let him within twenty yards of Thomas. You have to trust him, okay?"

I swallow hard, panic making my pulse race.

"I need you to stay calm so we can get out of here. With them distracted and riding the high of a perceived win, this is the best chance we have. You the praying kind?"

"I am."

"Good. Then bow your head."

I do as he says.

"Lord, we ask that You protect Thomas. Send your angels to shield him from this danger. Please guide the team, Lord, and lead us out of here. God, we pray this in Jesus' name, amen."

"Amen." Peace washes over me as Sawyer's prayer sets in.

God will protect my boy; I know He will.

And now I pray that I'll get the chance to see him again —so long as it's not anywhere near Earnest or this place.

Chapter 26

Garrison

It's been almost two months since I saw Zane Knox. And the relief I feel seeing him and Tessa walk into Anastasia's coffee shop is strong enough that it beats back the guilt I feel since they cut their trip short and hopped on a plane home.

"Zane." Anastasia rushes over to him and wraps her arms around her big brother. She's been an absolute wreck since I told her that the blood is more than likely Sawyer's. There's no way they would have been able to grab them unless he was injured.

"Hey, sis," he says as he squeezes her gently. Releasing her, he turns to me. "What's the latest?"

At that exact moment, my cell rings. Reaching into my pocket, I withdraw it and check the readout. "Hey, Elijah," I answer, placing it on speaker.

"I've got something."

"Tell us."

Zane and Ryker move in closer while Tessa wraps an arm around Anastasia.

"Victor Marks is Katelyn's husband. But they never divorced."

"They didn't?" It's news to me, but if she was on the run and he died before she got the chance, it's not really a surprise.

"No. He died ten years ago. Heart attack. The file is rough, though. Looks like she was with him when he died —the only witness."

"What do you mean?"

"Based on the witness reports, he barged onto the elevator with her and her son, then shoved an elderly man off before the doors closed. The elevator emergency stop was hit, trapping her and her son inside with him."

I clench my free hand into a fist, the realization hitting home that this is why she's not a fan of elevators. It's not the small space but whatever trauma happened to her inside.

"They heard screams from her and the young child, but it was twenty minutes before firefighters arrived to get the doors open. When they did, she was bloodied up pretty bad —hers, not his—and doing chest compressions on him."

She still tried to save him.

Even after he tried to kill her.

Oh, Katelyn, where are you?

"The brother—Earnest Marks—blamed her for it and

tried to pursue criminal charges. None were filed for obvious reasons, especially when the security footage of the elevator was recovered. He didn't have a leg to stand on, and Katelyn was cleared of any wrongdoing."

"Earnest Marks," Zane repeats. "Why do I know that name?"

"He's the owner of the West Coast Wranglers football team. The same team Victor played for up until his death."

"He was a football player?" I question.

"A popular one," Elijah replies. "Had a bright future straight out of college."

A future that was paid for by Katelyn's.

"I'm guessing he didn't let it go?" Ryker asks.

"Not even a little. I did some extra digging, got into some records I won't mention, but it looks like he's had a private investigator looking for her for quite some time."

"Which explains all the moving around," I say. "She was hiding from him."

"So it would seem." Elijah sighs. "As far as I can tell, though, the guy and his team are at training camp in Southern California. He hasn't even been out of the state since last year when he went to Hawaii."

"It has to be him," I say with absolute certainty. "If it were random, they would have left Sawyer for dead."

A strangled sob leaves Anastasia, and we all turn toward her. She's turned into Tessa, who has both arms wrapped around her. *Way to go, Holt.* "I'm sorry," I tell her. "I—" What else can I say?

"The important thing is that they didn't," Zane replies. "If they took him, then they clearly wanted him alive for some reason."

We look at each other, though neither of us says what we're really thinking. Taking Sawyer could have been a way to torment Katelyn. After all, forcing her to watch her friend die would hurt her more than death ever would.

Friend.

Katelyn's friend. "Hey, Elijah, is there any way to find out who Katelyn roomed with at college?"

"Let me see."

"What're you thinking?" Zane asks as the clicking of keys becomes background noise.

"Katelyn told me that her roommate died in an accident the day after she met Victor."

"Do you think that has any connection?"

I nod. "I can't tell you why unless I believe it's pertinent, but trust me."

"I always do," Zane replies.

"Yasmin Hernandez," Elijah says. "Looks like she died in a car accident on her way to work. Brake's failed."

"Intentional?" I question.

"The report says they looked like they were cut, but no charges were ever filed."

So he killed her. Earnest Marks had Katelyn's friend murdered because she knew the truth about what really happened that night.

"Try to find a connection to that accident and Earnest."

"The trail is long cold, but I'll try. Lance wants to know if you need backup. He and Jaxson are geared up and ready to head your way. Same thing with the Hunts. I told Tucker I was giving you a call, and he said both Dylan and Riley are ready to hit the ground."

"Maybe. I'll let you know."

"Sounds good." Elijah ends the call, so I shove my phone back into my pocket and cross my arms, the information rolling around in my mind.

Earnest Marks was trying to salvage his brother's reputation.

When he died while assaulting his wife in a public space, Earnest tried to throw Katelyn under the bus, desperate to make his brother look good even in death.

Which tells me he will stop at nothing to get back at her.

And the best way to do that is—*Thomas.* "He's going to send someone for Thomas."

"What makes you think that?" Ryker questions.

"If he's going through all of this trouble, it's not going to be enough for him to get his hands on Katelyn. If he wants her to suffer, then he's going to want her to know that he has her son, too."

"We need to get to the ranch." Zane turns to Tessa. "You guys go to Leopold. Tell him what we found out and let him know he needs to send a car."

"On it." Tessa releases Anastasia and kisses Zane. "Be careful."

He flashes her a smile. "I always am."

By the time we've gotten to the truck, I've already dialed Weston.

"Anything?" he answers.

"It quiet out there?"

"Kyle Harding got here a few minutes ago, but that's the only update I have on my end."

I'd texted Weston to let him know that I asked Kyle to drive out and check in on Thomas. I thought he could use a friend, and instead, I just sent another kid into danger.

"We're on our way out there now," I tell him.

"Any particular reason?"

"We think that someone may be coming for Thomas, too."

He's quiet for a moment, likely because he's checking windows. "That your headlights?"

Dread slams into me. "We're still twenty minutes out."

"Then it looks like company is here. I've got the fort. Just get here when you can."

"Weston—"

"I'll protect him, Demo. Just get here." The call ends.

"Someone's there." The words make my skin crawl. *This can't be happening.*

Zane slams on the accelerator, and we race off into the night. I only hope we get there in time.

Lord, please be with them.

Zane brings my truck to a sliding stop right as Weston steps out onto the porch. He throws a body down the steps into the dirt, then crosses his arms. Aside from his shirt being untucked in the front, he doesn't even look like he broke a sweat.

"Thomas?" I demand as I rush out, weapon drawn.

"He's fine. I was just taking out the trash."

The man he just threw down groans, but Ryker is already flipping him over onto his belly and zip-tying his hands behind his back.

"There's another one inside, though I wouldn't expect that one to wake up anytime soon. Took a nasty fall face-first into the counter."

"Where's Thomas?" I sprint up the steps.

"In the cellar. Kyle's with him."

Without wasting another moment, I rush inside and rip open the floorboard that leads down into Weston's cellar.

Kyle's standing just below the stairs, a broken bottle in his hand. Thomas is behind him, both boys wide-eyed and terrified. Pride swells in my chest at the sight of Kyle taking such a protective stance over Thomas.

"Garrison!" Thomas pushes past Kyle and throws his arms around my neck, his entire body shaking.

Thank You, Lord. Thank You. Tears sting my eyes as I hold onto him. I press a kiss to the top of his head, so beyond grateful that he's okay.

Kyle's still frozen, eyes wide, a broken bottle in his shaking hand. I reach over with one hand and gently take it from him. After I toss it to the side, I pull him in for a hug, too. Both boys cling to me, terrified but safe.

"You guys are okay. You're okay," I tell them.

"Did they take my mom, too? Why is this happening?"

"We're going to get her back, okay?" I pull away from them and look into Thomas's wide, terrified eyes. "I promise, Thomas. For now, we need to get you both somewhere no one will think to look, okay?"

"Okay."

"We can go to my house. They don't know me. Mr. Hayes can come, too," Kyle offers, likely wanting to keep Weston around for safety.

It's a solid plan, but not this time. "That's a great offer, Kyle, but I can't risk putting you and your family in danger any more than I already have. I'm so sorry. If they don't know you, we need to keep it that way."

"Okay," he says, standing a little straighter now.

"Thank you, Kyle. Thank you for protecting him."

"I didn't do anything."

I reach forward and place a hand on the back of the kid's head. "You would have. And that's the same thing." Outside, sirens wail. "Come on. Let's get you two checked out."

Chapter 27

Garrison

A man sits at the interrogation table, wearing a dark sweater, dark pants, and an annoyed expression. His head is shaved to the scalp, his face clean-shaven as well. But as he stares straight ahead, I have the sick realization that I've seen him before: standing outside the coffee shop.

"Do you recognize him?" Leopold asks me.

"I've seen him before. He was lurking outside the coffee shop. He'd been on the phone, and a woman had been with him, so I let it go."

"His name is Andrew Thorn. He's a professional football player," Jack offers. He's been here roughly an hour, arriving right as Leopold was booking this guy. The other one is still in the hospital under guard. Apparently, it'll be a while until he's drinking through anything but a straw.

Thank you, Cowboy.

"Let me guess. West Coast Wranglers?" I growl.

"That would be the one. I have a team searching Earnest Marks' place right now, but so far, they don't have anything."

"They won't find him there. He wouldn't have gone far. Not when he still wants Thomas."

Jack turns to Leopold. "You feel like seeing if this guy can give us a location?"

"It would be rude to keep him waiting," Leopold responds. "We'll be back," he tells me right before he and Jack leave the room.

"We'll get them back," Zane tells me.

I nod, unable to speak. I have no doubt that we'll find Katelyn and Sawyer…but will they be alive?

The door to the interrogation room opens as Jack and Leopold step in. The guy sitting at the table grins at them, then leans back in his seat, arrogance pouring from him. "My lawyer arrive yet?"

Leopold takes a seat across from him while Jack remains standing. "Not yet, his invitation must have gotten lost in the mail," Jack retorts. "Tell you what, until then, how about we chat?"

"I ain't saying nothing without my lawyer."

Jack leans forward. "You remember that guy who messed you up? You know, when you were trying to kidnap Thomas Ellis? Well, he's right on the other side of that glass, and I know he would *love* to come visit."

"You can't touch me. I know my rights."

"Yeah, I bet you do." Jack opens the file in his hand. "Over a dozen arrests in the last two years alone. Assault. Driving while intoxicated. Your lawyer must be working hard for that retainer." He tosses it onto the table.

"I tell you what. Since you're not feeling overly chatty, how about we paint a picture for you?" Leopold's demeanor changes as he sheds his nice guy tone and show-cases why he's the guy people count on when things go sideways. He leans forward and clasps both hands in front of him on the table. "Your boss decided he wanted to make an example out of an innocent woman and her son. You, being the dedicated employee that you are, jumped at the chance. You came here to abduct them but ended up taking her and a highly trained member of a Navy SEAL team. Great idea, by the way. That's going to go over super well."

At that, Andrew's mouth twitches. *A crack.* He didn't know who Sawyer was.

"Now, three other members of that same team are standing just on the other side of that glass," Leopold points toward us. "You met the fourth earlier. He was the one who made smoothies your buddy's new meal of choice." He drops his hand. "Now, the three that are here? They would just love to tear you apart, limb by limb, until you sing like the canary we both know you are. Two lives are at stake, and I'm the only reason they haven't ripped you apart yet."

"You. Can't. Do. Nothing."

Leopold stares at him a moment, then glances up at

Jack. "Up for a coffee break? He's clearly not going to talk."

"Sure thing. We'll be back when your lawyer shows up."

Taking that as the invitation I sincerely hope it is, Ryker, Zane, and I leave the viewing room.

"You've got five minutes with him," Leopold says. "Please don't break anything," he adds with a pointed look at Ryker.

"I'll do my best."

We step into the room, and Andrew's eyes go wide. "Hey! You can't do this!" he yells.

Zane closes the door carefully behind him, then crosses over to take a seat at the table. There's a reason he's the leader of our group. And not just because of the rank he once carried.

Zane Knox is as level-headed as they come.

He can face down sure death and still not break a sweat.

Right now, all I can think of is extracting information by brute force, but Zane will get there faster. And the information will be more reliable because it wasn't disclosed out of desperation.

"You took something of ours," Zane says calmly.

"I ain't saying nothing."

"You will," Zane replies.

Andrew snorts. "Not a chance."

"You're going to tell me everything I want to know, or I'm going to unleash Tank on you. Then Demo, here, will finish off the pieces. See, you didn't just take our brother; you took his girl, too."

Andrew snorts. "Your girl is a tramp. Always has been."

I lunge forward, hands clenched into fists, but Ryker pulls me back by gripping my arm. I take a deep breath, trying to calm myself. He's baiting me, shifting the attention from him to me in an attempt to buy time.

"You're not getting the kid," I tell him. "You're not getting out of here because we have proof that your boss was responsible for this kidnapping and the murder of Yasmin Hernandez." The last one is a bluff, of course. Elijah hasn't actually been able to find a connection, but based on Andrew's face? It's one hundred percent true.

He murdered Katelyn's friend to keep her quiet.

"You can't prove that."

"Oh, I can. The FBI is tearing apart his life as we speak. How long do you think it'll be before we get to you?"

Andrew looks from me to Zane, who's crossed his arms and is watching every subtle move Andrew makes.

"Sing, canary," Zane says. "It's your only chance to save yourself."

CHAPTER 28

KATELYN

"You doing okay?" Sawyer asks me. His tone is strained as he slowly works the bindings on his wrists. I've been doing the same, but so far, I've done nothing but bloody up my hands.

"No."

"We're going to get out of here," he tells me.

"How can you be so sure?"

"Because I've been in far worse situations than this and survived."

"When you had a team that knew where you were. They don't know where we are, Sawyer. What if—"

"You have to stay calm, Katelyn. Do you trust Garrison?"

"Of course."

"Then trust that he will tear apart this world to find you.

I'm just lucky because that means he'll find me, too." He winks, trying to lessen the tension.

"How do you know?"

Sawyer stops tugging at his restraints and looks at me. "Because if it were Anastasia, nothing short of death would keep me from bringing her home." It's the closest I imagine he's ever gotten to admitting his feelings. "Besides, Garrison *loves* to save me. Just you wait; he'll never let me live this down."

I smile, feeling a bit of relief thanks to his optimistic outlook. Still, what if he's wrong? What if they don't find us in time?

The door opens, and Earnest walks in, a furious expression on his face.

Which only fuels my joy. "You didn't find him." *Thank You, Lord. Thank You for keeping him safe and bringing Garrison into our lives.*

He doesn't respond to me, just reaches behind him and rips a gun free from a holster at Leo's waist. His muscle looks honestly surprised—and slightly annoyed.

I hold my breath as he turns, leveling it on Sawyer's face. "Talk. I'm done playing games."

"I—"

"Not an answer." He drops it and fires. Sawyer grunts, the bullet tearing through the flesh of his shoulder. Blood saturates his chest, dripping down from the wound like nasty red teardrops.

"No! Stop!"

"Talk."

I open my mouth to respond, to beg for Sawyer's life even as I'm sure it won't do any good. But before I can, an explosion rattles the building. The floor shakes violently beneath us. The lights flicker, and dust sprinkles down on top of us.

"What was that?" Earnest demands.

Sawyer grins. "Boom, baby. That would be Demo. I hope you're ready for war, Marks. Because it's on your doorstep."

"Not a chance." Earnest shoves Leo's weapon back into his hand, and he re-holsters it. "I'm not having this ruined by some has-beens playing soldier. Cut her loose."

This is my only chance. I remain perfectly still as Leo cuts my legs free, but the moment my last wrist is free, I lunge forward, kneeing him in the chest and reaching for the gun at his waist.

Someone yanks me back by my hair, and pain explodes along my scalp. My vision goes blurry, and I stumble backward, losing my balance.

"You're already in it, Marks! Let her go!" Sawyer yells. "Hurting her will only make it worse for you!"

"Kill him. Find the boy. If the team is here, they left him unprotected."

"No! Let me go!" I fight against his hold, but Marks pushes me against Bradley's chest, and I'm dragged from the room.

Sawyer's gaze is wild as he thrashes against the chair, his focus on me and not the man currently closing in on him—a knife in his hand.

CHAPTER 29

GARRISON

We clear the hangar with the speed and precision we had when we were still in the field, but it doesn't feel like enough. "Anything?" I ask through my coms. Rubble decorates the floor, thanks to the hole I put in the side.

"Not yet," Zane answers.

"I'm moving through the back." Weapon trained straight ahead, I shove open a door and head down the hall.

There's a room on the right, so I offer Ryker a nod. He comes around and slams his boot into the center of it. The door flies open, and we move in just in time to see a man raise a knife to Sawyer's throat.

I squeeze the trigger.

The gunshot echoes through the room, and Sawyer's attacker falls to the ground.

"Eagle, we've got Cable Guy. Send in the cavalry," I order through the coms.

"Coming in hot," Jack replies.

"It's about time. Epic entrance, by the way," Sawyer says as Ryker cuts him loose. "Real hero stuff."

"Where's Katelyn?"

"Marks just took her. He and another guy are trying to get out. He ordered the others to go after Thomas."

"We've got him protected. Jack's bringing a team in."

"For once, I think I might be happy to see him," Sawyer says. "You bring me something? Let's go get this guy." I reach down and withdraw the holstered pistol on my hip, then offer it to Sawyer.

"Let's go."

Heart in my throat, I move out into the hall and continue down. We're just emerging into the main part of the neighboring airport when the sound of helicopter blades fills my ears.

My stomach drops. If he gets her in the air, I won't find her again—of that I'm sure.

"He's making a run for it!" I rush forward, sprinting as fast as I can out onto the tarmac where Katelyn is being held inside a helicopter already in the process of leaving the ground.

"Garrison!" she screams.

I don't stop. Instead, I drop my rifle on the ground and strip out of the Kevlar vest weighing me down.

Pushing my body as fast as it can go, I race forward.

Someone fires a weapon my direction, but I don't slow my pace. Not even when the chopper is nearly out of reach.

Right as I reach it, I jump forward and fling myself into the cockpit. I'm immediately assaulted, a fist connecting with my jaw. But I spin out of reach, gripping the overhead railing to steady myself as I fight to remain in the now airborne chopper.

The man raises a gun, so I slam my arm into it, knocking it to the side, right before I plant my boot in his chest. He stumbles backward—falling from the helicopter with a terrified scream.

Heart in my throat, I raise my gun and face off with the man holding Katelyn. The steel barrel of a pistol is pressed to her temple. A single tear runs down her cheek. Her eyes are wide and terrified, her skin pale. "Take us down, now," I order the pilot.

"You don't take orders from him!" Earnest yells.

"You're going to want to if you don't want to face felony kidnapping and assault charges."

"Taking us down," the pilot calls out. We start to descend, but since the ocean is right below us, I know it'll be a few minutes before I have backup.

And in those minutes, everything could change.

I shift my attention to Katelyn. "You okay, baby?" I ask her.

"How sweet," Earnest sneers. "Does he know he's risking his life for a killer? Do any of these men know what you are, Katelyn? Or does your beauty blind them to the truth?"

"The only killers here are you and me," I say. "You kill for sport and self-preservation, and I won't hesitate to kill you if anything happens to her. So, think about that before you pull that trigger."

"You're a fool," Earnest snaps.

"You're delusional. Let her go. Now."

"Let her go?" Earnest repeats, his tone giving away his next action even before I've had time to fully process the threat.

"Easy, Marks," I warn. But it's too late. My gaze travels around, looking for anything I can do to save us both. Unfortunately, there are no fast ropes in a personal helicopter.

Maybe—

"You did tell me to let her go." He pushes her closer to the open door of the chopper, and she clings to his arm, her lips trembling.

"Garrison," she cries.

"It's going to be okay, Katelyn. We're going to be on the ground soon, Marks. The FBI already has enough on you to lock you up; don't add another murder to that list." If I shoot him now, he'll drop her.

If I make a move toward him, he'll drop her.

My only hope is that I can stall long enough that backup will arrive.

"What's one more, right?" He shoves her toward the

door, and she screams as her eyes go wide and she falls backward—out of the helicopter.

I leap forward after her, abandoning any desire I have to see Marks in cuffs. She's all that matters.

Katelyn's mouth is open on a scream I can't hear. But I can see her panic as she tumbles backward.

The only sounds in my ears are the hammering of my pulse and the wind rushing past me. I stiffen, keeping my arms at my side. *Steady body position.* Normally, in a descent like this, I'd have a parachute to save us; this time, I've only got me.

But if I can reach her, then I can absorb at least some of the impact.

My gaze locks on hers—wide and terrified as she free-falls.

God, please save us. Please. We can't survive this without You.

I reach for her, pulling her against my chest and spinning us right before we slam into the icy depths of the Atlantic.

Chapter 30

Katelyn

The air is ripped from my lungs as we slam into the wall of water.

It's dark. Cold.

I fight to break the surface, kicking my legs as my lungs burn from lack of oxygen. I break through and scan the inky surface. "Garrison!" I scream, panicked. He jumped after me.

He took the hit.

What if he didn't survive?

"Garrison!" I shout again, then dive back down into the water, searching for him. My hand brushes against something hard, and I grab, tugging his weight up to the surface. He's completely limp.

Is he even breathing?

We break the surface. "Garrison!" I yell, shaking him as best I can while I fight to keep both of us above the water.

Frantic, I scan for land. How far are we from shore? It can't be that far, right? We weren't in the air that long. Cold water laps at my neck, and it takes strength I didn't know I had to keep us above water.

Lord, be with us. Deliver us from this, please, God.

The shadow of land in the distance gives me hope, so I wrap an arm around him and swim. I've never been more grateful for the early morning practices of my college swim team than I am right now. Still, it's been a long time since I was in the water, and I'm feeling every bit of that.

Using every inch of strength left in my battered body, I swim us both toward shore. When we're finally close enough to the beach, the waves take over, shoving us forward even as they try to rip us back.

I fight them, my only focus on saving a man who risked everything for me.

God, please don't let him die. Please, Lord. Tears stream down my cheeks, and I scream in frustration as I fight the current to pull him free.

"Katelyn!"

Someone screams my name, giving me a surge of hope as I struggle to keep Garrison's head above the water. "Over here!" I yell. "Please! We're over here!"

A man I've never met sprints forward alongside Jack. Both men reach us in quick strides. They tug Garrison to shore. I fall to my knees in the sand and shove them aside to feel for a pulse. It's faint. Too faint.

I press my ear to his mouth. "He's not breathing," I cry,

then pinch his nose, tilt his head up, and cover his mouth with mine. I breathe into him.

God, please. Please don't take him.

Still, Garrison doesn't move.

Fear threatens to consume me. He can't be gone. I can't lose him. *Focus, Katelyn.*

I lean down and breathe into his airway again, urging his body to take over. *Come on, Garrison, breathe.*

Still, nothing.

People surround us, but I refuse to give up.

Just as I'm pulling away again, Garrison's eyes fly open, and he coughs, water spewing from his mouth.

The man who'd rescued us alongside Jack turns Garrison onto his side and breathes a sigh of relief.

Garrison's body seizes as he fights for air, but after a few moments, he rolls onto his back and stares up at me, lids heavy. "Caught you."

I cup his face. "You almost died."

He grins. "Worth it."

"Thomas?" I whisper.

"Safe and sound. Your boy is a tough one," he adds with another grin.

"Thank God." The weight on my chest lessens, even as the adrenaline begins to wane and my body trembles. *Thank You, Lord. Thank You for protecting my boy and for keeping Garrison safe.*

"You and I are going to have to talk about these near-death experiences, Demo. The cry for attention is getting a little outrageous," Sawyer says as he sinks to his knees beside us. His shoulder has been crudely wrapped, but at least the bleeding looks to have stopped.

Garrison smiles softly, still out of breath. "I'll work on that."

"Please do because I can't lose you," I tell him.

He reaches up with a shaking hand and brushes hair out of my face. "Okay…I guess we're up to five lasagnas now." I collapse beside him, resting my head on his arm as paramedics and police flood the scene.

I'll have to move soon, but right now—everything in my world is right.

Because Thomas is safe.

And Garrison Holt is mine.

CHAPTER 31

GARRISON

A couple of cracked ribs and a concussion later, and I'm spending one night in the hospital. Turns out, my injuries are a lot less than they should have been. I sent Katelyn home earlier with Weston, who'll sleep on the couch and make sure she and Thomas are safe.

They caught up with Marks, and Jack said they have enough to put him away for a long time, but it'll still take some time before I'm confident Katelyn and Thomas are safe. She would have stayed here if it weren't for her son. He'd refused to leave without her, which was the final straw in her agreeing to go get some actual sleep.

Aside from some bruises on her face and injuries to her wrists and ankles where she'd been bound, Katelyn was in the clear. As I'd hoped it would, my body absorbed most of the shock from the fall.

Thank You, Lord. He saved us out there; there's not a doubt in my mind.

There's a soft knock at my door, and it swings open. Dressed in a hospital gown, using his IV pole for a cane, Sawyer walks into the room. He peeks behind him, then gently closes the door and crosses over toward my bed.

"You supposed to be up?" I ask him.

Without answering, he slowly lowers himself into the chair. "I hate hospitals."

I laugh. "I'm not overly fond of them either. How are you feeling?"

"Alive. Thanks to you." He's quiet for a moment, something unusual for Sawyer most days. "I'm sorry, man. I tried to save her. They came up on us so fast. And then there was the gun—"

"Are you seriously apologizing?" I sit up a little straighter, hissing through clenched teeth when the movement jars my injured ribs. "You did save her, Sawyer. She's alive because you put yourself at risk and took the hits. If you hadn't been there—" I shake my head. "I don't know what would have happened to her."

"For a moment there, I really thought I was done." He takes a deep breath and looks up at me. Behind his sarcastic exterior, Sawyer Maddox has a heart of gold.

"Katelyn says you were Mr. Optimistic."

He snorts. "Yeah, well, can't lose my charm even in the face of death. I have a reputation to uphold." There's a weight on him now that's not typical.

"You talk to Anastasia yet?"

He shakes his head. "I told Zane to tell her I wanted to rest."

I arch a brow. "Really?"

He shrugs. "She's with him now, and I think it's time I start coming to terms with it. He's all right, I guess. And he cares for her."

"Sawyer—"

"Nah, it'll be fine. I'll survive." He forces a smile. "After all, it's just an infatuation, right? I mean, if it were love, I would have already said something. Look at you, friend-zoned for what—a week—before you did something about it? I keep hesitating, and I think it's because I know we're better off as friends."

"You sure about that?"

He takes a deep breath. "No. But I'm going to work on getting okay with it."

The door opens, and Rose storms in, a frustrated look on her face. "Sawyer Maddox. What do you think you're doing out of bed?"

He winces. "Busted. I'm sorry, Rosie, I just needed a walk." He fakes a pout, the old Sawyer slipping back into place. But I know him well enough to still see the heartbreak. I'm honestly not sure how he does it. I spent three months pining after Katelyn, and most of that time, she barely knew I existed.

I couldn't imagine seeing someone every single day.

Being friends. And loving them while they loved someone else.

"Yeah, well, you can take a walk right back to your room, boy."

"Get him, Rose," I say with a smile.

She shakes her head as she helps Sawyer to his feet, but there's a smile toying at the corners of her lips.

"You get some sleep, Demo," Sawyer says. "See you tomorrow."

"See you tomorrow," I reply. "And Sawyer?" He glances over his shoulder. "Give yourself more credit. You know what you feel. Don't convince yourself it's something else unless you're absolutely sure. Otherwise, you're missing out on a whole lot of life."

He offers me a half-smile, then leaves the room, Rose right behind him.

As I settle back against the pillows and close my eyes, I think back to all that I've been through in the past two months.

Being stabbed and almost dying.

Getting pepper sprayed.

Falling in love.

Falling—literally—out of a helicopter.

The list is a lot longer than it should be, and yet I'm still here. All because God has a plan for me.

I just seriously hope that plan includes Katelyn and Thomas, too.

"You sit," Katelyn orders as she locks the apartment door behind us. Since Kyle and I managed to get most of her furniture moved in before she went missing, it's her stuff in the two-bedroom apartment while mine is next door, ready to be arranged and unpacked.

"Yes, ma'am," I reply with a grin that only Thomas can see. His own smile widens as he takes a seat on the chair across from me.

After yet another night in the hospital, I am more than ready for an actual shower and some real sleep. So long as that sleep is here on the couch, because I have no intention of leaving Katelyn and Thomas just yet.

"How you feeling, Mr. Holt?" Thomas asks.

"Kind of like I fell out of a helicopter without a parachute."

He snorts, his joy returning now that his mom is safe. The kid has been glued to her side ever since last night, and I absolutely love seeing it. With the two of them together, order is restored in my world.

"But I've had worse," I add.

"You know, Sawyer said that same thing after he was shot. Just because you've had worse doesn't negate what you're going through now." She hands me a cup of water. "You almost died."

Her face is bruised, her right eye bloodshot, but she's alive. My beautiful Katelyn. I'd happily take that fall over and over again if it meant she walked away. There's not a hit I won't take for her.

"Worth it."

She shakes her head and takes a seat on the couch beside me.

"I think I'm going to go call Kyle, see if he wants to play some video games." Thomas jumps up and rushes off to his room, leaving Katelyn and me on the couch alone.

I set the water down and turn toward her. "Hey. Did I tell you I bought you a present?"

"You did?"

I point toward the bookcase, at the brown bag sitting on the bottom shelf. "I set it there after Kyle and I finished moving everything in."

Her brow furrows, and she gets up to cross the living room. "I didn't even notice this. I'm sorry."

"Don't be. I wanted you to open it with me, anyway."

Katelyn carries the bag over and takes a seat on the couch beside me once more. "Can I?"

"Please."

With a wide grin on her face, she carefully opens the brown bag and withdraws the Bible. "Oh, Garrison," she says softly, running her fingertips over the HOLY BIBLE printed in gold on the front of the floral cover. "You bought me a Bible."

"You said you didn't have one anymore. I wanted to make sure you did."

She looks over at me, tears shimmering in her eyes.

"You have no idea what you've done for me, Garrison. From the moment we met, you've been healing what you didn't break. Thank you so much. For this. For everything."

"Baby, I wish I could take the credit, but that's all God. He is the ultimate healer. I'm just grateful He put you in my life so I could show you what you deserve." I reach out and run my fingertips over her cheek. "Which is everything, Katelyn."

She smiles, and a single tear rolls down her cheek. I wipe it away with my thumb, then lower my hand. "So, listen, I also had some time to think."

"Oh yeah?" she laughs, setting the Bible on the table in front of us. "When was that? In all your downtime over the last forty-eight hours?"

Laughing, I angle my body toward her. Pain shoots through my side at the awkward movement, but I push through it. "I love you, Katelyn Ellis. I know it doesn't make any sense since we haven't known each other long, and it's okay if you don't feel the same yet. I just want you to know that I have fallen madly, helplessly in love with you."

Her eyes fill with tears, and she leans forward to press her lips to mine. "It doesn't make any sense," she whispers. "But I'm in love with you, too."

I breathe a sigh of relief. "That's good to hear. I was a bit mortified there for a second."

She laughs, but it's cut short when I pull her in and press my lips to hers. The feel of her against me, her soft curves and silky hair, is so familiar even as it's completely new. As she pulls away and settles her head against my chest, I press a kiss to the top of her forehead and close my eyes, feeling peace settle over me for the first time in a long, long time.

Epilogue: Katelyn
Three Weeks Later

A dinner date with Garrison.

Even as I stare at my closet, trying to figure out exactly what I'm going to wear, I can't keep the smile off my face.

We spent the last three weeks having dinners in while we both healed—he more so than I. Our evenings have consisted of Garrison, Thomas, and me all sitting in the living room watching a movie, or gathered around the table laughing and talking about our day. They've been the best nights of my life.

And this morning, I made the decision to reach out to my parents. Something I plan to do tomorrow, once I've figured out just what to say to them. How do I apologize for lying to and then abandoning them? For keeping their grandson from them for the last thirteen years?

One step at a time, Katelyn. I breathe deeply, trying to

calm my nerves and set that aside for now. I want to enjoy tonight.

It seems so surreal, but in a matter of a month, my entire life has changed. My routine. And I am so beyond grateful for it.

Garrison Holt.

Navy SEAL. Ridiculously handsome neighbor.

The man who risked his life to save mine and my son's.

I'm in love, and oh, does it feel so good.

I lift a cream-colored sweater with a scooped neck. Not low enough to show what it shouldn't, but enough to reveal the silver cross I wear around my neck. I love this shirt, but will Garrison?

Someone knocks on the door to the apartment.

"Who is it?" I call out.

Thomas waits a beat, then calls back, "Miss Knox!"

"Let her in, honey!" I replace the sweater, then make sure my robe is closed before opening the bedroom door. "Hey, Anastasia, what's up?"

"I am here to offer my services as best friend," she says, then holds up a garment bag. "And I brought backup."

"You are amazing. Come on in." I close the bedroom door as she lays the garment bag on my bed and unzips it.

"Since you told me that you weren't big on dating before, I assumed you probably didn't have much."

"That's accurate."

"Well, I have three great choices here, and since we're the same size, they should fit you like a glove." She takes a seat on my bed as I go through the bag, selecting a navy-blue dress with a modest neckline and partially open back.

"This is gorgeous."

"It's all yours," she replies with a smile. "Go, try it on!" She ushers me into the closet—*my* closet. Wow, still feels weird to think that.

"How are you doing? How's Jack?"

"He's okay. Busy." She's quiet for a moment. "Have you talked to Sawyer lately?"

I finish slipping into the dress, then draw the side zipper up before stepping out into the room. "He came over for dinner last night. Why?"

Anastasia leans back against my pillows. "Just curious." But it's more than that, and I think we both know it. "Girl, that looks *amazing* on you. Keep it. I genuinely cannot wear it now that I know it looks that good on you."

I laugh. "I cannot keep your dress." Turning, I study myself in the mirror, my grin spreading as I realize that I really do look nice.

Not "cute diner waitress."

But nice, with a capital 'N'.

"Garrison is going to lose his mind." Anastasia winks. "And my work here is done." She stands. "Have a great time, don't do anything I wouldn't do, and best of all, enjoy being in love with a wonderful, strong, amazing man who would do anything for you."

"Thank you so much, Anastasia."

She pulls me in for a hug. "Anytime, honey. Have fun. Need me to run Thomas over to Weston's?"

The two bonded during the attack that nearly claimed my son and Kyle. So much so that he's been spending at least three days a week helping Weston on the ranch he works at.

"That would actually be great, if you don't mind."

"Not at all."

I step out into the hall after her. "Hey, honey, Miss Knox is going to take you out to Weston's. Is that okay?"

"Sure thing!" Thomas sets his controller down, then turns. His eyes widen when he sees me. "Wow, Mom! You look beautiful!"

My eyes fill. "Thanks, baby."

"Seriously. So pretty. I hope you guys have fun tonight."

"You, too. No junk food before dinner."

"Mom, I don't even think Weston knows what junk food is."

"It's true," Anastasia confirms.

I laugh. "Still."

"All right, come on, kid. Let's get out of here before your mom's big date." Anastasia winks at me as Thomas jumps over the back of the couch and pulls me in for a big hug. At almost fourteen, he's nearly as tall as I am already, but he'll always be my baby.

My sweet, wonderful boy.

We've talked a lot over the last month. About Victor

and Earnest, and why things were so rough for us for so long. While I didn't go into the details, he handled everything I did tell him with incredible maturity.

It lifted yet another weight from me.

"I love you."

"Love you, too, Mom." Thomas pulls away and grabs his bag, then bounds out the door before Anastasia. I'm just heading toward the bedroom again when it opens.

"Did you forge—" But I stop mid-sentence when I turn around and see Garrison standing there in the doorway—staring at me as though I'm the single most important thing in the world.

"Wow," he whispers. "You look amazing."

I study his dark jeans and a button-down nearly the same shade as my dress. He's wearing a pair of boots and has styled his hair. "You look amazing, too." Attraction burns in my belly, a warmth that spreads through me as I look at him.

Oh boy.

"I'm starting to think that I'm underdressed." He crosses over toward me, closing the distance in long, easy strides, until he's standing only a few inches away.

I rest my hand on his chest and look up into those gorgeous eyes, so full of joy. Of love.

"You're perfect."

He leans down and captures my lips with his. A gentle kiss that stokes the fire that's been burning within me for far longer than I want to admit.

"I wanted to wait, but—" He trails off and reaches into his pocket. When he withdraws a small velvet box, my heart begins to hammer. And when he drops to one knee, the world around me tilts on its axis, spinning wildly out of control in the best way.

"Garrison."

"I know it's soon, but I can't wait, Katelyn. I can't wait for you and Thomas to be a part of my everyday. I want to wake up with you in my arms and go to sleep the same. I want to eat dinner with you guys every single night and spend our evenings together—as a family. So, Katelyn Ellis. Will you marry me?"

Tears blur my vision, and I can't even see Garrison or the ring, but my heart is so, so full. "Yes. Yes!" I squeal, and he stands. I throw my arms around his neck and slam my mouth onto his, giving in to every bit of love I carry for him.

I never thought I'd find what I have now.

Never even dreamed of falling in love.

And now I not only have a love for me but someone who loves my son as his own. Someone who will never lay a hand on me in anger and will love me until the day I leave this earth.

Garrison is an answer to a prayer I didn't know I had. I guess it's a good thing God knows what's in our hearts, even when we don't.

Thank you so much for reading! I hope you loved Garrison and Katelyn's story! If you feel up for it, please consider leaving an honest review! They help so much.

And be sure to keep turning the pages for a sneak peek at Sawyer and Anastasia's story, SEAL of Courage!

Bonus Chapter:
SEAL of Courage

Anastasia

Sawyer's shop is pristinely organized, every single tool in its place. Which makes it easy to navigate in the dark. I follow a path through the main bay toward his office. There's a single light on inside, offering a faint glow that gets brighter the closer I get.

Heart racing, I pause just outside the cracked door. *This is silly.* Sawyer Maddox is one of my best friends. So why do I feel so nervous?

Get it together, Anastasia. It's just Sawyer.

I knock on the door, then push it open. Sawyer is seated behind his desk, baseball cap on backward, a black t-shirt stretched over his muscled chest. How does he look so good even when there's grease smeared on his cheek?

"Anastasia," he says, eyes widening in surprise.

"So you remember my name. That's good." I walk in and take a seat behind his desk.

"Of course I remember you. Is everything okay?"

He's so cold now. Even though, technically, he's being perfectly kind. But this isn't the Sawyer I know. The one who would do anything to see me smile. Who'd hang out at the coffee shop whenever he had a spare moment so I'd have someone to talk to when there was a lull.

"Everything's fine. I just dropped Thomas off at the Westons' and thought I'd check in and make sure you're okay."

"I'm fine." He glances back down at the papers he was looking at when I came in.

"Are we—"

"We're fine, Anastasia. I'm just busy. You've got Jack and the shop; you know how it goes."

Jack.

"Yeah, I guess so. You're okay, though?" Ever since he was released from the hospital, Sawyer's been in his own world. He's even missed dinner at my mom's a couple of times over the past few weeks, which is completely unusual.

"Of course." He flashes me a smile, but it's not *his*. "Why wouldn't I be?"

"Not sure. Just figured I'd ask."

He goes back to his papers, so I stand. "Well, I guess I'll get going then."

"Okay. It was good to see you. Thanks for stopping in." He offers me another smile, so I push out of the room, my heart sinking with each step between us.

There was a time I thought Sawyer might be *the one*. As cheesy as it sounds. But then, as time passed and he never acted on what I thought was between us, I moved on. I had to, right? I couldn't wait around forever.

We'd definitely had a spark.

A connection.

Even after I started dating Jack, we'd maintained a friendship, which only solidified my thoughts that a spark was all it was. After all, if he truly felt for me what I thought I felt for him, he'd have said something, right?

Then he'd gone missing.

Those hours when I thought I'd lost Sawyer were the worst in my life. I'd been devastated by the loss. Desperate to get him back. And then I did. Except—this isn't him.

"No," I snap and turn toward him.

"No?" He looks up at me.

"No. You don't get to do this. You don't get to be cold. I didn't do anything to deserve it." I cross my arms.

Sawyer stands and crosses his, too. The tattoo on his right arm flexes with his muscles, drawing my attention for a brief moment before it shoots back to his face. "I didn't realize I was being cold."

"You're not being *you*." I throw my hands up in the air. "You know exactly what you're doing."

"I'm not trying to be cold, Anastasia. I'm just trying to be respectful."

"Of what?"

"Your relationship with Jack. He's a good guy. I was

wrong, so I took a step back." His tone is ridiculously level—lacking all emotion.

I glare at him. "Is that what this is about? We were friends long before I ever met Jack. I didn't realize that having him in my life meant I'd lose you." The very thought makes my stomach churn. Emotion burns in my throat, an unyielding lump that will strangle me if I let it.

Why does this hurt so bad?

Sawyer comes around his desk. "You didn't lose me. I'm right here."

"No, you're standing here, but you're not really here." Tears burn in the corners of my eyes. "I miss my friend."

"I haven't gone anywhere."

"You almost—" I trail off, swallowing down past the lump in my throat. "You almost died."

"It's not the first time," he replies.

I shake my head, the hurt deepening with every moment I spend standing here in front of him.

"Look, Anastasia, Jack is your boyfriend. If I were him and someone was hanging around you the way I was, I'd not be happy about it. The last thing I want to do is cause you problems."

"Sawyer—"

"Now it's my turn to say no," he interrupts, frustration taking over and erasing the emotionless façade. "You don't get to stand there and pretend that you never saw the way I looked at you. Everyone in town saw it. Now, I'm moving on, and you don't get to come in here, demanding answers to anything. You chose him!"

His words slam into me one after the other, like waves battering a rocky shore. *"You don't get to stand there and pretend that you never saw the way I looked at you."*

But I didn't see—not really. "You never asked!"

Sawyer swallows hard. "And that's something I must live with. But I'm moving on, Anastasia, and I suggest you do the same."

My cell phone rings, and Jack's name lights up on the screen.

"Look at that, you're already halfway there. I'll see you around, Anastasia."

"Don't bother." With tears in my eyes, I rush out of the shop and out onto the dark street. With trembling fingers, I try to get the keys out of my pocket, but they fall to the ground. "Come on."

When I've finally retrieved them from the ground, I straighten, my vision so blurry I can hardly see anything. And then—bright headlights. Too close.

I scream.

Strong hands rip me back against a heavy body. We go to the ground as the car continues speeding off into the night.

The hard body beneath me is unfamiliar, but the scent of motor oil and pine is one I'll never forget. "Are you okay?" Sawyer rolls me over and pulls me to my feet, then runs his hands over my arms.

Body trembling, I can't catch my breath. *What just happened?*

"Anastasia, are you okay?" He cups my face and forces me to look at him. His caramel-colored eyes are wide, his unruly hair a mess without his ball cap.

Was it knocked off when he took me to the ground?

"I—think so."

"We need to get you inside. Come on."

"No." I shove him off, anger and hurt pushing through all logic that I probably *should* have him make sure I'm okay. But I can't do that. I can't face him again. Not yet. Not until I've fully pushed past this crush that threatens to destroy me. "I'm fine. Thanks."

Sawyer takes a step away from me. "You almost got hit."

"I was too close to the road." I look at where I'd parked. It's no wonder I was almost hit. In my nervous anticipation of seeing Sawyer, I'd practically parked on the street.

"Please come inside; let me look at you in the light. Make sure you're okay."

"I'm fine," I snap. "I'll just call Jack and have him fly in." The moment the words are out of my mouth, I want to rip them back.

Sawyer's expression goes cold. It's surreal, really, to watch his worry fade away, replaced by a cool façade that is so not the Sawyer I know.

But I put it there.

I put that pain on his face with my harsh words.

"I'm sorry, Sawyer. I'm just rattled. Thanks for saving me. I really am okay." But I'm anything but. I'm shaken—my entire body trembling as the understanding that I could have died settles over me.

"Yeah. Well, I'll call Zane and let him know what happened anyway. You may want to get checked." Without another word, Sawyer turns away, lifts his baseball cap from the ground, and heads into the shop, his powerful shoulders slumped…defeated.

And it's all my fault.

Thank you so much for reading! I hope you loved Garrison and Katelyn as much as I do!

Be sure to keep an eye out for the next book in the Iron Tide Brotherhood: SEAL of Courage, featuring Sawyer and Anastasia!

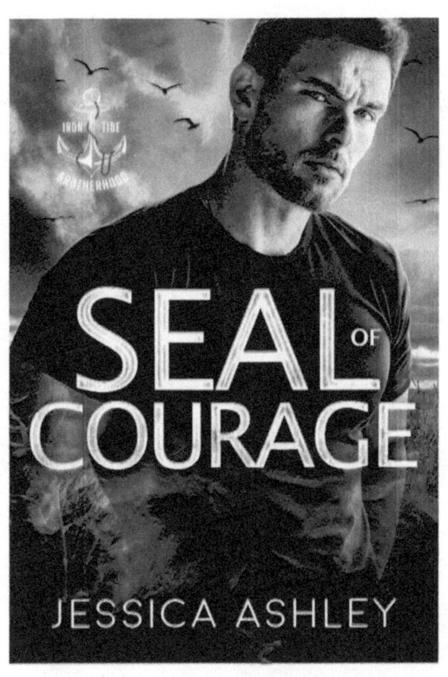

He loved her in silence…because loving her out loud was never an option.

Former Navy SEAL Sawyer Maddox has spent most of his life protecting others from the shadows. Calm under pressure. Loyal to the core. And painfully aware that the woman he's always cared about is completely off-limits.

Anastasia Knox is the little sister of one of his best friends…and the one woman Sawyer has never been able to forget. She's built a quiet life in their small coastal town, doing her best to be content with a relationship that looks right on paper. But when anonymous messages turn into late-night threats, that fragile sense of safety shatters.

Sawyer doesn't hesitate. He moves in. Steps closer. Putting himself between Anastasia and the danger—no matter the cost. Even if it means crossing lines he swore he never would.

Because the longer he's near her, the harder it is to ignore the truth.

She doesn't belong with the man she's with.

She belongs with him.

A gripping romantic suspense about faith, sacrifice, and a soldier who will risk everything for the woman he never meant to love.

About the Author

Jessica Ashley started her career in 2016 writing romance novels for the secular world, before feeling the Lord pulling her in a different direction.

She is now a three-time award winning author of Christian romance, and has published nearly twenty novels and novellas since 2024.

She is an Army veteran, who resides in New Hampshire with her husband and their three children.

You can find out more about her and her books by joining her newsletter via her website: https://jessicaashleybooks.com/ or by joining her Facebook group, Romance, Redemption, & Rescue: Jessica Ashley Books.

Member of the ACFW.

Awards won:

- *First-place in the Romantic Suspense category of the Firebird Q1 2025 Book Awards. (Pages of Promise)*
- *Readers' Favorite Gold Medal Winner for excellence in writing. (Bravo)*
- *Literary Titan Gold Book Award Winner. (Echo)*

Bravo: Bradyn Hunt

Echo: Elliot Hunt

Romeo: Riley Hunt

Tango: Tucker Hunt

Delta: Dylan Hunt

<u>Hunt Brothers Short Novels</u> *(Website Exclusives)*

Lima: Lani Hunt

<u>Hunt Brothers Holiday Novellas</u> *(Website Exclusives)*

A Hunt Brothers Valentines: Bradyn & Kennedy

A Hunt Brothers St. Patrick's Day: Elliot & Nova

A Hunt Brothers Easter: Riley & Jules

A Hunt Brothers Thanksgiving: Tucker & Alice

A Hunt Brothers Christmas: Dylan & Emma

<u>Iron Tide Brotherhood</u>

SEAL of Honor: Zane Knox

SEAL of Bravery: Garrison Holt

SEAL of Courage: Sawyer Maddox

<u>Standalone Novels</u> *(Website Exclusives)*

Critical Velocity: Beckett Wallace